MURDER IN THE SLAUGHTERHOUSE

Tom Crowley

ALSO BY TOM CROWLEY

Matt Chance Thrillers
Viper's Tail

Non-Fiction
Bangkok Pool Blues

TOM CROWLEY

MURDER IN THE SLAUGHTERHOUSE
A Matt Chance Thriller

Down & Out Books
3959 Van Dyke Rd, Ste. 265
Lutz, FL 33558
www.DownAndOutBooks.com

This is a work of fiction. Names, characters, places, and events are either the
product of the author's imagination or are used fictitiously. Any similarity to
real persons, living or dead, events, or locales is coincidental and not intended
by the author.

Cover art and design by JT. Lindroos

ISBN: 1937495736

ISBN-13: 978-1-937495-73-2

Dedicated to Krue Nang, Khun Samran and all the other selfless social workers around the world, who work daily to protect our children.

Thank you and God bless you.

Prelude

The pick-up truck careens along the mountain road. Forest cover hangs down to the road on one side, but on the other side there is a hundred foot drop.

Inside the pick-up are four kids—fearful and hopeful but mostly just curious to see what's beyond the next corner. Previously, thirty minutes was a long trip for them; the five hours on the road thus far is an impossibly long time. The children are from Lisu hill tribe homes in a remote northwest corner of Thailand. The vehicle is a battered Toyota pick-up with an extended cab. The male driver and a woman they just call Auntie sit in front, the four teenagers sit in back. They are all young and slight of build. It isn't crowded even with the carry bags they were allowed to bring along with some changes of clothes and a few other personal possessions. They have been in pick-up trucks before, but this is the first time any of them have ridden inside the cab. When the groups from their hill tribe villages went to market, the kids lucky enough to go along sat in the open back of the pick-up, exposed to the sun and rain, but happy and excited. This luxury of riding inside is new to them.

The four teenagers don't know the driver or Auntie. The arrangements for the trip had been made by their parents, or in the case of the twin fifteen-year-old girls, Aom and Nang, by their stepfather. Their mother had cried but agreed as the money to be gained from their jobs working at a restaurant in Bangkok would be a big help now that she had two younger children from her new husband and couldn't work as much to earn money. Also she knew, though she had never said anything, that her new husband had been molesting Aom, who had become increasingly quiet and withdrawn, over the past two years. Aom's mother thought her daughter would be safer in the city. Their stepfather had even been paid an advance on their salary, a large amount of money: twenty thousand baht, about six hundred and eighty dollars.

Of the two boys, Joe is bigger and taller than Pan and has broader shoulders indicating that when he fills out he will have a strong body. Pan is not only of much slighter build; he is attractive, almost pretty, in his good looks. The boys don't know the girls or each other though Joe remembers seeing the twins at the farm market the previous summer. The Lisu girls in their colorful clothes had stood out for that as much as for their cuteness. For hill tribe girls, fifteen was not too young to be thinking of marriage. Joe had been too shy to approach them initially and by the time he had snuck around and had some mountain whiskey to drink and built up some whiskey courage, they were gone. The boys are from different villages, but of the same mountain-dwelling Lisu hill tribe group as the girls. They are also fifteen years old. For some reason, the payments to the boy's parents were only half of those paid for the girls since they were from different villages. This was not general knowledge. The important point to each family is the promise of money flowing back to the village from Bangkok. All of the children had finished school with the sixth grade since it was deemed to be enough education.

In the cab of the pick-up truck, they sit divided—the boys on one side and the girls on the other—with the girls' bags in between them as a barrier. They haven't spoken to each other very much at all. Then Joe speaks to the girls in the Lisu dialect asking what village they are from. Aom, still cast in the role she has taken with her stepfather of protecting her sister Nang, replies and names her village. The Auntie turns around and yells at them to keep quiet, adding that if they have to talk they can only speak Thai from now on. Startled, the children all nod in frightened agreement. Nang starts crying softly. Aom holds her and comforts her, telling her it will be okay.

The road continues to twist and turn and finally descends to the city of Tak and the broad plains covered with rice fields. It is the first time the mountain born and bred teenagers have seen open countryside and now the sense that they are going to a different world and life gains strength within them.

At Tak the pick-up joins the North-South highway. Shortly afterwards, the driver pulls over to a rest area. The kids are let out but told to stand next to the pick-up and not wander away or go inside the food mart. Auntie takes the twins to the restroom and then brings them back. Then the driver does the same with the boys. After that they wait while Auntie goes inside and buys drinks and snacks for all. No food orders are placed. The kids will eat and drink what they are given and do it as the pick-up drives along. As soon as their food and drink arrives, they are ordered back in the pick-up which proceeds south on the highway, through the ancient capital of Ayutthaya, and on to Bangkok.

The shadows from the receding sun grow longer as the pick-up races down the highway and darkness is falling as they come to the northern outskirts of Bangkok. The kids have all fallen asleep as they ride through miles of lush green rice fields. The driver curses as he slows suddenly to pay a toll and they catch up with the remnants of the evening rush hour on the city's expressway. The kids wake up, eyes wide open at the number of cars and buildings and lights. It's a Disneyland without joy. They had never imagined there could be so much of everything. Finally, after several toll stops, starting and stopping and more cursing at traffic by the driver, they come to the exit indicating the port area of Klong Toey.

It's complete darkness now. The bright lights of the upmarket areas of the city are left behind as the driver winds through congested, dimly-lit streets, across a railway track and pulls up in front of a dilapidated three-story Chinese shophouse which has a few colored Christmas lights hanging outside to mark it as a night spot. The ground floor has some tables and is being used as a bar. Men are sitting around several tables drinking. A small shrine, lit by red lights and an altar with a picture of a Chinese Buddha, is set up in the far corner. This is primarily a Chinese slum area in the port district. Stairs in the back of the shophouse lead to the upper floors. The driver and Auntie herd the kids to the front area and Auntie asks a question using a strange dialect the kids don't understand, not Thai. One of the men grunts at her and points a finger up the stairs. Auntie leads the kids around the small tables; the men drinking and playing cards are all looking closely at the hill tribe kids. One man picks up on the fact that the girls are twins and makes a comment to those at his table, resulting in raucous laugh from all. The kids don't understand the language but Aom is familiar with the nature of the look. The man could be as dangerous as her stepfather. She puts her arm around Nang in a protective gesture as they walk along.

On the second floor, there is a hallway with doors to three rooms, a bathroom and in back a kitchen area with a table. The stairs continue up to a third floor divided into the same arrangement. Auntie leads the kids to the kitchen table where five men are drinking and playing cards. One of the men, a bit more carefully dressed than the others and a bit older, in his mid-fifties, looks at Auntie and the kids. He speaks to Auntie in a Chinese dialect.

"These are the hill tribe kids? Do they all understand Thai?"

"Yes, it was all we could get on this trip, but I have two or three more whose parents I'm still talking to. Maybe on the next trip."

Auntie turns to the kids and tells them to come closer so the old man can inspect them. He deliberates for a few seconds, walking around the kids to look at them from behind. As he does so, Aom reflexively puts her arm around Nang's shoulder again as if to shield her from the old man's gaze. This move is noted. The old man thinks to himself, "*This is her weakness. She'll do anything to protect her sister. Well, we'll give her a chance to do everything.*"

Then he turns back to Auntie, "It's okay. They will do. Put the two girls in the same room to start. We'll put the pretty boy in the room next to them. Make sure they get some food and get washed up, especially the girls. Show them how to wash their pussies. I'll see to the boy myself. We'll start training them later. There will be a lot of customers interested in playing with the twins at the same time. They'll bring in good money."

Turning to the driver the old man gestures to Joe, "This one isn't pretty enough for our customers. Get him a meal and then put him back in the truck and take him down to Ranong. He goes to work on the fishing boats in the morning. We have people down there waiting for new crew. You know where to go."

He reaches into his pocket and gives the driver a handful of blue pills. "These will help to keep you awake on the drive down."

The driver and Auntie both nod and turn away with the kids. It's time for the kids to start their new life; though it will not be the life their parents have been promised.

Act 1—Thailand

"Let the little children come to me, and do not hinder them, for the kingdom of heaven belongs to such as these."
—*Matthew 19:14*

Chapter 1

In most cities of the world, you could say as the dawn eases its way above the horizon that the city begins to stir. In Bangkok, that wouldn't be precisely correct. The mystical mix of the city's night beat continues through the verge of dawn and the pace of the city only hesitates. There is a somewhat perceptible pause in the city's life movements as the often desperate human night activity slows to a crawl, around dawn, as the night people complete their retreat with the last of the seductively clad sex workers and transgender beauties scurrying out of the growing light into the back of taxis. But the beat is taken up virtually immediately with the morning traffic of the day people as they begin to reclaim the city.

As the sun's first rays reflect from the many pieces of colored glass and Chinese porcelain embedded in its structure and pagoda towers, Wat Arun, Bangkok's ancient temple of the dawn, glows and provides a show of dancing light from its location on the west bank of the Chao Phraya River. The lights provide a beacon to the boat traffic on the still dark river below. Not all of the City of Angels shares this brightness, however.

At the slaughterhouse across the river, miles to the east in the city's largest slum area, Klong Toey, the sun is also just breaking over the horizon. Long shadows cast from two blocks of run-down apartments just to the east interrupt the first streams of light to find the rough concrete floor of the old structure. The building is open on the sides with only a sheet metal roof above to keep out the rain and a four-foot high, rusting, iron-railed fence around the pens to hold the pigs and secure the killing ground. Concrete gutters run down the sides so the blood not captured for pig's blood soup, and the other liquids expelled by the dying pigs, could drain down to the outlet. Water hoses used at the end of the night's slaughters ensure the waste washes completely through the gutters and the outlet drain and into the nearby canal. The canal itself is bordered by slum shacks which provide their own donations to its septic waters as it seeps into the Chaophraya River. It has rained the night before. The moisture hangs in the air and a mist rises from the wet concrete as the early morning sun warms the air. The rank odor of blood lingers and grows stronger with the warmth of the sun.

It is quiet now. The squealing of the pigs, the shouting of the laborers gaffing, slashing, killing and rendering the pigs ended hours before, around midnight. The trucks loaded with pig carcasses then immediately departed for the fresh markets throughout the city. Now there is the silence of dawn. Birds, magpies mostly, are hopping along the gutters and floors picking at loose remnants of flesh caught in the rough concrete. The rats, competing with the birds for the loose bits of flesh, are becoming more hesitant as the light slowly increases. They are dashing back to hide in holes in the drains, watching beady-eyed for moments, and then dashing back for another morsel to carry to their den. As the light intensifies, they will leave the killing ground to the birds and wait for the next night's slaughter to begin.

Twenty yards away, up the rough concrete ramp leading out of the slaughterhouse to the road above, commercial life is beginning to stir. The sidewalk vendors selling plates of rice, bowls of noodles, fried chicken and pork and morning snacks and drinks are setting up their stands and starting to cook the food the morning crowds, on their way to work in the city, would need. However, down below, one carcass still remains sprawled just inside the rusted rail of the pen nearest the exit to the road adjoining the slaughterhouse. The carcass is on its back, one leg sticking out under the lowest of the iron rails, a bare foot pointed towards the road above. It is the body of a tall, slim boy—a teenage boy. His corpse is nude and he is lying with his head thrown back and hands out to the side, his adolescent genitals exposed. The body seems posed for a crucifixion, awaiting a cross. His head is unnaturally thrown back probably due to the gash cutting almost completely through his throat. There is a gaff, one of those used to hook the pigs and pull them to the slashing, stuck in his mouth and his blood has drained out and pooled around his body. His eyes gaze up sightlessly, not squinting from the early morning sun. Except for the birds strutting their macabre dance around his body, there is no movement at all.

Chapter 2

Matt Chance squinted towards the lamp table next to his bed. His mobile phone was ringing. It was just seven AM. He had thought he could sleep late. His girl, Noi, had pleaded she was too busy at work to spend the night and had left him to himself. He doubted that was the only reason. They had had some disagreements of late. It seemed to be something about commitment. In any case, he had thought a late morning's sleep would be the consolation prize. Obviously that was not to be.

He grunted into the phone not quite ready to talk. The caller's tone was urgent, "Matt, it's me, Somchai. I need your help. Now."

This brought Matt awake. Somchai was an important friend, his coach in Muay Thai, really his mentor in all things Thai as he struggled to relearn what it meant to be Thai after spending all of his adult life in the West, and much of that as a U.S. Army Ranger serving in Iraq and Afghanistan.

Somchai had influenced Matt greatly as he sought to get his feet on the ground—physically, mentally and emotionally—after returning, burned out from the wars, to his mother's homeland. If Somchai was in need, Matt would respond.

"Matt, are you there?"

"It's okay, Coach, I'm awake. Where are you? What's wrong?"

"I'm down by the slaughterhouse in Klong Toey. I need you here, Matt. One of my boys has been killed."

Matt could hear the edge of panic in the coach's voice. The violence in the coach's life was the controlled violence of the ring. This killing, whatever it was, had unnerved him.

"Okay, Coach. I'm on my way. Twenty minutes or so."

Matt ran through the shower, brushed his teeth, skipped the shave and was actually outside in fifteen minutes, but it was still going to be a struggle through traffic to get from his mid-town condo to the slum area in which the slaughterhouse was located. He decided not to try driving and waved down a motorcycle taxi trusting the bike would cut through the chaotic rush hour traffic much faster. The motorcycle guy wasn't eager to go over to the slums until Matt offered to double his fare to one hundred twenty baht from the normal sixty baht. That did the job and Matt hopped on the back.

The adrenalin rush of weaving through the morning rush hour traffic, with Matt riding pillion trying to anticipate the driver's frantic twists and turns, ensured he was fully awake when they got to the slaughterhouse. As they pulled up to the entrance, Matt could see a crowd had formed on the street above the ramp which led down into the area of the holding pens. People were delaying their departure for work, pushing to get a look at the scene below, some eating the fried chicken and rice they had just purchased from the street vendors, and exchanging comments on what had possibly happened. Matt pushed through the crowd and came to a police barrier where a local cop from the Port Authority police station was keeping people back. Matt held up an ID for the Department of Special Investigation, DSI. The ID had been authorized for him by his DSI friend, Neung, a foreign officer buddy from their time together in U.S. Army Ranger training. The cop raised the barrier and waved Matt through.

The sun was higher in the sky now. The direct sunlight heated the pools of rainwater and the air was wet and carried the rancid odor of death. Matt walked down the concrete ramp. He could see some eight to ten people gathered next to one of the pig pens below including a foreigner, a fat older white man, dressed in baggy blue jeans and a rumpled T-shirt, who was yelling at the police and the officer in charge. As Matt approached, he could understand what the foreigner was upset about. He was shouting at the police for leaving the body uncovered for the crowd to gawk at. The officer in charge, probably the head of the Port Authority police station as the port was only a few hundred yards away and this area was within his jurisdiction, was standing stone-faced and not replying. Matt looked beyond the group and he could see the boy's nude body exposed to all. A couple of officers were in the act of covering the body with a sheet. All the senior police officer did, when the foreigner paused for breath, was to hold up his hand to signal the foreigner to stop for a second and then he nodded towards the boy's body. It was now covered and the two police officers who had covered it were standing aside. The foreigner looked towards the body, said, "Okay," threw up his hands and turned and stalked past Matt going back up the ramp.

Coach Somchai was at the edge of the group around the police officer and saw Matt walking towards him. Matt waved to him to step towards him so they could talk privately without the police overhearing. Matt gave Coach Somchai a respectful *wai*, hands clasped together in front of his face.

"Coach, what's happened? You said this is one of your boys?"

"It is, Matt. You know him. It's Yod. He was one of the boys from the Metta Home for street kids that we would see at the Muay Thai training camp. Somebody killed him and left his body here last night."

He nodded towards the pigpens. "He was only fifteen years old. He had no parents or at least none claiming him."

Matt asked Coach Somchai, "How did you get brought into this?"

"It was Tarn, the head house mom at the Metta Home. The police called her to come and identify the boy as they thought it might be one of her kids. She came down and identified him and then left immediately as she couldn't stand to see him like this. She phoned me right after and asked me to come down and talk with the police to make sure they treated the case with respect. She was afraid they would just say it was an amphetamine-related drug case and let it go at that. She swears the boy wasn't doing drugs, either buying or selling."

Matt nodded, "Well, I understand why the police would think that way, Coach. Even the motorbike guy who drove me over here asked me why I wanted to go anywhere near Jet Sip Rai. He said it was dangerous. He said it was just for people buying and using amphetamines or Ya Ba as he called it."

The nearby Jet Sip Rai slum was a strip of run-down housing built by squatters on land owned by the Port Authority. The slum was immediately adjacent to the port where truckers from all over Thailand came to pick up goods shipped in from abroad. The drivers brought Ya Ba from suppliers at the port to keep themselves awake for the long hauls up and down country delivering the goods. Pinning the cause of the murder on drugs would be the default mode of the police on any investigation in the port area as drugs were involved in ninety percent of their cases.

Matt looked back towards the crowd watching from the entrance to the slaughterhouse. "What about that guy?" he asked gesturing towards the foreigner up above the ramp who was still talking with the crowd.

"Oh, that's Father Paul. He's an American missionary priest who is in charge of the Metta Home. He got the call about the boy and came to see for sure that it was one of the boys from Metta. He's made his point here and talked to the crowd. He'll go home soon."

Sure enough as they watched, the priest stopped talking to the crowd and walked towards the van that had brought him to the slaughterhouse. A man wearing an Australian bush hat who had been recording his activities put away his camera and joined him.

Turning back to the death scene and pointing towards the police, Matt asked, "What do we do here, Coach?"

"Just join me in talking with the police colonel in charge, Matt. I want to let him know we have worked with the boy and haven't seen him involved in drugs at all. After being yelled at in public by the priest, I'm sure he's not in a good mood so we don't argue with him. Let's just try to plant a seed of doubt in his mind that we can exploit later."

"Okay, Coach. Lead the way."

Somchai turned and walked over to the officer and waited politely as the he gave some instructions to the police on the scene. The colonel finally turned to Somchai and Matt.

Somchai gave him a polite *wai* and started to introduce himself. He was interrupted, "No need to introduce yourself, Coach Somchai. I know who you are. I was a fan of your boxing. When I was younger my dad would take me to the

Lumpinee stadium. I saw you fight. You were a great champion. What can I do for you?"

Somchai was surprised and happy to be recognized. "Thank you, Colonel. It makes an old man feel good to be remembered."

Turning to Matt, Somchai introduced him. "Colonel, this is Kuhn Matt. He and I have been helping Krue Pip of the Penang 96 Muay Thai camp train some of the boys from the slum. This boy, Yod, was one of our boys. We want to find out what happened to him. He was not a Ya Ba boy, Colonel. He didn't use or sell amphetamines."

The officer didn't answer but looked at Matt for minute, studying him. Matt was used to this. As a *luuk krung*, literally half child, the name given to Thai with a Western parent, his appearance, Thai but not quite Thai, always caused a bit of a pause with a Thai audience.

Matt responded to the once over by showing respect, giving the policeman a *wai* and a traditional Thai, "*Sa wa di krup*," greeting with his hands clasped in front of his face.

The colonel, always conscious of his high position, returned a halfhearted *wai* and nodded back. After staring at Matt for a moment, the colonel said, "I believe I've heard of you, Khun Matt. You have friends in the DSI, I believe."

"I helped out the DSI last year as a consultant on a case where some American scientists went missing, but only as a consultant." Matt was playing it low key and humble knowing that anything that indicated that he felt he was important could cause offense.

"I think it was a bit more then consulting. I heard you were with the team that shot it out with the drug runners and finished them off. It was a good job. Well, both of you are welcome here but my officers have the situation in hand. The boy's throat was cut no more than four or five hours ago. It rained last night but this happened after the rain. As you can see he bled out here so it was done here. We are waiting for the medical examiner to arrive so that she can take charge of the body. Then we will learn more."

As he said this, a white van followed by a Mercedes coupe pulled up on the street above.

A camera truck from one of the TV stations pulled up at the same time.

"Ah, here she is now. It must have taken her a while to get her make-up and hair right and alert the press."

A slender woman in her mid-forties, dressed in black slacks and a pink shirt, stepped out of the Mercedes. True to the description, she looked ready for an audience: make-up just right and with a modish, almost punk hairdo, her short black hair mixed with patches tinted blond and swept up. At the same time, she projected a no-nonsense approach, pulling on a pair of rubber gloves as she walked down the ramp and calling behind her for her staff to bring a box of medical equipment down for her. This was the fashion-conscious, very PR-aware, but very competent and strong willed national medical examiner, Khun Wattana. From the second she was on the scene, she clearly considered herself in charge. Matt could tell by the body language of the police officer that he was not comfortable but was also not about to publicly challenge the lady.

The colonel turned for a last word to the Somchai and Matt, but nodded to the coach. "Let my officers perform their investigation. Any information they learn about this boy, whether Ya Ba was involved or not, as well as what this lady has to say, I will share with you. If you learn anything of substance from your contacts, please feel free to call me. Now if you'll excuse me, I will try to find common ground with this lady."

He walked towards the body but stopped short and waited for the medical examiner. Both just nodded to each other, no exaggerated formal respect was to be shown by these two. The medical examiner had locked horns with the police before, publicly disagreeing with their theories on murder cases too often. Both were aware that this case could be the occasion for more contention.

Matt turned to the coach. "Come on, Coach, let's get out of here. We can't do anything for Yod and these guys will find whatever there is to find here."

The coach nodded slowly and turned to follow Matt. He found the scene overwhelming. For Matt violent death had been too common a scene yet he found it overwhelming in different ways.

They stopped on the street above the entrance ramp. The crowd was still growing, especially now that a TV van had arrived. Matt took the coach by the arm and led him away from the crowd.

"What do you want me to do, Coach? The police will handle this."

"Matt, once the TV cameras go away the police will put this on the back burner. You heard what he said about Yod, 'this boy.' Yod is not important to them. The case will slowly disappear. You know how to do these things, Matt. You have friends in the Department of Special Investigation. You worked with them last year and helped to track down the yakuza gang. Ask some questions. Don't let them bury this."

Matt looked back at the scene, the TV truck and the crowd up above, the police and the medical examiner below. In a few hours the body would be gone, the pigs for the evening slaughter would start arriving on trucks from the countryside and the slaughterhouse would be back to its normal business. Three to four hundred pigs would be slaughtered by early morning and the cycle would go on.

"Okay, Coach. I'll try. Who do I talk to? Who will know about Yod?"

"Start with Tarn, the house mom at Metta. She should be there now waiting for a report from me. Go talk to her. I can't do it. This sort of violence is beyond me. You have experienced war and death. She should know about Yod. She is the one who got him off the street and back into school. I'll phone her and tell her to expect you."

Chapter 3

The slaughterhouse slum was built between a canal and a main cargo road, and it was a short, five-minute motorbike ride across that road and the adjacent railroad tracks to the Jet Sip Rai area next to the river. Jet Sip Rai slum was on a strip of land owned by the Port Authority. Forty or more years earlier during the Vietnam War, it was a large tract of undeveloped land, mostly swamp, which presented a great opportunity for the poorest of families to move in and squat there. The Port Authority had not fought the squatters much over the years, but now they had plans for development and were slowly pushing them off the land.

The Metta Home was the largest structure on a narrow street or soi. The soi was flanked by a series of rundown Chinese style shophouses. Stray dogs wandered the street. A walkway, too narrow for two people to walk side by side, ran over an open ditch filled with sewage and led to rows of shacks behind the main road.

As Matt arrived at the entrance to the Metta Home, there was a large number of young children, boys and girls aged six to twelve, all dressed in their school uniforms filing out to get into vans and go off to their various schools. All were laughing and joking with one another and peeking in curiosity at the stranger entering their home. It was a scene full of the children's joy of life and anticipation. A dramatic counterpoint to the vision of death and despair Matt had left behind just minutes before at the slaughterhouse. He felt somehow lighter and more hopeful just seeing the children. Ahead of him the principal building of the Metta Home was three stories tall with walls of concrete block. The exterior was painted a tan color, and it was built around an open courtyard. A slim forty-something woman dressed in black slacks and a white blouse was waiting just above the steps up to the entryway which led to the wide interior court yard of the building. As he walked up the steps she came forward and welcomed him.

"Are you Khun Matt?"

"Yes, and I guess you are Krue Tarn."

"Yes, Coach Somchai called and said you would be here and let me know what is happening about Yod. Please come inside and sit down."

Krue Tarn led Matt through a glass door on the side of the entranceway to the courtyard and into an office. There was a window looking out on the courtyard which had several trees, a small grass space and some tropical flower beds. It gave a calming air to the building amidst the bustle of the children heading out to school.

As he sat down and accepted a cup of tea from Krue Tarn, Matt looked around and thought it was like being back at school in the principal's office. Her office was quite clean and spare with pictures of children and paintings by children on the walls. On her desk was a stack of files Matt presumed to be case files of the children in the home.

Matt was still uncertain what was wanted of him with regard to the boy's death, so on the way over he had decided to probe a bit first to find out just what, besides the death of one of her wards, were the concerns of Krue Tarn. But first he thought he had best let her know he was acquainted with the boy.

"Krue Tarn, I should let you know I had met Yod and worked with him a few times at the Muay Thai camp at Penang 96. Coach Somchai is my teacher and he and I help out there at times with the coaching of the young boxers. My impression was that Yod was a good boy. He was not a natural at Muay Thai and lacked some confidence, but it seemed important to him so we all wanted to help him. I'm very sorry about his death."

"Thank you for that, Kuhn Matt, and thank you for coming now. You're right. Yod was not a confident boy. He had some serious issues like most of our children." She reached over and patted the top folder on the stack she had on her desktop.

"I can share with you some things about him we don't normally provide to the public. Now that he is gone, it won't matter and may help you understand my concern about how the police handle his death."

She took the top folder, laid it down on her desk, opened it and looked at it for a few seconds. Then she sighed heavily and looked up at Matt again.

"Many people refer to the Metta Home as an orphanage but that is not true. I would guess only about ten percent of our one hundred eighty kids are without any family. Most of our kids are here because they are not safe with whatever family they have come from or the family exists but has fragmented for differing reasons and cannot be found. We spend a lot of time, often years, and effort looking for extended families for the children and when we can we help them to go to that family situation."

She sat back in her chair and folded her arms across her chest in a way that seemed to emphasize the gravity of her words.

"Most of our kids come from abused or at-risk backgrounds. The court makes them our wards until a safe family situation can be found for them. Sometimes we get children as infants; sometimes they can be fourteen or fifteen years old. Yod came to us when he was ten years old. We found him in the Patpong bar area, he had been sitting outside a gay go-go bar begging, and one of the more responsible bar owners in the area, called us and asked us to come and take care of him. He didn't know what happened to his family just that he was in Lumpini Park and some bar workers on their way to work in Patpong took him along when he asked them for money for food."

She leaned forward now, not being dramatic but wanting Matt to listen and understand.

"We found that Yod had been sexually abused for some years, apparently by a male relative, who brought him to Bangkok and sold him to another man. Yod was afraid of the new man, saw a chance and ran away. We haven't had problems with Yod. He was happy here for the most part and happy to go to school. However, as you might imagine due to his treatment, Yod has had problems with himself. We try hard to control it but this can be a rough place in terms of the kids teasing and taunting each other. Some of the other boys at times called him gay and tried to get him to perform sex acts with them. We do have some gay boys here who band together, but Yod usually didn't join them. He was trying hard to prove he was a 'real man.' The Muay Thai training was part of that."

Matt felt as if he was swimming under water and couldn't find the surface. All of this was so far from his experience and reality that he couldn't find a frame of reference for it. He felt he had to reach out and grip something so he asked a question.

"Krue Tarn, I'm lost. Do you feel this is all somehow related to Yod's death?"

"I'm not sure. It may be. We understand that recently Yod has formed some kind of relationship with a man. What that relationship is we don't know, but Yod has had some money in his pocket, five hundred baht notes, that he didn't get from here. I learned of this from one of the other boys, a member of the gay group, who said Yod had shown him the money and said he had found a new friend. He said he had seen Yod and another boy from the local community talking with the man after school several times recently before coming back to the Metta Home at night. Then last night Yod didn't come home."

Matt was surprised at this turn, but at the same time felt a bit of relief.

"If that's the case, the police should be told. I'm sure they can track this man down and see if there is anything there."

Krue Tarn shook her head at Matt.

"No, you don't understand, Kuhn Matt. It will be just the opposite. The officers in charge of the port police station have been friendly to us, but the police here are not trained to handle crimes against children. They most probably don't want to bother with this case already because it's just one of 'those people.' One of our kids, who have no value because everyone believes they must have done something terrible in the last life to be born into such misery in this life. The police, at least those not specially trained to deal with sexually abused or trafficked children, for the most part don't want to be associated with our kids in any way. Most of the people of Bangkok feel the same way. This belief is one of the little discussed dark sides of our religion that prevents people from caring for poor or abused children except from a great distance. Also, if the police hear about Yod getting money from outside, they will just assume he was hired to run Ya Ba for one of the drug dealers infesting this place, that he took too much of the product himself and got into some crazy fight ending in his death. It'll be just another reason to write him off."

Matt was getting schooled on life in the slums and he wasn't really comfortable with it. Once the lady had laid things out, he knew she was probably right, but he didn't see a path for him to be of any use.

"Krue Tarn, I accept what you say, but what do you want me to do that the police can't or won't do? Also I saw this foreign man you work with, Father Paul, down at the slaughterhouse. Doesn't he have the connections to push for a complete investigation?"

Tarn laughed, a quietly disappointed laugh. "I'm afraid Father Paul's connections are that he has managed to offend most of the police and high officials in this district over the years. They don't like being corrected, especially not in public. You saw him at the slaughterhouse. Was he pointing out to the police what was wrong on the scene while a video was being made?"

"Well, yes."

"I don't think he'll be involved further. Actually to give him his due, his public activities are a great help in attracting donations from overseas donors."

"Oh."

Now Krue Tarn's face softened. "Yes, oh. That's the way it is. Let's not worry about it."

She shifted back in her chair, her eyes boring into Matt. "Kuhn Matt, Yod was abused enough as he came into life. I don't want his departure from this life to be the source of more abuse. He didn't do drugs. He was afraid of drugs. He wouldn't do anything to hurt another creature. You saw him in training. That is why he wasn't good at Muay Thai. He just didn't have the spirit to attack another. He was a sweet boy."

Then, remembering from Coach Somchai's description of Matt being a Muay Thai student and coach, as well as a former combat soldier, she apologized. "I'm sorry. I hope I didn't offend you."

Matt smiled at the irony, all his life, since his father's death at the age of eleven, he had been looking for people to praise his warrior spirit and now someone was apologizing for saying he might have one.

"It's okay, Krue Tarn. I understand not everyone likes Muay Thai as a sport, but sports are a very good way to help young people build their self-respect. From what you say that was a real need for Yod."

Krue Tarn nodded but she was not a lady to drift off the subject and she came back to Matt to push for what she felt she needed from him.

"Kuhn Matt, what would help is if you could just ask a few questions following in Yod's footsteps these past days. I am not just concerned about what people will say about Yod, I am also concerned our other teenage boys may be at risk. You can talk with our boys; they may be more responsive to you as a man and a coach than to me as a woman. Ben was the boy who said Yod showed him the money he was given. We should find out who Yod was seeing and what they wanted of him. Can you at least ask around about these things? People here in the slum respect the Muay Thai coaches, Coach Somchai and Krue Pip. You can use their names. People will talk to you."

Matt found himself nodding yes. This was a strong-willed lady behind the pleasant exterior.

"Okay, Krue Tarn. I'll do my best."

Chapter 4

The location of the meeting later that morning was one of the many safe houses used by the spy agency in the general Bangkok area. It was located in Pak Kret, an area that until recently was considered a country area, across the Chao Phraya River and out of reach from central Bangkok making it a relatively safe location. Formerly, the quickest way to the area from Bangkok was to drive to a ferry located on the east side of the river. It would take you to a pier adjacent to a temple across the river and you could then take a motorbike to whatever location you wanted. The recent completion of a nearby bridge made it easier and quicker to gain access to the area by car. Now, even though a small building boom was in progress, the safe house was still relatively isolated and useful. The house, surrounded by a banana plantation tended to by farmers in the area, was unimposing and fit into the country scene. It was two stories, had a front courtyard with a small fountain in the middle and was surrounded by a concrete block wall six feet high topped with broken glass. There were security cameras on the corners of the house, not unusual for homes of those with a bit of wealth in a secluded area.

The meeting was between two key people in the operation, code-named Desert Breeze. Bashir Bechara was Lebanese and Sunni Muslim by birth. His given name meant the educated one. Today, he was meeting with the head operative and the man with overall responsibility for Desert Breeze, Jake Chavez.

In an organization addicted to pseudonyms, cover stories and names and nicknames, both men had alternate tags. Bashir was known as the "Camel Driver" in reports, simply because the agent he was running was named Hamel, whose cover name was "The Camel." Thus, Bashir became the "Camel Driver." The handful of people involved with the operation found the nickname humorous. Both of those tags were used as cover IDs in official correspondence. Bashir, who worked as a private businessman in Thailand, was not an employee of the organization, but operated under the status of an unwilling contractor. Several years earlier, while conducting export-import business between Thailand and the Middle East, he had been providing various favors for jihadi groups using Thailand as a place to meet or transit. While he was not trusted with any key operations information, the jihadis considered him sympathetic and a useful fixture on the Thai scene, which was an important place for meetings, support documents, equipment and occasional money laundering. Over the years, Bashir had earned the trust of various new jihadi groups as he assisted their requests in these areas. Unfortunately, while attempting to smuggle in some drugs from Pakistan as part of his import business, the Thai police had caught him. Documents of intelligence value related to possible terrorist activities had also been found in his bags and the police had informed the intelligence services, and they had quietly taken the matter to an international ally. After some discussion, it was decided that Bashir could be useful as a double agent if allowed to continue his activities in place. Though at first reluctant, Bashir soon became enthusiastic when confronted with the alternative: a painful interrogation and death.

The man Bashir was meeting, Jake Chavez, was officially known in communications about the operation simply as COS or Chief of Station. However, though it was not official, he too was known by a different name. Behind his back, he was called "The Snake." All his colleagues knew his reputation for treachery, both within and without the organization. He was not a popular man but his bosses in Langley valued that he got the job done, no matter how dirty, or especially if it was dirty. If there was collateral damage in his operations, and there always seemed to be, it was really not a concern to him or his bosses as long as the damage was a long way from Washington, D.C., and covered under the guise of plausible deniability.

The Snake was waiting, drinking coffee, seated at a table in what was the dining area of the house. He was going over some papers as the man known as the Camel Driver walked up to a security guard, was patted down for weapons and then proceeded through the front door of the safe house. The Snake didn't bother to get up, but waved the other man to a chair opposite him. He pointed to a carafe of coffee on the table.

"Good morning, Bashir. Would you like some coffee?"

"Thanks, Jake, I would. It's been a busy few days."

Bashir was referring to the activities surrounding the Camel's visit from Pakistan.

"Well tell me about it. What is the status with your friend?"

Bashir put a folder on the table. "His first need was twenty new blank passports—here are copies of the passports. They all have the new tracking tags inserted. We provided copies of Philippine passports this time. Not difficult for the people here to do."

"What else?"

"We are also providing mobile phones. I will give him the special ones provided by your staff. I am meeting him tomorrow afternoon to arrange for the pickup tomorrow night. He is on a plane back to Pakistan the next day."

"Where are you meeting him?"

"At a restaurant on Soi Arab. He is staying nearby at the Grace Hotel as usual. He feels he is more easily lost in the crowd of Arab customers there. Also, the Pakistani Embassy is just across the street. I believe he has an intelligence contact there."

"Has he had any special demands or requirements?"

"No, just the usual. Like many of these people who so publicly practice their religion at home, he likes the nightlife here and feels this is one place he can indulge himself without worrying about what his more religiously strict companions in Pakistan might think. I don't get directly involved, but have made some calls to get him what he wants. We made a secluded private home available to him for his activities. He has always been discreet. He loves his trips here too much to jeopardize them in any way."

The Snake looked at Bashir. Letting the silence build. It was one of his favorite tactics. If people had something to be nervous about, silence somehow made them more nervous. After a few minutes, the Snake picked up the file and looked through it.

"He made no mention of special days coming up, anniversaries such as 9/11 to be celebrated, anything like that?"

"No, though he is still hinting at a special meeting to be held here in a couple of months. Apparently he has been told to organize a safe place to bring some fellow jihadis from Indonesia and the Philippines for instruction. Nothing has been decided or fixed though."

"How about his payment for the services you provide? Is he still providing drugs as well as cash?"

"Yes, he delivered both at the pickup transfer point after his arrival. He doesn't question the cost of these things. He is much more concerned about the quality of the goods we provide. He also has stopped pushing me to identify the sources of the documents and equipment here in Thailand. This time he provided more drugs than before and less cash and said that would continue to be the case. Apparently one or more of their international sponsor nations are becoming somewhat squeezed for cash and trying to substitute the drugs in all their black activities as payment in kind. As you directed, I didn't resist. I told him it was okay and that I would find routes to unload the drugs. I followed up and delivered the packages as you told me."

"Okay, Bashir. Good work. Let me know if anything special happens and confirm once the pickup is made and once he has left country. When you talk with him, I want you to focus on the meeting of overseas jihadis here in country. Let him know you can't expect to make secure arrangements for him and his guests if he lets things go to the last minute. Got it?"

Bashir nodded and got up and left. He was always relieved when a meeting with the Snake was over. This snake was not the kind to give warning before striking and though he himself had been spared so far, he had heard how deadly the Snake's strike could be when he felt he was being crossed. Their relationship was based on Bashir's fear of the man and what he might do. There was no room for small talk or the slightest opposition.

Chapter 5

Matt had gone back home and finished cleaning up after he left the Metta Home. Then he decided he would go on to his office and try and gather his thoughts. His workplace was in a high-rise office and condominium building with an upscale shopping complex on the first six floors. He really hadn't wanted it—his work as a part-time training consultant to the National Forestry Department and National Parks Authority didn't necessitate it—but his mother insisted on it as a matter of family face. Matt's mother, Lek, had met and fallen in love with Matt's father Rick Chance, a case officer for the CIA, when she had worked as a translator for the Embassy while studying at Chulalongkorn University.

Unfortunately for Lek, her lover, Matt's father, though on an unaccompanied assignment, had a wife and two children in the U.S. When Lek became pregnant, she defied her family's wishes and had the baby out of wedlock. The situation caused an uproar at the Embassy when Rick Chance acknowledged the boy was his child, in an effort to ensure paperwork would be processed to guarantee his son could someday have a U.S. passport. He achieved his goal, but was immediately reassigned out of Thailand to the Middle East Division of the Agency. Lek had never married, raising Matt by herself. Rick Chance had found ways to return and visit her and Matt over the years until he was killed in the Iranian-sponsored bombing of the U.S. Embassy in Beirut in April of 1983 when Matt was eleven years old.

Lek finished school and working on her own, starting with some family properties she shared, invested in real estate. As Bangkok had boomed over the years, she had done quite well and had an ownership interest in the building housing Matt's office. So following her wishes, Matt came to have an office with an upmarket Sukhumvit Road address overlooking a small park. Now, going over the events of the morning, he leaned back in his chair and looked out the window at the children running in the playground in the park below and tried to gather his thoughts.

Coach had said Matt was more accustomed to violent death, but it wasn't true. Coach was wrong. You never become accustomed to violent death. You just learn to control your outer reactions. Of course it mattered if the death was that of the enemy or if it was the death of one or more of your buddies. The death of the "bad guys" was not a cause for mourning but one for relief, though there were those who celebrated, sometimes in morbid ways. The emotional impact of the death of buddies could be very strong and would never go away. However, seeing the helpless, sprawling nude body of the young boy had shocked Matt and the picture stuck in his mind. This wasn't right. This wasn't combat. Kids were supposed to be protected, not slaughtered. Matt felt a growing anger. Coach and Krue Tarn were right. From the beginning, through the accident of birth, an innocent boy had been denied any opportunity for a happy life. To some extent with the early loss of his own father, Matt could identify with that. At the very least, Matt could help ensure Yod's death had some meaning by helping catch those who did this to him and protecting the other boys who might be targeted for this sort of treatment.

Matt had interviewed the boy at Metta— the one Krue Tarn identified as Yod's friend who had knowledge of his after school habits. Matt had picked up something to work with. Ben had identified the older man he had seen Yod talking with, and who might have been the source of the money Yod had been flashing, as a local man called Uncle Choi. That was all the boy knew or was saying. Matt had no idea who this man was and how he fit into the scene. Through his past cooperation with the DSI, Matt had some knowledge of transnational crime figures in Thailand. But the local crime scene—drugs, local mafias controlling crime—was not an area Matt had real knowledge of.

He needed help on this matter and he thought he knew the first place to go. There was a private investigator, an older American who was one of those left over from the Vietnam

War. His name was John Scales. His military service had been in the 7th Special Forces, a group involved early on in Vietnam and then eventually moved to operations in Laos when the 5th Special Forces took over the responsibility for assisting the involvement in Vietnam of anti-Communist groups, specifically the Hmong hill tribe people.

John had stayed on after the war and retired in Thailand from the military. Many of his old contacts had become generals and in one case he was working with a general who was the son of one of them. He found himself called on to consult and often mediate on issues where the military became involved with civilians or the police. He was associated with a Thai law firm and both he and the firm had become accepted as impartial mediators. He also had assisted the Thai police in identifying who the criminals new to Thailand were, as the migration of mafias from around the world to Thailand had taken place over the past thirty years. John was "old school" exposure for Matt, and Matt found he liked it. One time he had invited John to accompany him on a visit to the Kaeng Krachan National Park while he carried out a training contract he had from the National Parks authority to work with the park rangers and develop their land navigation skills. John had insisted on driving and the primary CDs he had brought along for the two and a half hour drive were Joe Cocker and the Rolling Stones though he did throw in some John Handy to keep Matt off balance. That was John. Matt had anticipated him and brought along a couple of his favorites, Santana and Dire Straits, which John accepted. None of Matt's alternative sounds would have been allowed.

Now Matt called John, gave him some background and asked for a quick meeting pleading the urgency of the case. An hour later they were meeting in the Starbucks on the lower level of Matt's office building.

John was waiting for him when Matt went to the coffee shop. Matt was on time. John had a habit of arriving early and casing the scene, even for meetings with friends. John was five ten, thinning gray hair but still slim and fit-looking. His physical and mental discipline had carried over from his military days and he projected a quiet, controlled manner. That manner appealed to Matt. He was always uncomfortable with people who felt they had once been something and insisted on letting you know about it.

As the lunch rush had passed, the coffee shop was only half full. There was space to talk. Matt sat down across from John, thanked him for coming, gave him a synopsis of the case and stated his problem.

"John, I'm more than a bit out of my depth here. If this was a case of tracking someone in the jungle or the mountains or somehow related to combat or even transnational crime, I would feel more comfortable. I know nothing about the local drug scene, abused kids and local mafias selling drugs and using kids, any of it. I don't even know where to start with this guy Choi the kid mentioned. What do I do? Go around looking for him? Where do I look? Should I confront him directly? How do I take this on? I guess what I'm saying is how would you proceed?"

John leaned back and sipped his coffee giving Matt a bit of an amused look.

"Slow down, cowboy. This isn't all that hard, it will take a bit of work, but for sure you don't need to fix bayonets and charge, much as that seems to be more in line with your experience."

Matt was forced to laugh. This military style language and direct approach was a great help. None of his Thai contacts would have called him "cowboy" to point out his inexperience concerning the task he was undertaking. They would have danced around the subject and have just shown sympathy by saying it would be a difficult job.

John went on, "Listen, you've proven both in the military and here with your part in the operation against the yakuza last year that you know how to think on your feet. You can do this. The first thing to do in looking for someone, especially if you're working a murder case, is to get as much background as you can before you try bumping into anyone who may be directly involved. There are a large number of dangerous people in this town and they may be doubly dangerous if you involve them in a surprise confrontation. In this case, don't start by looking for this guy Choi right off the bat. Start by speaking with people who might have some background on him. Can you think of any of your contacts in the slum or contacts of Coach Somchai who might have some background to share?"

"Well, yeah, I have just met him a few times, but Coach Somchai knows Krue Pip, the head guy at the Penang 96 training camp in the Klong Toey slum pretty well. They are the same age and go back over thirty years in the Muay Thai world. Krue Pip grew up in the slum. He would know most everybody and where they fit in. I think he would be open with me if I approached him along with Coach Somchai."

"Okay, why don't you start there? Also, Matt, you said you talked with the boy at the Metta Home who knew Yod and said this guy Choi had given Yod money. Is that right?"

Matt immediately saw where John was going with this and felt a bit uncomfortable. John was pointing out his interrogation of the boy might not have been complete.

"Well yeah, he said Choi would sometimes visit a computer games shop where the boys would go after school and he saw Yod talking with him a couple of times. After the second time, he said Yod showed him some money Choi gave him."

"Did you ask the boy you talked with if he or any of the other boys had been given any money by Choi?"

"Yeah, I did and he said no."

"You might go back and double-check this with Tarn the house mom and then again with the boy. It's very probable that he or some of the other boys had taken money and had some idea of what Choi wanted, but he didn't want to say so to you. The boy felt relieved when you finished questioning him. It was easy to finger Yod, but he could be in trouble if he said he took money or identified some of the other boys. Go back and check that out. On a second interrogation people are often afraid you found out they didn't give the whole story the first time. Handle it right and if he has more, it will come out."

John paused to let this basic interrogation primer sink in and see how Matt was taking it. Matt just nodded. Then John went on.

"Right, now let me give you a little background on the name which might help put this guy into perspective. Choi is a Chinese name and in this case it's a somewhat unflattering

Teochew dialect nickname. That indicates this guy is part of the extended Teochew Chinese sect resident along the Bangkok waterfront. You know Thailand is fifteen percent Chinese and for the most part have not assimilated. From generation to generation many stay within their clan groups.

"The Teochew community speaks its own dialect of Chinese and comprises roughly half of the Chinese population in Thailand. The biggest financial and agricultural corporations in Thailand are family organizations with a Teochew background. At the same time, a Teochew family also leads the biggest mafia on the Klong Toey waterfront. The leader is known simply as Black Chan or Black Face. The nickname of course is never used with him directly; it comes from the wine colored skin patches that cover much of his face and upper body."

John paused and Matt took the chance to voice a bit of the rising dismay he had been feeling.

"So, John, what you're telling me is that looking for this boy's killer may well involve some confrontation with a local mafia?"

John shook his head sympathetically and said, "I'm afraid that may be the case. If it happened in the Klong Toey slum area, it happened on their turf. There must be some involvement or point of contact within the gang. Check it out but be very careful when you are doing the checking. These guys are dangerous, and down on their own territory, along the port, even the police don't want to take them on if it can be avoided."

Matt sat back, shook his head and laughed without a smile. "Nothing's easy, is it?"

"Yeah, nothing's easy. Matt, go ahead and take the first steps. Find out what the background is and then we can talk again. Definitely don't go around trying to find this guy Uncle Choi directly. He may find you first, and that could be a problem."

"Okay, thanks, John. You've given me a couple of starting points and a lot to think about. I'll check back with you."

"Anytime, Matt. Be careful. I wish I could give you more, help but I don't kid myself that I can still operate on the street anymore. You can do this. I've got to go now, but I'll be available if you need me."

John left and Matt sat staring at his coffee trying to sort out what his next step should be.

Chapter 6

Noi was the one with the busier schedule, or at least a schedule driven by clients, so unless it was a special occasion, Matt would defer to her on where and when they would meet for dinner. Tonight she had opted for a light dinner at a noodle restaurant set in an open area off a hallway in the basement of the Erawan Hotel. The restaurant was called You & Mee. It had one of her favorite meals, *Khao Soi*, thick white egg noodles and chicken in a curry sauce with coconut milk.

The relationship with Noi had endured a year and a half now, about a year longer than any of Matt's previous relationships. Of course in his previous life in the military, many times not spending more than a year in one place, contributed to that. But also Matt had partially bought in to the old military joke: if the army had wanted you to have a wife they would have assigned you one. He really felt he had to have his mind free when going into combat. It was tough enough in the field without going nuts over an unfaithful girlfriend or wife back in the States as he had seen happen with soldiers many times. Now however things were different. He was, for the first time since he was a teenager, settled down.

It had been a good relationship from the very beginning, but his activities assisting on the case involving the Japanese mafia, the yakuza, the previous year had put some strains on the relationship. Matt had tried to shield Noi from much of the violence that had occurred, but he couldn't hide from her he had been shot in an assassination attempt while going to meet one of his contacts on the case. He was able to blame the attempt on his life on a drug gang that had been put out of business by the Thai military, thus ending any further threat, but for Noi it had still come as a real shock. For her the world of violence was something encountered in movies. Though it was not discussed, he also got the impression from little things she'd said that her dating experience at school in Australia had exposed her to some men who were quick to fight and she was very uncomfortable with it. Noi shared in the Buddhist belief in the sanctity of life. Her first reaction to Matt being wounded was very strongly protective and caring, which moved Matt deeply. After he had healed and as they put the incident behind them, she had let him know on several occasions his past life of violence was one she was very uncomfortable with. In any case, the unspoken request was for no more such events.

Noi was even a bit unnerved with Matt helping coach the slum kids in Muay Thai. Buddhists believe *those kids* must have done something wrong in the last life to be born into this life with such problems. This was a very conventional view held by many amongst middle and upper class Thai society. It was a self-serving belief for those who also saw their success in this life as proof of how good a life they had led in a past incarnation. The culture did not encourage reaching out to the poor in any way. The major Thai assistance program to the poor is for the rich to buy their votes at election time.

Now Matt was worried she would react negatively when he told her he had committed to helping find out the facts behind whatever had led to the death of the boy. At the same time, he needed to be open with her. Clearly with Noi, deception was the biggest possible sin. She would forgive many things but wanted honesty, possibly the hardest thing to give at times.

Matt arrived early and found a corner table where their conversation would be less exposed to those sitting around. Noi arrived on time, which Matt appreciated. For the Thai in general, and especially Thai women, time was relative and being twenty or thirty minutes late for an appointment was par for the course. Noi had gone to university in Australia. Possibly due to her education overseas or her involvement in managing her own computer software business, Noi was usually on time. She also had the nice principle of forgetting about work the minute she sat down. Today she was sporting the professional look, but it was the business professional look not the government or totally buttoned down business suit big corporate look: black slacks, a white blouse open at the collar with a loose blue scarf that passed for a tie, black shoes with low heels. She had clothes sense and one of the things she had done for Matt was to help him discover that cargo pants might be fine for the jungle but not necessarily for everyday use. Other touches had followed and Matt had watched his makeover and bought into it with a detached sense of amusement. As always between the sexes though, the question was how far the makeover could go. In a sense, it was going to be part of the conversation tonight.

Matt smiled as Noi arrived and sat down. Actually Matt smiled whenever Noi was around. As he had confessed to her at one point, she was good medicine for him no matter what was worrying him, she arrived and he smiled. All things suddenly seemed manageable. She smiled back when Matt said hello.

"Hi, babe, you look great. You have the young professional look down, but still with a personal touch."

"Thanks. It's been a busy couple of days. I haven't had time to add any special touches. You've been busy, too. I want to hear about it. Let's get some noodles and catch up."

Matt called over a waitress and they both ordered. As the waitress left, Matt looked down for a second to gather his thoughts. Before he could speak, or possibly because he didn't know where to start, Noi prompted him.

"What's worrying you? It seems like you've got something big on your mind."

"Well, I've got something going that's a bit out of the norm. Let me run it by you."

Matt recapped his day starting with his morning wake-up call from Coach Somchai and going through his afternoon meeting with Jack Scales. Noi put her hand to her mouth and said a soft "Ohhh" when Matt described the scene with Yod lying in the pigpen with his throat cut. Matt didn't tell her Yod was nude or any other details. She would see the press reports the next day. Enough was enough for now.

Then a smiling waitress walked up with the dishes they had ordered. This was enough to restore a sense of normality to their talk and break the depressing mood.

Noi was overwhelmed by Matt's story, but managed a rueful smile. "Well, I think I've lost my appetite, but let's be practical and eat first. Maybe with a full stomach, we'll think better."

For Noi, eating was a serious business not to be bothered with conversation. They both addressed their meal in silence with Matt more or less playing with his food. When confronted with problems, he tended to lose his appetite. Amazingly, for such a slim woman, nothing deterred Noi's appetite. When the food was finished, the waitress refilled their drinks, ice tea for both of them. Matt watched Noi, apprehensive as to what her response would be. He wanted her support but he knew she wouldn't be comfortable with his diving back into the black world again.

Noi picked up her drink and sipped on it slowly, looking at Matt over the rim of the glass. Then she set it down just as slowly. One of the things Matt greatly appreciated about her was her analytic mind. She might be uncomfortable with his brushes into the underworld, but she could put that aside when he asked for her help and put her very organized, businesslike mind to work. This she did now.

"You've been asked by Coach Somchai and Krue Tarn to help and you said you would?"

"Yes."

"They both think you are in the best position, outside of the police, who may not be fully motivated, to get to the truth of the boy's death?"

"Yes."

"And you take your promise to these people seriously?"

"Yes."

"Are you qualified to do this? It's more like police work than anything."

"Not really, you're right. I will need friends like John and Neung to help out."

"Whether qualified or not, you are going to give it a try because you keep your word?"

"Yes, and I think the boy deserves to have someone care about what happened to him."

"Well then, we know the answer don't we, Matt? Just be sure to call on all the help you can, okay? I don't want to provide any more after-action nursing service. I like my heroes healthy."

Matt, knowing it was possibly the wrong response, couldn't help himself and smiled broadly. "But your nursing service was so good."

Noi shook her head as if she was dealing with a child, but couldn't help but smile back. "I think I'm out of practice. Should we have a refresher course?"

Matt knew he wasn't completely off the hook on getting involved with investigating Yod's murder but was relieved, for now, things were okay. She would back his play. He nodded enthusiastically.

"Let's do that."

Chapter 7

The next day Bashir Bechara, the man known as the Camel Driver, was waiting inside the coffee shop on Soi Arab off the main Sukhumvit Road. He was sipping an espresso and smoking a hookah. The soi was crowded with coffee shops and restaurants selling halal food to Middle Eastern customers.

It was two twenty PM and he had been waiting for twenty minutes for his contact to keep the appointment. He was not happy. The Camel Driver was in his mid-forties, medium height, substantially overweight and with a medium complexion; he had a Middle Eastern appearance including a carefully trimmed beard. His Lebanese background was useful in that, depending on how he presented himself, he could be considered acceptable to all parties involved in the Middle East conflicts and terrorist activities as a fellow traveler and support person. In reality, he was a successful merchant who was always on the lookout for ways to squeeze some extra money out of whatever transactions came his way. He had no religious or political agenda other than the promotion of Bashir Bechara.

Finally, the man he was was waiting for appeared and took the seat opposite him. Hamel Fahan was in his mid-thirties, thin, medium height, dark complexion with a moustache, goatee and a hooknose giving him a strong appearance though his rimless eyeglasses offset it to some extent. His identity documents said he was Jordanian, but he was actually a Saudi by birth and had denied his home country long ago. When they first met, Hamel asked what he should call him. The Camel Driver had responded with a joke; one emphasizing both of their security concerns, "Just call me *habibi*," this is an Arab term of endearment between lovers or very close friends. Then, after Hamel had laughed politely at his joke, he told him it was okay to call him Bashir as this was the name he was known by with their common friends.

"You're late, Hamel. It's not a good habit."

Hamel delivered a soft rebuke. "Ahh, Bashir, my friend, you forget about the obligation to pray. I was called to pray and came as soon thereafter as possible."

"This will be our last meeting on this trip. Have all the arrangements of the past few days worked out as you desired?"

"All has gone well, my friend, as usual you are efficient and thorough, especially on the personal details. Thank you for your help."

"Well I am happy to say all the items requested have been produced and are ready for your pickup this evening."

Bashir slid a piece of paper and a key across the table.

"Here is the house number and the key to the front door. Go alone after seven PM. No one will be there but we will have it under observation for security purposes. The outside gate will be closed yet unlocked. Go right in. After you unlock the door to the house, leave the key in the door. The package will be on a table just inside the door. Take it and go. There will be a white scarf tied to one of the bars on the bottom of the gate as a safety sign. If it's not there, don't stop, keep going. You can contact me at the emergency number and I will provide a secondary place for the pickup."

Hamel didn't speak. He just nodded, picked up the key and paper, got up and walked away.

Chapter 8

Matt arranged with Coach Somchai to meet at the Klong Toey market, a major source of fresh seafood, meat and vegetables for restaurants in central Bangkok. From there they would walk over together to the Muay Thai training camp in the slum area called Penang 96. Matt had learned on his first visit Penang 96 was a very different world from the Bangkok he knew. The camp exists in the crowded squalor of slum huts and open sewage drains under an overhead expressway and alongside dirty train tracks, in the poorest area of the sprawling city of eleven million people. Coach explained the camp is home to a tribe of warriors whose training for combat starts early in life and never ends. It's a family-oriented clan and passes the warrior tradition down from generation to generation. In all cases these families have no wealth other than this golden tradition.

The members of this group have homes, albeit for the most part these are squatter's slum shacks. They work at a variety of basic labor and security jobs and the children go to school every day. But the training ground is very much the center of their existence and identity. The training ground is a small lot no more than sixty feet wide and ninety feet long. It's surrounded by a chain link fence and has some rough concrete toilets built in a corner at one end. At the other end, taking up almost the full width, is the boxing ring, standard size, three feet above ground with a fence of ropes around the sides. This has been the training ground for generations of Muay Thai devotees and the home of champions.

On the walk over, Coach Somchai provided Matt more information on the background of Krue Pip.

Coach explained the family angle was important. Krue Pip was now in his late-fifties, but over thirty years ago he was a competition fighter taking on the best in Thailand at the famed

43

Lumpinee Muay Thai stadium, the pinnacle of Muay Thai competition in Thailand. After retiring, he trained his son, Be, and others, mostly relatives, some starting to learn as young as the age of ten. Now Be is in his thirties, working as a security guard and Krue Pip is training, along with many others, his granddaughter, Ink, who is fourteen and has won a national championship in a children's Muay Thai competition, as well as his grandson, Chuan, who is thirteen. There were certainly more offspring and more championships in the offing. Coach Somchai told Matt to let him do the talking. Krue Pip, even though Matt had come down and helped out before, would be more open to being questioned by a man his own age.

As they approached, Matt saw that there were around fifteen teenage children working out on the dozen or so large dilapidated kick bags hanging from four iron frames set up around the gym grounds. The ground itself was rubber covering over the concrete. In an effort to emulate the composite floor covering of modern gyms, they had cut up old truck tires available from a cross-country truck lot nearby and flattened them out as much as possible, making a floor for the gym to protect the children to some extent when they took falls. The tires were not flattened very well and it would be easy to trip on edges and bumps when just walking around the gym.

Today there were six older males, most in their fifties, in attendance sitting on the side, former fighters, all now carrying excessive weight and no longer in the boxing form they were once were. One older guy looked to be in his sixties and wearing Muay Thai trunks and gear was sparring and playing around with the kids. He had a punched-out look and manner, both gruff and kindly, that reminded Matt of the trainer for Rocky Balboa in the motion picture series.

They stopped at the open gate entrance to the camp and Krue Pip saw them from inside the chain link fence. He gave a big smile and *wai* to Coach Somchai and Matt and walked over to greet them.

"Good to see you, Coach. You want to work with some of the boys today?"

Coach Somchai laughed; Krue Pip worked nonstop at getting help for his efforts at Penang 96, whether it was financial assistance or help in kind such as coaching from Coach Somchai or Matt.

"Thank you, Krue Pip, but today I'm afraid we have a different mission. We were wondering if you had some boys from the Metta Home training nowadays."

Krue Pip tilted his head to the side, his body language more on the negative side.

"Yeah, we have a couple of boys who come over from Metta but they are not consistent. Apparently they don't have a man in the home to help keep them focused. We welcome them and help them to get equipment, but without a consistent effort they won't really make any progress."

He waved over to the boys training, "There aren't any boys from Metta here today."

Coach Somchai nodded and said, "That's why we're here. One of the boys was named Yod. You remember him?"

"I heard he's the boy they found over in the slaughterhouse, right? That's lousy. Yeah, he was a good boy, but not really meant for boxing. These are great kids we've got here, but they're tough kids. Yod was a bit soft hearted. Frankly some of the boys thought he was a bit gay and was just trying to prove something to himself."

"That may have been right. We're not sure. The lady in charge at Metta, Krue Tarn, asked us to try and find out any background we could on how the boy ended up being killed. Did he have any problems here or was he mixed up in anything that you thought was wrong?"

"No, like I said, he was good boy. Just a bit too soft for all this." The last said as Krue Pip nodded at the boys intensely kicking bags and sweating.

Matt, as bad as the behavior of interrupting two seniors talking would be, was tempted to interrupt and get to some more pointed questions, but Coach Somchai saved him.

"Have there been any outsiders hanging around trying to talk with the boys? We heard Yod was seen talking with an older man outside one of the video game shops in Jet Sip Rai a few days before his death."

Krue Pip was a veteran, not just of the Muay Thai world, but also of fifty plus years in the slum. He knew where Coach

Somchai was going. He lifted his head and looked his old friend straight in the eyes. To most people he would have said no and ended the conversation. To Coach Somchai, after a pause and with a bitter smile, he said, "Do you mean that old asshole Choi?"

Coach Somchai nodded and his expression showed his thanks for Krue Pip's friendship and trust in him. Giving out information in the slum could be dangerous. Krue Pip was taking a big step for him.

"Yeah, that's the name we were given. What makes him an asshole?"

Krue Pip laughed, a disgusted laugh.

"He's part of the Black Face gang. He could be doing anything. He handles Ya Ba, the crazy medicine, and tries to get young boys, ten years old or so, to deliver the packages for him. He never gets caught, only the people he uses get caught and they are scared to say anything for fear of what Black Face will do to their families. He also has some connection to the sex trade. He came around here once, about a year ago, and tried talking to our kids after practice." Waving towards the group of former fighters sitting on the side, he added, "We told him directly that this neighborhood and our kids were off limits for his efforts and to never come back. We haven't seen him since."

Coach Somchai nodded. "You did the right thing. We have to protect the kids."

Looking to Matt, he told Krue Pip, "My young friend Matt here is going to try and find out what's behind what happened to Yod. Please let us know if you hear more about this guy Choi or anything about Yod."

Krue Pip nodded quietly and looked over to include the older men sitting on the sidelines watching the boys training, "We will."

Then he smiled as he asked for some payback. "Next week on Wednesday, we have several new boys coming in for a beginner's camp. Would you like to come down and help us get them started?"

Both Matt and Coach Somchai laughed at being put in a position where they couldn't say no. Coach Somchai answered for the two of them.

"We'll be here. We're looking forward to it."

With that they waved goodbye and started walking away. As they walked, Coach Somchai put his arm around Matt's shoulder.

"Matt, this business of Choi being part of the Black Face gang is serious. He may not be dangerous himself, but the gang is very dangerous if Black Face Chan decides you are a threat to his business interests. Don't try and confront him directly until you have gotten your government friends behind you, okay?"

"I understand, Coach. I'll give Neung a call and see what he has to say. I am not sure the DSI will have any jurisdiction on this but for sure he should have information. Thanks a lot for today, Coach."

Chapter 9

The Camel had one of the helpers assigned by Bashir pick up the packed bags he had left at the Grace Hotel and check out for him, paying cash. His bags were now at the safe house he would use for the night prior to catching his plane in the morning. There was no specific reason for his moving, but he had formed the habit early on in his work as a courier of spending as little time in one place as possible. Besides which, the hotel was a distraction. Over the past ten years, it had become increasingly besieged by foreign whores who were part of the human residue of the breakup of the Soviet Union. The women were all over the age of thirty—very old by Thai sex work standards—some working voluntarily, some trafficked by the mafias, Russian, Ukrainian, Uzbekistani, etc., who had inherited the opportunities and benefits of the new disorder in eastern Europe. The Camel found the whores blatant and disgusting, but the sex tourists from the Middle East treasured their services and found their plump bodies and blond hair attractive. The women, and their handlers from various mafias, had a profitable business.

The only dangerous parts of the exchanges between the Camel and Bashir—in reality his handler though he didn't know—were the times when the drugs and money were dropped off and the products he was shopping for were picked up. His passages through Bangkok's Suvarnabhumi airport were arranged by Bashir's contacts with the customs authorities and always the specially marked bags were eased through. The Camel presumed it was all just part of the facilitating payments that Bashir made in the normal course of his export-import business.

The drop off of the payment, drugs and money was made after the Camel was picked up at the airport. The car would swing through a residential area of Bangkok—to ensure it

48

wasn't being followed—go to the parking area of a mall—a different one every time—the Camel would take his clean bags and get into a waiting car with a driver and leave the payment packages behind. The new car and driver would take him to the hotel and he would check in completely clean.

His pickup of the goods he had ordered would be handled once again with a car and driver assigned by Bashir. The car would take him from the hotel through a residential area, drop him off at a safe house and then another car and driver would pick him up with his bags and take him to a different safe house to check the goods and spend the night awaiting his flight. He had always found Bashir's arrangements efficient and his sense of security above reproach.

Tonight's run was as uneventful as always. The car pulled up to a gate of a private home on a quiet street. There was no security in sight and the gate was partially open. There was a white cloth attached to the gate. His driver went in, picked up the goods and soon they were on their way.

Chapter 10

Krue Tarn called Matt a day later to let him know the coroner had released the body and they would be holding the prayers and cremation ceremony in the afternoon starting at four PM. Normally these ceremonies would involve at least three days of prayers by the monks at the chosen temple, but for the slum children the costs of paying for three days of praying and then cremation was too much. It always came down to a one day event, an hour or so of prayer followed immediately by the cremation. When children of the Metta Home died, they used the nearby slum temple Watt Saphan on a road just up from the slaughterhouse and next to the bridge crossing over the Prakanong canal to perform the ceremonies. The monks there always gave the Metta Home a lower price. When a child died, the head monk or abbot would also take time afterwards to talk to the children and help them to understand that all life was transient and an illusion in an effort to build their understanding of their religion and to lessen their pain at losing a brother or sister.

Matt and Krue Tarn had agreed to meet at the temple. Coach Somchai was up in the North Eastern Isan area visiting a Muay Thai camp. When Matt pulled up at three forty-five PM, Krue Tarn was already there. A group of monks were sitting in line on a small stage in one of the prayer halls or *salas* next to a wooden casket, and a large picture of Yod in his school uniform was placed next to it. The children and staff from the Metta Home were seated in metal chairs facing the monks. Krue Tarn was apart from the hall sitting on some chairs underneath a tent that had been set up in front of the cremation building for the audience to view the ceremonies that would precede the cremation. Matt walked over and joined her.

"Thanks for coming, Khun Matt."

"No need to thank me. It's the least we can do for Yod, to see him off from this life in the correct manner."

"Well I have learned some things I need to share with you which I don't want to get out to the public. Please sit down."

It was a serious occasion and she had a serious look on her face, but Matt could see it was more than that. She looked worried. Matt sat next to Krue Tarn and waited to hear what she had to say.

"I got a call from the medical examiner. She had several things to share. She said they would be in the official written report she gives the police, but she wanted me to know in advance. First, it looks as if Yod had a struggle with whoever killed him. He had bruises on his chest and face and his knuckles were bloody. He had been fighting with someone. Also, though the cause of death was loss of blood from having his throat cut, he apparently was unconscious at the time. He had a bloody contusion on the back of his skull. He had been hit hard, probably knocked unconscious with a blunt instrument. She couldn't say what."

Matt thought of the police officer's comment about the possibility of Yod using amphetamines or Ya Ba and looked at her as she paused. He then said, "Krue Tarn, I know you don't believe he was using Ya Ba but this crazy type of fighting is often the result of using Ya Ba, isn't it?"

"That's right, Kuhn Matt, but in this case there was no Ya Ba in his blood. It's something else, worse in a sense. The medical examiner says he had a bit of alcohol in his system, but not much. What she did find was a large dose of ketamine. This is not a slum drug, but apparently it is being used increasingly here in Thailand, both on the club scene for young people and in the sex industry. It's probable someone had drugged Yod with ketamine."

Matt asked, "Does anyone else know about this? Has there been previous use of this drug by your kids or on your kids?"

Krue Tarn paused and looked over at the staff assembled in the *sala*. "No, this is the first I have heard about this. I am not telling all the staff right now, but I will talk with one of our staff who works a lot with kids on the street at night to see if she has any background."

She looked back at Matt, "Khun Matt, this scares me. This is new to us. In the slums we know about Ya Ba but little about this drug and its effects. I am afraid someone may be targeting our kids. Can you look into this for us?"

Matt groaned inwardly, this lady had no hesitation in adding to the load. At the same time, he understood her feelings. This drug was obviously linked to the boy's death in some way. If Yod was a convenient target, maybe other teens from the Metta Home would be also. He would have to find out how Yod came to be targeted if he was to get the answer as to why the boy had died.

"I'll see what I can find out and let you know. Actually, one of the things I would like to do today is to talk again to the boy I spoke with the other day, Ben, the boy who said he saw Yod receive some money. Is that okay with you? We can do it here after the ceremony and after all the other kids have left so that nobody sees us talking. I can drop him off near the Metta Home afterwards."

"That's okay, Kuhn Matt. I'll talk with Ben and make sure he stays behind to meet with you. It won't be noticed." Now Krue Tarn paused, "One more thing when you talk with Ben. We've had a couple of occasions recently where he didn't come home at night after school. We found he stayed with an uncle who lives in a shack by the railway tracks. The uncle has been in jail twice for selling drugs and Ben is not allowed to be there. He was told if he stays out again, we will not allow him to return, but will turn him back in to the court."

Matt nodded and was about to get up and leave Krue Tarn go to her duties with the kids, when she reached forward and grabbed his arm to stop him.

"Wait, there's something else. I don't want anyone to know this, Kuhn Matt, but you have to know."

Matt was surprised by her intensity and sat back down.

"They did more than beat Yod. The medical examiner told me Yod had been sexually abused. Some man or men had raped him. She said she thought they used the ketamine to make him docile so he wouldn't resist or remember."

Matt was stunned, the murder of the boy and the way his body had been displayed were way beyond his understanding.

Now, learning of the additional insult of sexual violence was overwhelming.

"Krue Tarn, I don't have all the answers, but between us, Coach Somchai and I have enough friends that we should be able to find out what is going on. I promise we'll keep looking."

Krue Tarn thanked him and then excused herself to join the staff group in the *sala* where the monks were beginning to pray. Matt trailed behind and found a place in the very back trying to get his thoughts in order as the rhythmic Pali chanting of the monks washed over him.

After the praying and ceremonies accompanying the cremation, Matt waited under the tent where he had talked with Krue Tarn and watched the staff and children from the Metta Home depart. At the last, Krue Tarn brought over Ben.

As Krue Tarn left, Matt asked the boy to sit down opposite him. Except for a few stray dogs wandering around, the temple grounds were now deserted. The monks had gone back to their rooms, their *kudti* as the Thai called them.

Matt looked at Ben, the boy was fifteen years old, the same age as Yod but not as tall. He was slight of build and handsome, he had big eyes and thick eye lashes. He was almost more pretty than handsome. Ben sat in front of Matt his hands in his lap, looking at the ground. He was clearly uncomfortable; possibly it was the setting in the temple, possibly taking part in Yod's cremation ceremonies, possibly having to be questioned by Matt again or all three. Matt decided to use his discomfort without being too hard.

"It's not a happy day is it, Ben? Yod was your friend is that right?"

Ben just nodded, still looking down.

"Did you and Yod go to school together?"

Again Ben just nodded, still looking down.

This time Matt put a bit of force in his tone.

"Ben, we need to find out what happened to Yod. Do you know why?"

Ben looked up at him, just shaking his head.

Matt spoke with more force. "Because we can't let this happen again, Ben, can we? Do we want this to happen to another boy or girl from Metta?"

Ben looked up at Matt, shaking his head in agreement.

"Ben I need you to help me. Whatever you say will be between you and me, but I need the truth, you understand."

Again, Ben looked at Matt and just nodded his head yes.

Matt was ready. He spoke softly. "Ben, you took money from Uncle Choi, too, didn't you?" He paused. "It's okay. You can tell me."

Ben was looking down again and wringing his hands. Matt reached over and put his hand on top of Ben's to stop their motion. He spoke softly again.

"Ben, it's okay. I won't tell anybody, but you need to tell me the truth. Tell me the truth for Yod."

Ben looked up, his eyes moist, not quite ready to cry. "Yeah, Uncle Choi gave me some money, too, before he gave money to Yod, two times."

"Are those the times you didn't come back to Metta?"

Ben, surprised now, jerked back and looked at Matt with a scared expression. "How did you know?"

Matt just shook his head, trying to give the impression he knew everything.

"It's okay, Ben. I know, but I need you to be honest with me. What happened?"

Now Ben's eyes started to water. "It's my fault. I shouldn't have told Yod. When I told him, he wanted to make some money, too."

Matt continued, still speaking softly. "What did you tell him, Ben? What about the money? What about the nights away from Metta?"

Ben looked down again, he was crying, letting out his burden. "Khun Matt, you know Yod and I are gay. Actually, Yod was gay. I am a woman in my heart, but the staff at Metta, they don't understand. They don't like gay boys or ladyboys."

Speaking somewhat bitterly, he went on. "They like gay girls, Tomboys and Di's, but somehow boys can't be different, you know?"

Matt didn't know, but he nodded his head to show Ben it was okay to talk.

"We always see Uncle Choi around the computer games shop after school. He comes around at least once a week and talks to the kids and gives out small money so they can play the computer games. Sometimes he hires kids to carry Ya Ba for him. Sometimes he offers kids the chance to make money other ways."

Matt was speaking very softly now. "What other ways, Ben?"

Ben looked up at him, his eyes asking for understanding. "Uncle Choi told me I was very pretty. He told me there was a man who would like to meet me, that I could make a thousand baht just for going to have a drink and a talk with the man. I was scared, but I wanted the money. Uncle Choi had one of his guys drive me to a shophouse five minutes away from the port area. Downstairs there was a lounge area and some older gay boys were sitting around talking. They looked at me when I walked in, but nobody said anything. Uncle Choi's man took me upstairs and into a room with a bed and a chair and a bathroom. He asked if I wanted a drink and brought me a soda when I asked for it. He told me to wait and I would have a visitor. I drank the soda and was feeling a little drowsy and I must have fallen asleep on the bed. A little later an older man, maybe forty or so and a little fat came in. He sat on the bed and started to talk to me and play with me. I don't remember much after that. All I know is Uncle Choi's guy must have taken me to my uncle's house afterwards. They know my uncle from the drug business. That's where I woke up the next morning."

"What happened, Ben?"

Ben looked away. "He must have fucked me. My ass was a little sore. I really don't remember. My mind was really fuzzy the next morning. At first I was angry with Uncle Choi for not telling me straight, but I had the thousand baht in my pants pocket. Then I thought about it. Anyway, I'm a woman, I'm supposed to be fucked, right?" he said with a shrug of his shoulders. "I spent the money on games and things for the other kids. When Uncle Choi came back a week later and asked if I wanted to make some money again, I said yes."

Ben looked at Matt, seeing if he could stop talking. Matt didn't speak, but just tilted his head showing he expected to hear more.

"The second time was the same as the first except there was a different guy, older, and he smelled bad from cigarettes. I didn't want to take the drink they gave me, but Uncle Choi's guy made me drink some. He said it would relax me. The same thing happened. I got sleepy again and was just lying there when the old guy came in. I don't remember much, but the next thing I knew it was morning and I was at my uncle's house again. My ass was sore so I know I got fucked again, but I had my money and the old guy had put a couple hundred baht extra in my pocket as a tip. He must have liked me."

Matt knew where the story was going.

"And when Yod asked you about the money, you told him?"

Ben sobbing now, "He was my best friend, Kuhn Matt. When he said he needed money, too, I told him not to do it. It's different for me. I'm a woman. We must accept these things. It's my karma. Yod was gay, but he wasn't accepting of his karma. He was fighting it. I thought he would have trouble and I guess he must have. But why would they do this to him, Khun Matt? He was a good boy."

Matt had never been exposed to such human fragility and hopelessness. For the first time in a long time, since he was in the field in Afghanistan crying over the body of a buddy after an ambush, he felt like crying, too, but he controlled his emotions. It wouldn't help Ben. Ben was looking for someone to support him, not to join him in his grief.

He put his hand on Ben's shoulder and squeezed it hard to get him to focus. "Ben, it's not your fault. These people would have found Yod at some time. It's terrible we lost Yod but we won't lose you or any of the other kids at Metta. Do you understand me?"

Ben was still crying softly, but nodded.

"I'm going to take you back now. No one will know about this or what happened to you, but don't go with Choi's men again and stay away from the games shop, okay?"

Again, Ben just nodded.

Matt took Ben back to the Metta Home and dropped him nearby so the other kids wouldn't see he had been with Matt.

Before Ben got out of Matt's car, he paused and looked at Matt. "Thank you, Khun Matt. Will you come to see me some time? We have dance shows at the school mid-term holiday in a month and I am one of the dancers."

Matt was caught completely off guard. He had no thoughts of his taking on a parental or guardian role at all in life, much less for a mixed-up street kid, but there was only one answer possible to the fragile, suffering soul in front of him. "Yeah, I'll be happy to come down, Ben. Now, go to school and take care of yourself like I told you, okay?"

Ben smiled, "Thanks, Kuhn Matt."

As Matt drove away, he understood he couldn't easily leave the misery he had encountered behind him. It was going to stay with him. The pain and hopelessness he had discovered was just too much. It was occupying all corners of his mind. He couldn't think. He decided he needed to turn his mind off and there was one sure way to do that.

It was now after six. Matt decided to drive over to Jack's Pool Bar and find somebody to knock pool balls around with him for a couple of hours. Hopefully some clarity would come by not thinking about things.

Chapter 11

When Matt walked into the pool bar, he was happy to see it wasn't busy yet. It was still early evening; the real players wouldn't come in until eight or later. He needed the quiet. He needed to lose himself in the click of the balls and the action on the green cloth of the pool table and completely disengage his mind from all the ugliness and misery it had taken on in the previous few hours. He was also happy to see one of the players he liked to shoot against was there. A woman named Da who was a part-owner of the pool bar. Da had first learned cue sports by playing snooker and, as many snooker players could do, she was great at making long hard shots. Her weakness in pool sports was in managing the game and that was where Matt was able to beat her, but only half the time. Their matches were always competitive, which demanded Matt focus only on what was happening on the pool table. This was exactly what he wanted right now. Da was in her mid-thirties, slim and attractive—an Asian Jodie Foster—wearing her hair short and spiked up, as was the current custom with Thai women, or "tomboys," who took the male role in lesbian relationships.

Da was happy to see Matt also since she could count on a good match and because she knew Matt's girl Noi would probably come along later. Da had a relationship in progress, but was attracted to Noi and always took time to let her know. It was a feeling Noi seemed to reciprocate in a low-key way while always making it clear she was with Matt.

In this case, Da was right, Noi would be following along. While stuck in traffic on the road from the port area to lower Sukhumvit Road where the pool bar was located, Matt realized his knowledge of recreational drugs was limited. He needed to know more about the drug the medical examiner had said she found in Yod's system, ketamine. He phoned Noi and asked if she could have one of her staff, probably Plato the resident hacker without a life who would do anything for Noi, research what the drug was, how it worked and how it came to be in the system of a teenage boy in Bangkok. Noi was accustomed to these requests from Matt, who could handle a computer, but had gotten in the habit of deferring to Noi on all research matters since she was the one who owned a software company. Noi for her part was happy to accept the requests because it demonstrated Matt's openness to include her in his work. As Matt expected, Noi said she would assign the job to Plato. Matt agreed to pay for the job with dinner at Jack's when Noi finished work.

Two hours later, Matt was sitting on the verandah outside Jack's with a soft drink waiting for Noi to arrive. He was much more relaxed, the pool play had done the job as he knew it would. They had split the two nine-ball matches; Da winning the first—seven games to five—and Matt winning the second by the same score. He was satisfied with the outcome; he blamed the loss of the first set on the turmoil in his mind, which had taken a while to settle down. While he hadn't forgotten the investigation he had promised to carry out, he accepted he needed to answer some questions about the drugs and the people providing them before he could even start to think about what steps it might make sense to take.

Noi came walking up the small soi entrance way to Jack's place carrying a large handbag. Her dress was the usual office wear but with classy touches: low heels, black slacks, pink blouse and matching accessories. Matt suspected she kept the blouse fully buttoned in the office, but would open an extra button or two before their meetings. He was appreciative. The view was great. Matt greeted her with a wave and got up to give her a kiss on the cheek as she sat down. Before Noi could speak, Da was out the door to greet her and also give her a quick kiss on the cheek. Matt watched a bit amused, but he always suspected if he wasn't on the scene, Da would be immediately ready to turn up the volume, so to speak.

The crowd was building inside the pool bar, several foreign tourists had come to shoot pool and drink with the hostesses inside. The music level had been amped up. The busy main street was over sixty feet away up a narrow soi from the courtyard so none of the street noise came through. The porch outside the pool bar and the adjacent courtyard remained a quiet escape. Across the parking lot and courtyard from the pool bar was the back of the owner's house. Just outside his back door he had suspended two wooden birdcages, home to his singing birds, hanging on stands six feet off the ground. They were getting some cool evening air before the covers were put on the cages for the night. The songs of the birds provided a gentle accompaniment to a meal being interrupted only occasionally by a burst of noise escaping from the interior of the pool bar when the doors opened and the din within escaped into the courtyard. Matt thought the juxtaposition of sounds was a perfect comment on Bangkok itself, scenes of exceptional beauty set against the prevailing discordant backdrop.

Da took Noi's drink order and went back inside. Noi smiled at Matt, knowing he was just a bit jealous of the attention Da gave her.

"How are you doing, babe? It sounded on the phone as if you were having a stressful day. The boy's funeral got you down?"

Matt had not told Noi of his talk with Ben and the horrific tale Ben had shared with him. Instead he had limited the discussion to his talk with the head house mom, Tarn. He felt the revelation of the presence of the drug ketamine in Yod's system was grist enough for Noi to chew on for the moment.

"Yeah, I've attended funerals for adults before, but never for a kid, especially for a kid who died such an ugly death. It sticks with you. I don't want to attend any more funerals like this."

Noi just nodded. Matt was wondering if she was going to pronounce the Thai mantra that this was punishment for the boy's sins in the last life. He had never gotten it from Noi, but knew she had been raised with it. Matt, probably due to his Western education, couldn't find guilt in children. He believed we all started as innocents. Noi knew how he felt and whether she agreed with him or not, never said differently.

Instead Noi pulled out several sheets of paper, the result of the research.

"Let's talk about ketamine. Plato likes your research requests. He found this one interesting and so do I. Do you want a summary?"

"Please, my mind isn't feeling too organized right now. What is this stuff?"

Noi, looking down at her notes, started to recite. "Well first of all, it's a real medicine. It's actually a general anesthesia used on both humans and animals, especially horses. It has some very good uses and is increasingly used to treat depression and bi-polar disorder. Also the U.S. military has been using ketamine the past few years to treat severely wounded patients as it seems to help alleviate post-traumatic stress disorder."

Here she paused and looked up, anticipating Matt would make some comment. When they had first met, he had displayed quick flashes of anger, not at her, but at others. It had bothered her as it is not the Thai way to ever show one is angry or upset. The person who loses control and shows anger loses face. It's just not done. Knowing Matt had been wounded in the military, Noi had done some research and discovered post-traumatic stress disorder. She then talked to him, using questions she had about the syndrome to indirectly indicate she wanted him to work at controlling his anger. At first he was uncomfortable with her effort to help him manage his emotions, but then he had to admit she was right. He had always had a chip on his shoulder, but he had come out of his combat experience with a short fuse on his temper. He consciously began working on controlling it and he was grateful she cared enough to help him.

He gave her an ironic grin and said, "I guess I must have missed my dose." He waved his hand to indicate she should continue.

Noi looked back to her notes.

"As can happen with medicines, people have discovered new uses for ketamine. It's also called Special K or, here in Thailand, Ya K. It's a popular party drug that was used in developed countries as part of the rave and party scene in the 90's and found its way to Thailand over ten years ago. It went out of style for a while, but has come back big the past few years."

Here, Noi paused again and looked up at Matt.

"Actually, I think I heard of this drug when I was going to university in Australia. We were getting warnings on campus about date rape drugs such as GHB or ecstasy, which were often combined with Special K. We were told to be careful at parties or at nightclubs, to watch our drinks and make sure no one had a chance to put something in it. Apparently slipping a powder into drinks is how it is most often administered to the target."

Noi went back to reading from her notes once again.

"It's difficult to produce, requiring sophisticated laboratory equipment. The supply in Thailand comes mainly from Pakistan and India. It's a minor drug compared to amphetamines, but there has been a substantial increase in its presence in the country. It's used on the bar scene, by sex workers with clients and by clients with sex workers, to make the subject more acquiescent. The user is essentially tranquilized and rendered somewhat immobile making rape or unusual sexual practices easier for the person administering the drug. Often times, depending on the dose, the recipient may not remember what happened the next day, the only clues being cuts, abrasions or bruises from rough sex."

She paused, shook her head with a rueful expression and then said, "I have to add one more note from Plato. He says, based on his experience, people don't use Ya K by itself at bars, but combine it with ecstasy to prolong the effect of the ecstasy for up to ninety minutes or more. Probably, in this case, whoever was administering the drug wasn't worried about the boy's experience and just wanted him tranquilized for long enough to use him."

Matt interjected, "Well this explains why somebody used it on Yod. They wanted to make sure the boy didn't resist their sexual advances. He was gay, but young and inexperienced. He might have changed his mind and this way he wouldn't be able to. This tells me the man he was with was a practiced sexual predator. This was planned. It wasn't a spur of the moment thing."

Noi nodded. "It would seem so."

They stopped talking about the case and the drug as Da came back out with a smile, Noi's drink and a notepad to take their dinner orders. There were several waitresses inside who could have taken the order rather than one of the owners, but Noi was, for Da, a special customer. Matt noted Da also appreciated Noi's slightly open blouse yet somehow he couldn't really get jealous. If Da were a man, he would have been irritated. They placed their food orders—a cheeseburger for Matt and Thai noodle soup with pork for Noi—and Da disappeared back inside.

They both sat in silence for a few seconds, absorbing what they had discussed so far and then Matt came up with the question that he felt had to be answered.

"Okay, this wasn't an accident. Someone planned to use Yod and preparations were made to use this drug and they followed through with it. Why and how though did this evolve into a brutal murder?"

Holding up the research notes, Noi said, "Well, there may be part of the answer here. Apparently there are potentially serious side effects of the drug besides being a tranquilizer, such as sleepiness and memory loss. The drug can, with some subjects, have serious psychotropic effects. The person receiving the drug may become paranoid and may have frightening hallucinations."

Noi looked up at Matt. "That could be one part of the answer. At some point, possibly after the sex or during it, Yod may have started experiencing hallucinations and become unmanageable. You said he was slim but fairly tall. He could have been strong enough to make real trouble if he started struggling with the man using him."

Da and a waitress returned with their dinner, smiling and placing it in front of them. Noi put her papers aside and said, "Let's focus on the food. We can talk after if some ideas come to us." Matt had to smile; just eating would represent a small return to normalcy.

During the meal Matt's mind continued to follow his train of thought concerning the manner of Yod's death. As the waitress cleared away their dishes, he voiced his thoughts.

"Accepting the possibility that Yod may have become hysterical or unmanageable in some way and the killer may have felt it necessary to hit him and render him unconscious in order to control him, still leaves us with questions. Why was he killed in such a brutal manner? Why was his body left on display in the slaughterhouse?"

Noi agreed, but spoke slowly, seeing where Matt might be taking this. "You're right. There is something more here than just a violent fight started by his possible reaction to the drug. The problem is how do you get at the answer?"

"I only see one way. I have to talk to the people who were directly involved. Starting with this guy Choi, who was talking to the kids at the games shop and gave Yod money."

This time Noi's reply was very quick. "No matter what, don't you try to take this on alone, Matt." Then, referring to some of his Thai buddies who had gone through the Ranger training with him, "Get one of your military or police friends to back you up. Get some advice from Neung. He should have some ideas."

"Okay. You're right. I'll set up a meeting with Neung tomorrow. Let's leave it at that for now. I can't handle any more."

"I can't either. Let's go home and focus on handling more important things, okay?"

Matt smiled and nodded and said, "That seems a practical approach." To himself he thought, *I am one lucky guy.*

Chapter 12

The next morning, after sending Noi off to work, Matt phoned his friend Neung. Neung was a mid-level supervisor with the Thai government Department of Special Investigation, the Thai equivalent of the U.S. FBI. The DSI scope of responsibility comprised crimes of national import much like the FBI. The previous year Matt had become involved in the search for a missing U.S. research scientist who had disappeared in the jungle north of the city of Chiang Rai. The case involved the operations of the Japanese yakuza in Thailand and thus had become of interest to the DSI. Matt had worked closely with Neung and DSI agents reporting to him in eliminating the yakuza gang active in the Chiang Rai area. Neung readily agreed to meet Matt later that morning at their "usual place." That was a *sala*, a sitting area with a roof, next to the pond in the park adjacent to Matt's office.

Matt was waiting when Neung walked up the path to the *sala*. There was no special security reason for meeting there. It was just that the park was a green and quiet place where their only company would be joggers and Burmese and Thai nannies looking after the toddling children of white-collar foreign workers. The park was shaded and relatively cool with the *sala* far enough into the park so the street noise was left behind.

Neung was medium height and at forty the same age as Matt. He was a cat in his movements, not a tiger, more a leopard, still as wiry and fit as he had been when they had been going through the U.S. Army Ranger course together. He used the excuse of an outside meeting to dispense with the white shirt and tie required in the office and just wore casual black slacks and a black polo shirt. It was not the normal government look, which he tried to avoid whenever he could. He was sporting his signature heavy gold Rolex watch. He said hello and then sat down next to Matt asking, "What have you got yourself into now?"

"More than I can handle by myself, I'm afraid." Matt gave him a complete reprise of the case as it stood without indicating what he thought the next step might be, thinking Neung might have something to volunteer. Neung had not reacted during Matt's recital except when Matt mentioned Uncle Choi was supposedly a member of the Black Face gang in the port area. This was the first thing he addressed.

It was clouding up and a light breeze ruffled the surface of the pond. Possibly it was going to rain. Neung looked up at the clouds for a second and then back to Matt.

"Listen, Matt, the Black Face gang is serious business, but they are considered local operators not part of our scope at DSI. Their main sphere is gambling. Money lending, local sales of amphetamines and the operation of bars and sex businesses are also part of their scope. At the same time, they are not known for murder. They usually restrict themselves to a severe beating when people cross them or fail to pay their debts. Sometimes they will take a guy's wife in payment and put her into sex work to pay off his debt. Murder is just not good business, and if they do it, they usually do it with handguns not knives. The sex business part of this may well be them, but it doesn't explain the method used to kill this boy and display his body. This is a severe insult to the local police. That is not the gang's style; they try to accommodate the local police as much as possible."

"Neung, I accept what you are saying, but how can anyone track the boy's killers without starting with his last known contact? The point you're making is the one I'm afraid of. The gang may be accommodating the local police and in this case, the local police may be accommodating the gang by deciding the death of a street kid is not big enough for them to go all out and disrupt the gang in an effort to get to the killers. There is no indication at this time that they are making any progress in getting the boy's killers."

Neung got up and walked around the edge of the *sala* looking into the seemingly green water of the pond as the surface reflected the surrounding trees. "Let me ask some questions informally. I don't know the officer in charge of the police in the port area, but I know someone who does. We have to proceed carefully here. They will not appreciate outside interference in their case. Give me a day or so and I will get you an update. In the meantime stay away from the port area, okay?"

"Okay, I'll stay away for now but, Neung, I can't walk away from this. Whoever did this may do it again. I made a promise to the house mom at the Metta Home. She is afraid more of her kids may be in danger. We've got to stop this guy."

Neung smiled at Matt's use of the word "we." "Okay, buddy, I understand you."

Chapter 13

Of course, Matt couldn't wait. When he didn't hear from Neung the next day, he decided to check out Uncle Choi and the recruitment scene—the video games shop—the following day.

The main street of the Jet Sip Rai slum ran parallel to the river. As virtually all residents along the river were squatters, the buildings had grown up in a haphazard fashion over the years. Most of the original squatters were day laborers coming from the countryside to work at the port. The Port Authority had gone along with the development, even allowing several large apartment blocks to be built, as they secured payments for the building rights and shares of the rent for land they had no immediate plans to use. The result of the formula was to create an instant slum since there was no incentive to plan for the future but rather to put in the lowest possible investment and take out the returns as quickly as possible.

From the entrance road to Jet Sip Rai, driving under an expressway and crossing the railroad tracks bordering the slum on one side, somehow, in the space of fifty yards, the light seemed to dim. It could be a bright, sunshiny day in Bangkok but, as if a veil of poverty hung over this strip of land, the day became just a bit grayer while proceeding into the slum itself. Possibly in an attempt to brighten the atmosphere and increase hopes of prosperity, the merchants had invested in a six-foot high, gilded sitting Buddha. It was placed on railway land just before crossing the railway tracks.

The buildings on the main street consisted of a long row of three-story, narrow front Chinese shophouses. This building model went back hundreds of years to a time in China when taxes were charged on the street frontage of buildings and thus, to save taxes, it became the norm to build on a narrow front and extend deeply about five times the frontage to get the desired space. This model became the standard for construction for Chinese families throughout Southeast Asia from the 19th century through the 20th century. Generally, the bottom floor was open to the street and would hold the family business whatever it may be. In Jet Sip Rai many of the shops were restaurants with a myriad of other shops providing other services thrown in here and there. There was no usable sidewalk and the street was narrow and crowded. If cars parked on both sides of the street, there was barely room for a third vehicle to squeeze through between them and fight its way between the motorcycles, children playing and portable stalls for vendors selling roast chicken and other street food. Behind the main street, slum shacks were thrown up alongside open sewers and families of seven and eight people crowded into a room or two with a single bathroom. Amazingly enough, it was a relatively safe environment. By and large, unless drunk or on drugs, the Thai don't deal in crimes of confrontation. There were no shootings or killings unless the police had a drug crackdown in progress. The greatest danger at night on the dimly lit street would be purse snatching or, at the few homes that appeared to have some wealth, a burglary. Between the police and the mafia, most aspects of life for the very poor were controlled.

Matt had gone down to Jet Sip Rai at four PM. The slum kids would be coming home from school in their uniforms, as all Thai schools required uniforms, indicating which one they attended. It was early in the rainy season and Matt had found a seat under cover at a noodle shop on the side of the street opposite the video games shop and just a few doors down. It was raining when he first arrived but let up after a few minutes. The rain had cooled off the heat of midday yet it left the air an uncomfortable blanket of moisture. He intended to listen to the warnings he had been given about not confronting the man called Uncle Choi head on. However, he was still determined to get a first-hand look at the scene the kids had described. Matt had not come alone. Sgt. Major Chatri, his friend from the Border Patrol Police, was with him.

Over a year earlier, when involved in an operation against a yakuza camp in Northern Thailand, the sgt. major had acted as Matt's right-hand man during the assault on the camp. He had been wounded, receiving extensive flash burns to his back during the explosion set off by the yakuza leader that finished the fight. He had healed and stayed in Bangkok to be near continuing medical care. For duty purposes, he was assigned as a liaison to the Royal Guards Regiment commanded by Tommy, another of Matt's Ranger training buddies. Tommy was the organizer of the prior year's mission. Matt and the sgt. major had stayed in touch. When Matt explained why he was going to Jet Sip Rai, he also asked if the sgt. major would back him up; the sgt. major had immediately agreed to come along. The sgt. major was a significant physical presence. He was of medium height and also of nearly equal width, muscular and heavyset. He had faced many fights, both with weapons and without. He was dark skinned and had a three inch scar on his left cheek which ran down to the corner of his mouth.

The shop was crowded. Both men had ordered some noodles and were taking their time eating them. They were in the middle of the shop, but Matt had a direct line of sight to the video games shop. It was busy there, as many kids had stopped in after school. The crowd of school kids was almost totally boys, though every once in a while, an adventurous pair of teen girls would stop by and tease the boys. The ages seemed to be from twelve to eighteen. There was a municipal law barring kids under the age of sixteen from playing in video games shops, but the law didn't kick in until ten PM. After school the early teens attended in large numbers.

They had waited for over an hour and Matt was concerned they were becoming too conspicuous. The shop owner had approached them twice and they had ordered more food and drink as their ticket to stay. The sgt. major had no problem putting down any quantity of noodles. Then a car pulled up at the intersection and a man fitting the description of Choi got out while the car drove off down the street. He was late forties, medium height and overweight, balding with a moustache. His short-sleeved white shirt hung over his belt, black slacks and simple thong sandals instead of shoes. The simple dress look was mixed with a heavy gold chain and medallion around his neck and a big gold wristwatch. This was much as Ben had described him. He walked towards the games shop and stopped in front saying something to the boys standing around. It was a joke it seemed as they all laughed. The man went inside. Matt touched the sgt. major on the arm and told him, "When he comes back out, I'll talk with him. Just stay here and watch, okay?" The sgt. major, finishing his third bowl of noodles, just nodded.

After about ten minutes, Choi came back out of the shop with his arm around the shoulder of a young boy about fourteen wearing his school uniform and backpack. Choi leaned over and spoke in the boy's ear and then gave him a pat on the back and sent him on his way. The boy went running off. Matt interpreted that as a package of Ya Ba pills being delivered. Matt doubted Choi had ever touched the pills. A messenger had probably delivered them to the shop earlier. As Matt watched, he felt the anger boiling up inside him. Choi would never get his hands dirty by handling the drugs. He would never be caught. He would never do jail time. Only the kids and any drugged-out adults he used would be caught by the police. Choi watched the boy running off and then turned to talk to some of the other boys standing outside the shop.

Matt decided this was his moment and walked towards the front of the shop. Choi had his back to Matt and was talking to a slim, handsome boy of perhaps fourteen. He had his hand on the boy's back just above his buttocks. He was moving his hand softly back and forth and was talking quietly to the boy while two other boys watched. The two other boys saw Matt approaching and stepped back a bit, not knowing what was going to happen. Matt had no plan and if he had had a plan it would have been dissolved in the growing tide of anger and loathing he felt for this man. The one thing he knew he had to do was to make sure of his identification.

Matt called out sharply, "Choi."

The man straightened up from his pose over the boy and turned to Matt. "What?"

Matt, almost on top of him, spoke deliberately: "Are you Choi?"

Choi stood up straighter now, confident of his position on his turf, looking with scorn at Matt's approach. "Yes, I am, so what?"

Matt didn't pause as he closed the last half step, with his left foot closest to the target, he said, "So this, you pig." No Muay Thai moves, no orchestration, Matt just buried his right fist deeply into Choi's soft stomach. Choi doubled over and might have fallen at Matt's feet but he caught Choi by his arm and held him halfway up. Matt moved his feet out of the way thinking Choi might vomit on them, but he didn't. Choi was just dry retching for a few seconds, gasping for air. The boys had stumbled back out of the way, their eyes wide with shock. This was Choi's corner; he was the local *Pu Yai*, the big man here. No one challenged him in any way, for this to happen was unbelievable.

Matt now held Choi up, one hand gripping his upper arm the other grasping his belt, holding him so they were eye level, faces only six inches apart. "From now on, no kids, you understand me? You want to deal with drugs and sex you deal with adults. No kids, no one at the games shop here, you understand?"

Choi was still gasping, incapable of speaking so Matt helped him. "Just nod yes." Choi nodded his head. Matt, accepting the answer, was picking Choi up a bit further, preparing to throw him to the ground, when he heard a yell behind him and then was hit on the shoulder. Matt bent over and dropped Choi who fell to the ground in a heap face down. As Matt turned to his left to face the threat, he was hit again in the left side. It was one of Choi's helpers, maybe his driver, a man as tall as Matt but heavier, using a two-by-four from a nearby construction site where he had been watching. Matt turned into the blow and instinctively grabbed the board and held it to his left side, pulling the man closer, and then hit him in the face with his right fist. Behind the man two more men were coming to help him deal with Matt. He couldn't worry about them now.

Matt kept pulling on the board and the man wouldn't or couldn't let go. He was at a disadvantage with Matt using the board as leverage. Matt kept hitting him in the face with his right hand. Finally the man let go of the board and hit Matt in the face with his right hand. Matt let the board drop and used his left—one, two, three jabs—to set the man up and then came through with a right to the throat. No need to break his fist on the man's chin. He had learned in the rangers putting a man out of commission was the goal. No need for any classic punches. The throat punch was always effective, possibly wrecking the larynx. The man fell to his knees holding his throat and trying to breath. Matt looked for the other two. He saw them both lying on the ground with the sgt. major standing over them, not even breathing hard.

"Thanks, Sgt. Major."

The sgt. major grinned at him. "They're just street punks, Kuhn Matt. I doubt they've ever been in a real fight until today."

Matt looked down at Choi, still lying face down, trying to get his breath. A crowd had gathered in the street watching. The boys inside the shop were all collected at the windows looking out at the wreckage of the street thugs. Matt bent over the prostrate Choi and grabbing his collar, turned his face so he was looking at Matt, "This was for Yod. Leave the school kids alone."

Standing back up, Matt turned toward the sgt. major, "I think we're through here, Sgt. Major. Let's go home."

Matt's Toyota Fortuner was parked in an apartment block lot a short walk away. As they walked to it, no one followed. While driving away the sgt. major, with a small grin, asked "Khun Matt, was that the plan?"

Matt had to laugh. "I guess so, Sgt. Major, though I didn't know it until I saw that guy touching the boy."

"Are you okay? I saw you get hit with that board a couple of times. The guy got in at least one punch."

Matt thought about it for a second, his face was fine but his shoulder ached and then he smiled. The satisfaction of hitting the pig, Choi, was the best medicine. "I'm fine, Sgt. Major. Maybe these guys will think twice before recruiting kids again."

The sgt. major nodded, "Good enough, Khun Matt. You only made one mistake."

"Oh?"

"After you hit him and he was going down, you should have let him go and then kicked him while he was down. You could have delivered your message and had both hands free to fight."

Matt laughed again. He still had a lot to learn but he was lucky he had the sgt. major around to help teach him.

"Okay, Sgt. Major. Next time."

"And one other thing, Khun Matt."

"Yeah?"

"This is a serious loss of face for the people in this gang. They'll be looking for a chance to get even. I would stay away from the port area for a while and keep your eyes open wherever you go."

"I got you, Sgt. Major. Eyes open."

Chapter 14

The next morning Matt woke up feeling sore physically but refreshed mentally. His shoulder and side ached from the impact of the two-by-four he had been hit with and he had purple and yellow bruises developing from the impact. The red mark on his face was receding; the guy hadn't had much of a punch. It had been a quiet night. After dropping the sgt. major back at the enlisted housing at the Royal Guards camp, Matt decided to go on home and collect his thoughts as to how to proceed. Noi was busy with her work and they had no plans to meet for a few days so he was on his own. He had some training materials he needed to go over for an upcoming session with park rangers at the western forest reserve and he thought taking a couple of pain pills and going over those materials would be the best way to come down from his testosterone high from engaging Choi and his guys.

He was running slow and a bit behind but thought he would make his usual morning stop in his office. As he was preparing to leave his apartment at 9:30, he received a phone call from Neung.

"Hey, Matt, how are you feeling today?"

"Hi, Neung, I'm feeling fine. Why do you ask?"

"Well I have a report of a gang fight down near the port yesterday afternoon. Apparently somebody took on some guys from the Black Face gang and gave them a pretty good beating. You wouldn't know anything about that, would you?"

Matt knew there would be blowback from the fight yet he hadn't thought it would be this quick. Of course he had no choice but to be completely open with Neung.

"Well yeah, a little bit. Do we need to talk about it?"

"Yes, definitely, and there is someone I need to introduce you to. We need to have a quiet talk at a neutral meeting ground. Do you still have the family membership at the Royal Bangkok Sports Club?"

"Yes. You want to use that as the meeting place?"

"Yeah, you'll understand when I introduce you to my friend. How about meeting there for a quiet lunch? We'll arrive at noon. It would be good if you could get there about fifteen minutes early and be ready to have us brought in as your guests."

"Okay. I'll be there and arrange things."

The Sports Club, as its members refer to it in shorthand, is one of the oldest and most prestigious of clubs in Thailand. Matt's mom was connected to the club through her family. Technically ladies couldn't be members, but had "ladies privileges" extended to them. She had insisted on extending the membership to Matt after his return home even though he had little interest in it. Located in the middle of downtown Bangkok, not far from the Siam Square, Siam Center and Siam Paragon shopping complexes, the club existed based on a royal charter granted in 1901 for the purpose of holding equine sporting events. Other sports facilities had been added over the years. While there was nothing luxurious about the buildings or its interior, the grounds included a horseracing track and golf course. Membership was not expensive since the horse race gaming proceeds covered the club's costs. Being sponsored and approved for entry was the difficult part. Of course in Thailand, as elsewhere, the right family connections could make things happen.

The club was a very "hi-so" destination with limited membership and holding a meeting there was a discreet choice. Certainly no gang members from the port area would be in the vicinity. Also no questions would be asked of Neung and his guest as to why they were meeting with Matt.

After Neung hung up, Matt decided to go on to the office and do some work on the training plans he was preparing. There was no way he could anticipate whatever it was Neung had in store for him at lunch so best not to dwell on it.

At noon Matt was waiting at the security box alongside the entrance gate to the Sports Club as a police car drove up.

Neung and his guest were in the back seat. Matt had the guard clear the car through to the parking area.

Neung introduced Matt to the guest. "Matt, this is Police General Sombat. He works within the Crime Suppression Division of the Royal Thai Police and is in charge of a new bureau which covers both anti-trafficking and crimes against women and children."

Matt clasped his hands in front of his face in a *wai*, which the Police General politely returned.

"Pleased to meet you, General Sombat."

"And I'm pleased to meet you, Khun Matt. My friend Inspector Neung has told me of the good work you performed on the drug case last year."

His comment conveyed to Matt that Neung had given the Police General the sanitized version of the events of the previous year, limiting it to the version in which the yakuza were only involved in drugs.

"I was just a part of a good team effort, General."

"More than that I think. It seems now we have a new case to discuss."

Neung interceded, "Yes, we do, but let's go sit down first."

Matt led the way into the sports club and onto the restaurant terrace adjacent to the track. As it was midday, there were no horses training on the track and it was quiet. Small groups of golfers were making their way around the short course inside the track. The click of a driver hitting a golf ball was occasionally audible. Across the way, the Four Seasons Hotel was visible just outside of the club grounds as was a station and part of the sky train route, which ran past the club over Rajadamri Avenue.

After they were seated and had ordered food, Neung took the lead.

"Well, Matt, I don't know whether to congratulate you on your knockout or kick you for not waiting for my feedback before going into Jet Sip Rai yesterday."

"I'm sorry about that, Neung. I really just intended to go and take a look at the site where this boy was apparently recruited. Then this guy Choi turned up and, well things just got out of hand. I couldn't sit there and watch him playing games with another boy."

Neung laughed, "It's okay, Matt. The port police are a little unhappy with you, but I can manage that. More importantly the Black Face gang and Black Chan himself are probably very unhappy with you. I'm sure they are asking around trying to find out just who you are and where to find you. You had better keep a sharp eye out when you are leaving or entering your apartment or on the street at whatever are your usual places. That's one reason I suggested the sports club. I know you don't come here often."

"No, I'm not a golfer or a gambler and my Muay Thai training is a bit too 'low-so' for this club."

"This murder is not within the operational area of the DSI, but at times, in our special operations work on anti-trafficking, I have had the chance to work with Police General Sombat who operates as part of the Crime Suppression Division. I think he can help us to understand some of what is going on with this gang."

Neung turned to Police General Sombat, "General Sombat, why don't you brief Matt on your responsibilities and how what is happening in Jet Sip Rai is of interest to you?"

"First, Khun Matt, let me say please don't be too hard on the Port Authority police district if they have seemed to be insensitive to the child protection aspect of this case and are focusing just on the murder and potential drug aspects. The reality is they don't have officers who have had training in anti-trafficking issues and what to look for in cases of abuse of women and children. The Royal Thai Police are trying to advance in these areas. This is why my unit was established. We have a cadre of officers working on cases and we are assisting the training of officers in all districts in Bangkok and in the provinces."

Matt was in a tough place; on the one hand he wanted to laugh in the guy's face. What special sensitivity was required to understand the death of a boy who had been drugged, raped, beaten, tossed into a slaughterhouse for pigs and murdered by having his throat cut deserved some attention? At the same time, he knew Neung had some point in setting up this meeting and he had to go along if he wanted to find out what the point was. So he just nodded his head and listened.

"We have been watching the Black Face gang from the anti-trafficking angle for some time. They have been bringing in hundreds of men, women and children as young as fourteen years old to work as slaves in the fishing, shrimp and pineapple industries. Many are hill tribe people and many are from Burma. There are other groups involved in trafficking, but here in Bangkok, the Black Face gang is the biggest. The gang also runs some brothels, holding women, girls and boys as sex slaves. The prettier of both sexes are held back from the shrimp factory or fishing boat trafficking to work for the brothels. I can't disclose all our information or how we are getting it, but I can tell you we are very close to striking the gang in areas where they are selling the people they traffic."

The General had Matt's attention and he began to have some hope that this conversation was leading to something positive regarding Yod's murder.

"While this fellow Choi was undoubtedly a link in the chain bringing this young boy into the sex trade, he is a low level link. Also we doubt that he or his men had a hand in the boy's death. This was just too public for the gang. Black Chan has survived for many years because he knows to keep his gang's activities as low profile as possible."

Matt was trying to keep his response as respectful as Thai custom required. He would gain nothing by pissing off the Police General, but he couldn't help but press him a bit.

"Sir, if these guys didn't kill Yod, who did? And how do we get at them?"

The Police General smiled, the kind of smile showing he was a bit irritated by Matt questioning him.

"Kuhn Matt, we will follow the link from Choi and find out who he delivered the boy to. By we, I mean my friend Inspector Neung here and my unit. I ask you to be patient a bit longer. We will find the connection and Neung will let you know when we do. I promise you it won't be dropped. At the same time, it would be best if you avoided the Jet Sip Rai area until we have some results. Is that okay?" This last question was said with a smile yet it was clear that it was an order.

"Of course, sir. I'm sorry if my unintentional clash with Choi and his men has caused any problem for the investigation."

The police general laughed and this was real.

"Actually, Kuhn Matt, your action was of use. The fight was so public the Port Authority police had grounds to pick up Choi and his men and question them. They were moving carefully up to now as we didn't want to take the chance of compromising our trafficking investigation. This public fight was a completely different matter and thus picking up Choi wouldn't raise any suspicion on the part of Black Chan. While in custody, Choi identified the client to whom he had delivered the boy named Yod."

Matt sat back. The police general had his full attention.

"Does this mean you'll be able to go after these people?"

"It's not quite that simple, Khun Matt. Choi says he doesn't have any contact info for the man who ordered the boy. The man calls about every six weeks or so, using a different phone every time. Choi's men deliver the boys to a public location, in this case the McDonald's restaurant in the Lotus supermarket on Rama IV Avenue, and leave. The customer takes it from there. Choi and his men have never seen the customer or his men."

"Is there a name or some form of identification?"

"The only name Choi has is Kuhn Aram, which is probably a cover name. The man is a foreigner. Choi believes from something in the manner of speaking and accent that the man is from the Middle East. When he calls, the clients the boys go to are always from the Middle East. The payments are generous and sent back with the boys and the boys are normally left waiting, usually semi-conscious from drugs, in a parking lot near to where they were picked up."

"Did this guy have anything to say about Yod being killed?"

"Yes, he said he was shocked and I believe him. Not that he cared for the boy, but no payment was made and he felt the public nature of the killing was bad for business. His men went to the pickup site early that morning and the boy wasn't there. They waited until after the sun came up and then went back to report to Choi. He says they didn't learn of the killing until later in the day. What he didn't say, but I believe is true, is that Black

Chan gave him hell for having something that would draw so much public attention happen on their turf."

Neung stepped back into the conversation to bring it to an end, probably feeling Matt had pushed the police general as far as possible for the moment.

"Matt, I think we have to accept this for now and let General Sombat and his men develop their anti-trafficking effort to its conclusion. He'll keep me informed and I'll keep you informed. Okay?"

This ended the discussion about Yod's murder. For Matt there was no choice but to say yes. He had questions about how Kuhn Aram could be tracked down, but Neung was clearly waving him off for now. So be it.

They finished their lunch and Neung escorted the police general back to his car while Matt waited.

When Neung returned to the table and sat down, he held up his hand to indicate to Matt to hold his tongue for the moment.

"I know what you want. You want a road map on how to find this guy Aram and we'll work on it. Police General Sombat is a good man. He will pass on any information he gets, but his first priority is to ensure his team is able to close the trap on this human trafficking ring. They've been working on it for over a year and it's big and important. At the same time there are other places and people in Bangkok selling boys for sex. I have contacts that know of these places and there is nothing to stop me from going out and trying to find out more about Aram. I will start today. Okay?"

Matt just nodded his consent and with that Neung concluded the meeting.

As he was driving back to his office, Matt decided he needed a good workout. He skipped the office and went to Coach Somchai's gym to exercise and spend some time punishing the body bag. This would help him decide how to proceed. It would also allow him to work out the kinks from the fight in Jet Sip Rai. He liked Neung's idea of going to other sources to track down Aram. He also decided to place a call to John Scales. John had street contacts, people he used in investigations. They could possibly help turn up information on foreigners who were repeat customers. After that Matt thought he would take the advice given by both the sgt. major and Neung and lay low for a few days. He would let Noi know he would be out of town for a while on business. He could avoid explaining his bruises to her. Possibly it was a good time for a trip to one of the national parks and a hike in the jungle. He could test out some of his training materials on the rangers in the park.

Chapter 15

Bashir had asked for today's meeting with the Snake on somewhat short notice. The meeting place chosen by the Snake was a room in the Dusit Thani, an established older hotel in the mid-town Silom Road area. The Snake used hotels as impromptu meeting places quite often. In general practice, he considered it good security. However, his list of hotels was short; the only requirement was a great steak restaurant so he could combine a bit of culinary pleasure with his business. This made it easier for those watching him to put systems in place to alert them when he was using one of his favorite hotels. In the old cold war days when competing against sophisticated intelligence agencies, he would have avoided this poor security practice, but as the Snake liked to tell people, "Those days are gone. There is no real opposition now."

Of course he was wrong.

Bashir's knock on the door was answered by one of the Snake's security guards. He might have become sloppy in his clandestine practices, but he knew enough to have at least two security guards with him at all times except when he was meeting with one of the two women he kept.

"Good Morning, Bashir," said the Snake rising from a chair at the desk where he had spread out some of his normal paperwork. The room was large, not a suite but an executive room with a large desk. The Snake didn't like to be cramped. CNN was on the TV as white noise and the drapes were pulled.

"Your message said it was urgent, so here I am. What has come up?"

"Jake, there has been a very public incident which I am afraid may have involved our friend the Camel."

The mood in the room went instantly from carefully cheery to dark black.

Jake held up a hand to signal Bashir not to speak for a moment, turned, went back to his desk and sat down facing Bashir once again. Now his face was as set as granite and the black eyes had turned obsidian.

"What is the activity and what is the Camel's involvement?"

"Jake, right now, I don't know all the details. It's about this boy that was found dead in the slaughterhouse slum last week. Apparently, he was the boy I had arranged for the Camel to meet with two nights before he left. I got a call from one of my police contacts. The police at the Port Authority station picked up the supplier we use down there, a guy named Choi. There were two guys who beat him up a couple days ago while he was making his rounds in the slum. They mentioned the boy by name. Then the police brought him in for a talk. The police asked him if he was involved, as he was seen with the boy during the week prior to his death. It seems Choi gave the police the name I use when I order boys for our Middle East guests including the Camel."

"Do the police have any way to trace you?"

"No. I always use different mobile phones to call Choi and the others we use to arrange for the services. I got rid of the phone immediately after placing the order for the boy. He and his gang never see the pickup or drop-off. The Camel has a boy or two visit him at one of the safe houses during his visits. There has never been a problem. He never uses the same boy twice and I vary the contacts I use to supply boys for him to use. Everything was set up that night so our friend could have his reward for his cooperation. He was at a safe house in Klong Toey and I had the two security guards watching over him pick up the boy and take him to the house. Their orders were to take the boy back when our friend had finished and then go on back down south."

"Did the Camel indicate any problem when you met with him before he left?"

"No. When I met with the Camel the next day, just prior to his departure, he didn't mention a thing, so I thought all had gone as usual.

The Snake's expression was growing as black as his eyes. "Jesus Christ. If this murdered kid is really the boy you arranged for him, we got a hell of a mess on our hands."

"From what Choi said to the police, I think it must be, but I've been unable to get in touch with the two security guards we used. They're not my men. They had come up from the south, provided by one of the Camel's contacts down there to help out with his security for this visit. They were scheduled to go back down as soon as he left town. They are strict Muslims and don't object to the Camel's sexual preferences. The boy may have had a reaction to the drugs used to keep him calm and the situation escalated from there. Maybe he said or did something to offend them."

The Snake didn't deal in increased volume when he was angry, but he did increase the emphasis, and now he was biting off his words.

"Jesus Christ, might have or maybe, that's bullshit. We need to find out exactly what happened. You get somebody to go down south and talk to these two directly and find out in detail what happened."

"Yes, sir."

"I'll check with some police sources and find out what their take is on this. You see if you can get some background on the two civilians who beat up your supplier. Find out who they are and what their interest is in this boy. We can't afford to have this expand in any way."

"Yes, sir."

The Snake was very agitated; he stood up at the desk and then sat back down again staring for a moment at the papers he had laid out. There was silence except for the hum of the air conditioners and muted voices from CNN. When he looked up, he again spoke deliberately to underline his seriousness.

"This operation is followed at the very top of the company and briefed to the National Security Council. If we lose this man and the access he has to Al-Qaeda, no one will forgive us. Make sure this killing goes away and whatever happens, there can be no connection to this operation. That is the top priority. The operation must be protected by all means. Am I clear?"

"I got you, Jake. We may need to take some extra measures to make the two local guys go away. I assume that's not a problem."

"It's not a problem but see it's handled quietly. We don't want to draw any more attention to this then absolutely necessary. It is preferable to solve this without involving our local contacts. Understood?"

The Camel Driver smiled. What his boss was telling him was to make this problem go away, whatever it takes and at the same time don't involve him. Such was life within the bureaucracy even, or maybe especially, within spy agencies.

"I understand, Jake. I'll get on it now."

With that the Camel Driver turned and walked out the door.

Chapter 16

The Snake sat back and started thinking about his options. This current assignment was an important one within the agency hierarchy of field jobs. He was at the end of a clandestine operations career stretching over thirty years. He was a working class kid, whose Mexican immigrant dad had worked in a cattle slaughterhouse. Recruited by the agency from a small Catholic college in Nebraska, his first assignment was in the Asian division, working in Seoul, Korea. The station chief at the time was nicknamed the Undertaker for his role in the agency's political death squad activities in Vietnam. The man had been a mentor for the Snake, though he hadn't yet earned that nickname then, taking the young agent under his wing and sharing the background on the ugly and unlawful activities the agency had carried out in Vietnam and Laos. The Undertaker, seeing the possibilities in the young agent, had stressed the necessity of having men within the agency who would not balk at taking on the ugly acts required to see that the mission, whatever it was, was accomplished. The truth was whatever served the mission. Lying and misinformation were a way of life. There were no friends, only people to be used to get the job done, and the foes were anyone, no matter what the nationality, including American, who got in the way of the mission.

The Snake had learned the lessons well and practiced them as he became involved in covert operations in Nicaragua in the mid-80's, then Lebanon, Iraq and the Middle East in the 90's and after the millennium, in the U.S. invasion of Iraq. He had watched with callous indifference as the Bush administration had bullied the agency management into providing anything—any evidence at all no matter how flimsy—that could be interpreted as evidence of weapons of mass destruction in Iraq and Iraqi intentions to use them. He was part of the group in the agency who understood the mission was not the gathering of intelligence, but rather the gathering and *shaping* of information. Information which would help the highly placed war clique in Washington, D.C., justify their intent to invade.

After the invasion, the Snake was involved on the ground, leading a special operations group tasked to ensure groups fighting for power in the new democratic order in Iraq and most amenable to following U.S. direction came to have control. Working on a general staff level, but completely screened from public view for security reasons, he was able to request missions involving special ops units of the U.S. military.

This was where the Snake and Major Matt Chance had come to meet. Matt led a Ranger unit assigned to support the Snake. Background intelligence for any operation was provided by the Snake's briefers. The mission for Matt's Ranger unit was a simple one: a nighttime raid in an area housing a Sunni group who were the followers of a radical cleric. It was said the group was planning an attack on Americans in the newly formed Green Zone, an area of greater security for U.S. Embassy and related civilian staff as well as military offices. The operation was to be a preemptive raid with the goal of spoiling the planned attack and warning the group from attempting such attacks in the future. Matt raised some background questions with the briefer. Based on his previous understanding of the Sunni group, their opposition to the Americans was only the art of name-calling. On the contrary, they seemed more opposed to the Shia politicians the U.S. was beginning to favor since they were not connected to the previous government. The Snake stepped in and quickly closed down this line of questioning. He used the agency's most valued protective shield, telling Matt that more detailed background intelligence was available on a "need to know" basis and Matt and his Rangers had been provided all they needed to know to execute the mission. This included the mission not being an intelligence gathering opportunity and that no prisoners were required, or as Snake put it, "Don't worry about prisoners." Matt had been mightily pissed off at Snake's arrogant manner, but did not want to argue with a representative of higher command in front of his troops. He let it drop for the moment, but vowed to take it up with his chain of command after the raid.

It was a tough mission. Any mission at night, in a dense urban setting, is difficult. The operational imperative was to get in unobserved and once the shooting started, do the job and get out quickly. They entered quietly and raided the buildings as instructed. The problem is that when you break into a building downstairs, there are people upstairs, usually the people with guns, who are immediately alerted by the noise. They had four buildings to hit and they hit them all at the same time. The shooting was brief and intense. Matt had led the team going into the biggest building believing the opposition would be greater. Going up the stairs was the most dangerous part, several Rangers had been hit and one died at the scene. As Matt was checking to ensure the attack squads all made it back out through the cover of the back-up platoon, one of the squad leaders came to him and told him they had two prisoners, guys who didn't want to fight and who had begged for their lives.

"What should we do with them, sir?" Of course the implication was they could just waste them since no prisoners were needed and get back to base. Matt told the sergeant to restrain them and bring them along. Back at the compound and before reporting to the Snake's operations hooch, Matt had the translator join him in a tent so they could question the two prisoners. The prisoners were definitely Sunni and followers of the radical religious cleric. They professed however to know nothing of a planned attack on the Green Zone, but said they had been planning an attack on an opposition Shia group, one with which they were contesting control of the leadership of the new government. Now Matt knew what was going on. This had nothing to do with securing the liberation of Iraq. The agency guy—as the Rangers called him not knowing his nickname as the Snake—was using U.S. troops to weaken the Sunni opposition of the Shia groups he favored to lead the new government. Matt was outraged. This was essentially assassination; it was certainly not within the guidelines of U.S. military operations and illegal for the clandestine operations of the U.S. This was surely why the Snake had used the cover story of protecting the Green Zone. One of Matt's troopers had died in a spook's game being played by the agency to further its effort to gain control of one of the factions to be involved in the new government. Matt had no way of knowing of the Snake's background. This was extremely dirty business, but it was business as usual for the Snake.

Matt had charged into the debriefing hooch and confronted the Snake, calling him a son of a bitch and telling him he was on to the political assassination tactics the Snake was using the military for. The Snake's response had been dismissive. He played on his position as an intelligence operative and that his civilian government service grade translated into the equivalent of a brigadier general's rank in the military.

"Major, my operations are in pursuit of the overall objectives of the U.S. government. That's all you need to know. If you have a problem, take it up with your chain of command. Congratulations on a well-executed operation. Now, get the hell out of here."

Matt had restrained himself and left. He had subsequently gone to his own chain of command, but to no avail. No senior officer was going to take on the agency. Senior military officers don't get the stars of a general's rank by getting involved in intramural fights with other government agencies. The positive outcome was that a spotlight had been placed on the Snake's operations and his special operation requests were reduced in number and much more carefully looked at afterwards. The Snake had never forgotten being challenged by Matt. For his part, he carried with him his anger at the memory of his troops being used in the Snake's dirty political war by assassination. Matt had followed the Snake's career in Iraq as the Snake came to be an advisor on security and intelligence to the new government. Matt had also heard rumors of U.S. officials working with the Iraqi petroleum ministry earning small, undisclosed fortunes on the side. The Snake's name was occasionally mentioned in that regard.

Neither knew the other was in Thailand. Yet. For the Snake, the Bangkok job was the last rodeo. With all the dirt in his background, his career would never stand the public light of day and he would never be acceptable for a high-level intelligence post such as the National Security Council. At the same time, he couldn't accept riding a desk in Langley, except as a short-term transition to some worthwhile corporate security post. He had divorced his second wife before accepting the Bangkok assignment. She had stayed behind in Virginia and got the home in the settlement. She might still be there when he went, back but he wasn't really concerned. What he was concerned about was making sure he was comfortably set for a life outside of the government. He had significant, well hidden offshore bank accounts. The off-the-record financial opportunities his current post offered were in no way equal to the lucrative rewards of his advisor positions in Iraq, but still very important to him. He was determined that nothing and no one would get in the way of this operation.

Chapter 17

Matt was returning from three days camping in the Erawan national park, a part of the western forest complex of several national parks around Kanchanaburi and along the border with Burma. It had been a good outing and reaffirmed for him a key reason to be in Thailand: there were still great sections of jungle parks not yet destroyed. He felt his work with the forest rangers might help preserve these areas and was a worthwhile task for him.

Spending time in the forest always left him in a good mood. By and large, the Thai public didn't like trekking through the jungle. When Matt would go hiking and camping in the U.S., there were usually trails to follow, routes carefully laid out by park rangers and rules to keep to the concept of leaving no evidence behind of human intrusion. In Thailand it was just the opposite. There were seldom any marked trails into the woods beyond the park ranger's headquarters. A hiker would have to find and use animal trails wending in and around streams. Normally there would be a campground near the park headquarters and young people from the city would come out and pitch tents alongside one another, get out their guitars and music boxes and drink, eat and sing into the night without a desire to go further or seek isolation in the woods. This they called camping and wanted nothing more adventurous. The idea of going into the depths of the forest to perhaps see a hornbill close up or check the mud alongside stream banks for prints from tigers or Asiatic bears was completely unknown to them. At the same time, the headquarters area and nearby camping grounds were looked upon by the rangers running each park as their commercial opportunity much as any government employee in Thailand would have approached it. The rangers' wives would run outlets for soft drinks, packaged snacks and cooked food all at a healthy markup to the prices outside the park. People were not encouraged to go hiking. For the park rangers, people hiking and taking time away from the campgrounds, meant a loss of profit opportunity and the possibility, if the hikers got into trouble, of the rangers having to go into the woods themselves, a chore they avoided as much as possible.

For Matt it was always a great opportunity to get away by himself. His view, which he shared with a few like-minded friends, was that a walk through the wilderness was like entering a special cathedral. Silence and respect were the rules of the day. Any evidence of wildlife he came across he would photograph and share with the park rangers who would include it their monthly reports as their own findings, showing their management in Bangkok that they were on the job. For both— Matt and the park rangers—it was a happy arrangement. On this trip he had been able to photograph a gaur, a type of wild buffalo, at a waterhole. He took the pictures back to the park rangers and gave them the grid coordinates of the waterhole so they could use them in their reports. He had also found evidence of poachers cutting into sandalwood trees for the profitable core wood used for perfumes. He provided those coordinates as well.

Matt had stopped in Kanchanaburi, the nearest town and the location of the current-day tourist version of the famous *Bridge on the River Kwai*, for a quick lunch around noon and then drove back to his apartment in Bangkok which was a little under three hours away. He was tired and possibly a bit less observant than he should have been. He made it through the city traffic and turned into the entrance of the soi his apartment was on. If he hadn't been so tired, he might have noticed one of the motorbike boys parked at the end of the soi jump up and get on his mobile phone as Matt's vehicle turned off of the main Sukhumvit Road. The soi was narrow; there was room for just two vehicles to pass in opposite directions with just a few feet clearance on either side. If a vehicle was parked on the side or someone was wheeling a pushcart with food to sell through the soi, oncoming vehicles had to slow to a stop and take turns passing. Matt's apartment was one hundred fifty yards into the soi, half way down to the next main road. The soi curved to the right thirty yards from Matt's apartment, blocking his view from that point. As he went through the curve and was able to see further down the soi, he was getting ready to go around a car parked on the side when a pushcart was wheeled out of a lane on the other side of the road. The cart was about thirty feet in front of Matt. He braked and stopped waiting for the pushcart to clear out of his way. But it just stopped and the man pushing it turned and went back into the entrance of the lane.

Matt's internal alarm bells started going off. Something was wrong. He needed to act.

Matt threw the gearshift into reverse and looked back to reverse out. He saw a taxi had been following him and was now right behind his Fortuner. As he turned back to check the cart, two armed men stepped out of the lane and pointed automatic rifles at him. They were dressed in blue jeans and T-shirts and wearing black balaclavas. They paused for a second and stepped towards Matt's vehicle; the pause saved his life. It gave him a second to throw himself on the floor of the Toyota as the windshield disintegrated above his head. As he was lying on the floor, he reached underneath the mat. He always carried his sidearm—a Sig Sauer .357—with him on his forays into the jungle to protect against poachers. He had left it under the floor mat on the passenger side on his way back. As he pulled it out, he could feel the bullets impacting the vehicle. The first volley had gone over his head and through the windshield. He had the engine block between him and the bullets, but the shooters would be coming to ensure they had gotten him and to deliver the kill shots if needed. Matt reached above his head to the door handle on the passenger side and pulled. The door opened about half way and then banged against a concrete telephone and electric line pillar.

The opening was small yet large enough for Matt to slide through head first. With the gun in one hand, the other couldn't fully stop his fall and he smashed his head against the concrete as he tumbled out of the car. He was dazed for a second but he had a brief reprieve as the men were still shooting into the vehicle above him. Matt pulled around in the prone position looking under his vehicle facing towards the shooters. They had paused for a few seconds inserting new magazines. Matt could hear one of them shouting at the other in a dialect he didn't understand. As he looked forward, he could see one of them walking towards his vehicle. The shooter was coming to ensure the kill and put a round though Matt's head just in case that hadn't already happened. Matt's view from under the vehicle was just the black boots and trousers, about fifteen inches up from the ground.

Matt fired five quick rounds, aiming for the concrete about a foot in front of the man walking. His shots ricocheted upward off the concrete and threw up concrete chips towards the shooter. Matt wasn't sure whether it was the bullet fragments or the concrete chips or both, but the man screamed and went down backwards dropping his weapon. Matt let off two more shots as the man seemed to be pulled backwards by his companion. The shooting stopped. Matt held his fire and continued lying down, looking under the Fortuner to see if the shooters would approach again. He heard some yelling and then the sound of a motorbike starting up and driving off and then silence. Matt waited a few seconds and then started crawling backwards still watching towards his front. As he got to the front of the taxi behind his Toyota, he started to stand up, crouching with his gun still pointed towards the direction of the shooting. He looked over at the taxi driver who was frozen behind his steering wheel—eyes as big and wide open as a hunting owl at night—just staring at Matt. Matt started to tell him not to be afraid then suddenly felt dizzy, he slumped backwards, sitting in the alley, his back against the concrete outer wall of a private home. He was having trouble seeing and then he understood, his forehead was bleeding, the blood running into his eyes. He had cut his forehead when he threw himself out of his Toyota. Matt dropped his gun at his side and reached into a pocket and pulled out a handkerchief holding it against his forehead to staunch the bleeding. Then he blacked out. That was how the police found him when they arrived ten minutes later.

Chapter 18

When Matt woke up, he was lying in a hospital bed with his left arm handcuffed to the iron railing on the headboard. He looked down and could see he was dressed in hospital pajamas. Actually he had some memories, first of being loaded into an ambulance and driven away from the scene and then of a doctor talking to him and giving him an injection. How long ago—he had no idea.

He looked around the room and saw two men standing at the side of the room, one was a high-ranking officer in a police uniform and the other was in civilian clothes: black slacks, a white shirt and a tie. They were talking to each other in muted tones. A third figure, a police sergeant, was standing next to the door, seemingly as a guard. The senior police officer seemed to be briefing the man in civilian clothes. Matt had a major headache. He felt something on his head and reached up with his right hand to find a large bandage over the left side of his forehead. This movement caught the eye of the senior police officer who turned and walked towards Matt. It was the police colonel, the man who was in charge of the port police station.

"Khun Matt, how are you feeling? You are a lucky man. From what I understand not many people would have gotten out of that ambush alive."

"Thanks, Colonel. Right now I'm not feeling too lucky. My head is killing me, and these... " He gestured towards the handcuffs holding his left arm to the bedpost.

"Ahh, yes, I'm sorry about that, Khun Matt." Turning to the police sergeant, the colonel gestured him to come over. "Please unlock these handcuffs. This man is not going to be charged."

After the handcuffs were removed, Matt just looked at the colonel awaiting his comments. He was in no mood to volunteer anything. The colonel picked up on this.

"You must understand, the officers first responding to the scene were from the Lumpini police station, they didn't know who was who. Since you had a weapon and had been shooting—actually hitting someone according to the blood trail at the scene—they had to treat you as a potential suspect. They phoned to my station to alert us as we put a search paper out on you yesterday."

"Why were you were looking for me?"

"Where were you the day before yesterday in the early evening?"

At first Matt balked, he didn't want to answer without more background, but then his experience with Thai police kicked in. He essentially had no rights here. Not answering would only make things more difficult and he had a feeling he didn't need that right now.

"I have been out of town for the past three days, camping up in the Erawan forest area."

"Is there someone up there who can back up that you were there?"

"Yes, the park rangers. I checked in with them going in and when I came out this morning. Also I have some time-dated wildlife photos I took during the trip. Why?"

"Well that helps, but we will have to check on it. Khun Choi, the man you fought last week, was found dead yesterday. He had been beaten and then shot. His body was thrown into the Chao Phraya River. Actually the killers, we think there were more than one, had bad luck since the body should have just disappeared into the undercurrents. However, somehow his body snagged on a projection underneath a passenger ferry pier and hung there. Some passengers saw it there and called us. Of course we felt we had to talk with you as someone recently involved in a confrontation with him. If all this checks out, as I'm sure it will, we no longer have an interest in you, unless you have a comment or other information you want to provide on Choi's death?"

No matter how lousy he felt, Matt couldn't help but smile. Cops were cops. They would always throw you a curve, most often at the last minute like this. The game was to first reassure the person being interviewed that everything was fine and then drop an "oh, by the way" question. It was in their genetic makeup. They couldn't help it, but he didn't need to play along.

"No, Colonel. I have nothing to add. I hope you are successful in catching the killers."

"Well then, Kuhn Matt, I will leave you to the Lumpini police and I believe there are some others who might want to talk with you."

With that last comment, the colonel waved to the civilian who had been standing quietly against the wall all this time. As the police officer turned to go, there was a knock on the door. It was opened and Neung entered the room. He nodded to the man dressed in civilian clothes, who was giving him a respectful *wai* in greeting, and then to the police colonel.

"Good evening, Colonel. I am Inspector Neung from the DSI. I apologize that it took me a while to get here."

"No problem, Inspector, your man here gave me some background so I understand your interest. I think, for the moment, I can say we are not looking at Kuhn Matt for the murder of the Black Face gang member. For the shooting matter today, the Lumpini police may still have some questions."

"I'm glad to hear that. Thank you."

With Neung's dismissal the Colonel left the room. Neung noted the police sergeant stayed at his post inside the door.

"Sergeant, I take it you are with the Lumpini police?"

The sergeant nodded.

"Well you can take up your post outside the room. Your station has arranged for you to be relieved soon."

At first the sergeant hesitated, but then nodded and went out of the room. Neung turned to Matt.

"Wow, Matt, you have a habit of being in the middle of things. I understand you have been camping and then came back to town today. The doctor says you may have a concussion. Do you feel up to telling me what happened today in your soi?"

Matt nodded and proceeded to walk Neung through everything starting with his decision to get away and go to the forest for a few days and up until he woke in the hospital.

As he finished he couldn't help but ask, waving around the room—which was a fairly drab and not well-equipped hospital room— "By the way, what hospital am I in? This all looks pretty basic."

Neung laughed, "Not your style, huh? This is the police hospital on Rajadamri Road. The Lumpini police wanted to keep you in custody until they found out the full story of the shooting, so they brought you here. I've spoken with them and they're ready to release you. They have plenty of statements from witnesses, all of which clear you. The only real problem they had was the possession of the gun and I've been able to take care of that. Unfortunately, they want to hold on to it as part of the case evidence. I've brought you a replacement; it's locked up in my car. I'll give it to you later. I think you should be carrying it until this gets sorted out. Somebody is definitely out to get you."

"You think?"

Matt's head was really hurting and he leaned back against the pillow. He wanted to close his eyes, but he was looking for one or two answers before he did that. At the same time getting smart with Neung wouldn't help.

"I'm sorry. Who's trying to kill me and why? Got some ideas?"

"No, unfortunately all I have now is confusion and we're not going to talk about it here. The docs want you to stay the night. I want you to do so as well. You need to have a clear head when we talk. We'll leave guards here, including one of my men, and we'll pick you up in the morning."

Neung leaned over and pushed the nurse's button and almost immediately a nurse came in with a tray with some food and some pills.

Matt wanted to protest but then thought the hell with it. His head hurt too much to fight. Tomorrow would be fine. One last thing had to be done though. He had to call Noi and explain why he hadn't phoned on getting home. He wasn't looking forward to making that call.

Chapter 19

It was still too early for the hospital's daily operations to have started when Matt awoke. It was completely quiet. He just lay still for a few minutes, eyes closed, trying to assimilate all that had happened the previous day. Then it hit him: there was a scent of flowers in the room. He opened his eyes and looked around and found the source. It wasn't the presence of flowers; it was Noi's perfume. She was asleep on a small sofa on the side of the room. She had apparently organized a pillow and extra blanket from the staff. Noi had been upset when they spoke on the phone and wanted to come straight over. He thought he had talked her into coming in the morning, taken his sleeping pill and nodded off. In the Asian world, it would have been terribly wrong for her not to come and stay. The hospitals expected it and unlike Western hospitals made allowances for those close to the patients. Evidently Noi had arrived and taken charge. Even though he had told her not to come, it was still a great feeling to see her there. Despite still having a headache he couldn't help but smile.

Matt reached over to pour himself a glass of water from a carafe on the bed stand. The motion or the noise of pouring the water must have attracted Noi's attention. As he started drinking the water, she sat up, looking him over to see how he was doing.

Matt finished and looked over to Noi.

"Hey, you. Thanks for coming and staying with me."

Noi tossed her hair, running her fingers through it, trying to straighten it out from the tangle sleep had made of it and frowned at him. She threw aside the blanket she had been using and stood up. She was still dressed in her office clothes: black dress slacks, a conservative blue blouse and accessories. Apparently she had come straight from work.

"No, thank you for trying to get me not to come. I couldn't stay away. You should know that."

"I know it, babe. I'm sorry. I wasn't thinking very well last night. My head was hurting."

Noi sniffed a bit cynically. "Smart guy. Blame it on your injury and you know I can't say anything. How are you feeling now?"

"Okay actually. The head still hurts a bit but much better than last night. I'd like to get out of here."

"You will. We're taking you to get an MRI this morning and once that's done you're coming home with me."

Matt was a bit nonplussed. He had stayed over at Noi's before just not often. She had an older lady living across the hallway who closely monitored her coming and going. They had both decided not to give the old ladies' gossip mill too much grist to work with. At the same time, it was clear he had better avoid his apartment until they knew who was coming after him. He had thought briefly about finding a hotel room but knew it wouldn't fly with Noi.

"You're sure?"

"Yes, I'm sure. Where else are you thinking of going?"

Matt gave a small, submissive smile. It was time to retreat.

"Nowhere actually."

"Good, then it's decided. Neung said he would come and visit early this morning. Until then let me get you some breakfast and check with the nurses and see when they plan to change that dressing on your head. I'll be right back."

Matt leaned back and relaxed. This reminded him, in a way, of being in Army hospitals when he was wounded in Afghanistan. There was a certain luxury in giving control of yourself to others. The luxury of going from being a person who was action oriented, in charge and carefully controlled in most all things, to one who was dependent. In the Army hospitals it could be a bit anonymous; he had just been "the knee in bed six" as he had heard one of the nurses comment at one time. This experience was different. Now he found the effect of relaxed dependency was especially heightened when the one taking control was someone you loved and trusted. At the same time there was too much going on and too many unknowns about Yod's murder and the attempt on his life. He couldn't allow himself to relax for long, but decided he would enjoy the feeling.

With Noi's supervision, he had been able to have breakfast, shower and clean up. His dressing was changed for a much smaller one when Neung came in over two hours later.

Neung smiled at Noi and gave her a respectful *wai* in greeting. He knew she was important to Matt and though he found her a bit too independent for his liking, he also knew it wasn't his business. He turned to Matt.

"Well, you're looking much better this morning. How are you feeling? Are we moving you out of here?" He said this last bit looking to Noi to include her in the conversation. Noi answered for Matt.

"He needs an MRI first but after that, presuming it's okay, I'm taking him back to my place. He'll stay there until we are clear on things."

Neung just nodded. He understood Noi was in charge of Matt's welfare and that Matt needed her support.

"Good. Then let's talk about getting clear on things."

He looked at Matt, pausing expectantly, and then looked at Noi.

Matt was uncertain at first what Neung was getting at and then understood. He was hinting that Noi shouldn't be in the room. Noi also understood and stood by, stone-faced, waiting to see what Matt would say. This was not a woman who would volunteer to be excluded in any manner.

"No. She stays. I think the time has come to give her some background on all this. She has a right to know what is going on, especially if there might be any danger to her. What do you know?"

Noi went over and sat on the sofa. It had been established: she and Matt were a team. She didn't need to intrude on Neung's briefing in any manner.

Neung nodded accepting the reality and included her as he went on.

"Well some unusual things have come up. First the automatic rifle that was left behind at the scene by one of the shooters was an M-16. Looking at your Toyota and the shell casings left on the pavement it seems they were both using M-16s. That was good luck for you. The 5.56 caliber round from the M-16 is high velocity but has little penetrating power and the engine block was in the way. If they had used something with more penetrating power, well, it might have been different."

Matt nodded, remembering the flap about the M-16 and its successor the M-4 in Iraq. In urban fighting, when U.S. forces attacked insurgents hiding in houses built of twelve-inch cinder block, they were hard to get at. The light 5.56 caliber rounds were useless. Both marine and army units had requested and received permission to reissue the older M-14 that used the larger standard NATO 7.62 caliber round and weighed two to three times the 5.56 round in the M-16. Though the M-14 round had lower velocity, it had greater penetrating power and could smash through the cinder blocks and cause damage to the insurgents hiding inside. Matt remembered a Vietnam vet who cursed the M-16 for constantly jamming and praised the M-14 for never doing so even if you dragged it through the mud, and he had said the "damn thing could cut down trees." Matt imagined an M-14, or AK-47 using a shorter version of the 7.62 caliber round would have chewed up his Toyota and him as well.

Neung continued, "There is something strange about this particular weapon."

"What's that?"

"The serial number on this weapon traces it back to a batch of several hundred Thai Army M-16s stolen from an armory in Narathiwat in the south of Thailand back in January 2004. That means this weapon was in the possession of Islamic separatists in the South. How it comes to be involved in an attempted hit here in Bangkok is not clear."

"Could the Black Face gang have gotten it on the black market somehow?"

Neung sighed, shaking his head and showing a bit of uncertainty.

"We don't think so. We don't have any previous record of weapons stolen in the South coming up here. It's almost the opposite. The rebels down South have a tremendous need for weapons, and stolen weapons from other areas tend to flow in their direction. They are even raiding into armories in Malaysia for weapons to use against Thai troops. Of course the Thai army loses weapons from differing armories almost every year, but the weapons we find here in Bangkok and provinces to the North always come from armories around here. Also this type of hit seems much too public for the Black Face gang. Black Face Chan is known for preferring much quieter killings."

"Then what?"

"Well, and I hate to say this, maybe there is a third party involved in this matter of killing the young boy and maybe the third party has ties, somehow, to the South."

Matt thought for a second and then said, "For what it's worth, I don't think the guys who came after me were ex-military or police. The ambush was pretty amateur. They sprung it too quickly. They should have positioned the cart to stop me when I was even with the sub-soi they were hiding in. That would have been a better kill zone. Then they could have had clear shots right into the cab, right at me. Also I think experienced professionals would have hung in there when I started shooting back. These guys cut and ran quickly."

He looked to Neung who was absorbing the comment, "Police General Somchai did mention the man who ordered the boy from Choi was said to have a Middle Eastern accent and used the cover name Aram. Could it be there is an Islamic separatist or terrorist connection that's trying to cover up this killing?"

Neung looked off to the side indicating a level of frustration and uncertainty.

"It could be, Matt, and if that's the case, this matter has risen to a whole new level of sensitivity and complexity."

Matt understood what Neung was implying. If there were political angles to the killing it was no longer a simple matter of police work. Now the intelligence agencies would have to be involved, at least talked with and informed of the matter. In other words, it would be a whole new ball game and Neung's influence would be limited and Matt would be much more exposed.

"What's the next step? I would sort of like to have some idea of who came after me."

Neung noted the sarcasm but having soldiered with Matt was immune to it.

"I'll do my best. Let's start by being very careful. We have to presume you are still a target and start thinking of your security."

Turning to include Noi, he said, "You two don't let anyone know where you are going to be staying. Give me a day or two to try and get behind the veil on this."

Neung gave Matt a package, a cardboard box wrapped in brown paper.

"There is a replacement piece inside for your Sig Sauer and also a mobile phone. When I phone you, I will call on this phone. Hold on to it."

Then Neung turned to Noi.

"Don't give anyone here your name or address. I have a guy outside who will help you get Matt out of here and back to your place. Any contact info the hospital needs will be through my office. I need your apartment address. I will arrange to have some undercover guys rotating through the neighborhood checking things out just to be safe."

After Noi gave Neung her address, he left.

Matt asked Noi, "Are you sure you still want me? This could be a headache, babe." Then he laughed, "No pun intended."

"Yeah, I'm sure. Let's take care of things one step at a time. I'll cook and you wash the dishes. Agreed?"

"You got it."

Chapter 20

The attempted murder of a foreigner and a shootout in a residential area in the middle of Bangkok was in the newspapers, but not on the front pages. High-level police contacts had been in touch with the major newspapers and had been able to soften the coverage, yet the shooting couldn't be completely ignored. Though Matt's identity was not disclosed by the press, Jake knew it was Matt. The Snake already had a complete report from his police contacts.

The Snake had called the emergency meeting with Bashir and he was in a rage. Two things triggered his anger: the failure of the gunmen to finish the job and leaving behind a weapon as a trail to the Southern insurrection. Now he was standing over Bashir staring down at him.

"You son of a bitch. Don't you know the rules? The first rule of any hit is to finish the fucking job. These idiots have this guy pinned down and they run away and leave the guy alive because they discover he has a gun himself and one of them gets nicked a bit. To make it worse, they leave one of their weapons behind to give the police an idea of who they are."

Bashir was holding his hands above his head as if to ward off a blow.

"Jake, you know I had to use these guys. If I used local shooters, ex-cops or army types, the police would be on to them too quickly. The guys from the South are unknown up here and they are completely loyal. They can't be bought off. They see this as a holy war, as part of the *intifada*."

Jake was still angry but he knew Bashir was right.

"Yes, that's right, but do they have to be so damn incompetent? No wonder they're getting nowhere with their stupid separatist movement. The only people they can gun down successfully are unarmed schoolteachers and fruit vendors."

Bashir went on explaining, trying to get Jake to calm down.

"Also, I confirmed these were the two guys who killed the boy and started all this. This was their chance to make up for that mistake."

Jake had no concern about the teenage boy they killed, but as always, he was concerned about exposure of any kind.

"Did they explain why they killed the boy so graphically?"

"They said after our visitor left they went to the room to get the boy and take him back. He was not dressed, still naked, as our visitor had left him. He was suffering some sort of reaction to the drugs they used to put him into a passive state to make the sex play easier. The Ya K can have that effect. The boy was seeing things and paranoid. He went wild and hit them. He was slim but apparently strong. They said he called them pigs and insulted their religion. They both lost it. They knocked him unconscious and carried him out. Instead of delivering him to the drop-off site they took him to the slaughterhouse and cut his throat and left him there to rest with the pigs in retaliation for his insults. Then they just kept on going and ran down south. It took a few days, but I was able to threaten their leaders and they were ordered to come back to Bangkok and make up for their mistake. You have to understand. No one in their group in the South blames them for killing the boy. Insults to their religion are to be punished with death."

"Where are they now?"

"I didn't think it was safe for them to try going back down south. I sent them east towards the jungle areas along the Cambodian border. There are some Muslim settlements there in the rubber plantations in the hills. No one will report them."

Jake was stone faced. He just stared at Bashir for several moments and Bashir knew what was coming.

"Eliminate them. Have their own people do it as a punishment for their incompetence. Tell them the bodies should be left along the back roads between Chonburi and Pattaya. We need to give the cops here in Bangkok something for their cooperation. The police need to be able to say the killers paid for their crime against the boy. We'll make up a cover story. Tell their bosses we'll ensure the bodies of these guys will be discovered quickly and given an Islamic burial to satisfy any concerns their leadership may have on that regard."

"Okay, Jake."

"Let's talk about the guy they failed to hit. Matt Chance. He is potentially big trouble. I know him from past operations. He was an Army officer and a Ranger in Iraq. He has to go. He has connections both here in Thailand and in the U.S. that could threaten the operation and have both of us on the inside looking out. Do you understand me?"

Bashir didn't understand. He had been blackmailed when he was caught smuggling drugs into Thailand. The Thai government and the CIA forced him to enter into his role as their agent reporting on jihadis that he came into contact with and supplied. He had gone along because the alternative was jail and a death sentence. Until now he had considered Jake and his connections to the top of the security world in Thailand as untouchable. This sense of vulnerability on Jake's part troubled him. If Jake was vulnerable, then he, Bashir, was vulnerable, too. Of course, there was only one answer to Jake's question.

"I understand, Jake."

"Good. It's time we brought in the professionals. I can't use any Americans against an American target. Let me check some of my contacts in the Thai anti-terrorism black ops units. Maybe one or two of their graduates are available. We'll ask for a trained sniper, one of their 'men in black,' to do this job with one shot. Your job will be to find this guy and keep track of him until the snipers can be put in place. Put a watch on his apartment though I doubt he'll go back there. I'll check with the local intel service and get what information they and the police have on where he may be hiding. We have to get to him as quickly as possible before he has time to figure out what he's up against and starts his own planning."

"Got it, Jake."

Chapter 21

When he left the hospital, Neung had been unsure of what sort of barriers he would run into as he tried to push the investigation forward. He found out quickly.

When he questioned his boss at the DSI about tracking the M-16 and circulating information looking for the shooters, he was told to leave the case alone, that it was now a matter for military security. This meant the Thai civilian intelligence establishment in the DSI, which is normally involved in matters of national security, would have to defer to ISOC the Army's Internal Security Operations Command, an organization answering only to the Prime Minister. He was not too surprised, just the fact of one of their stolen weapons being used in a shooting in Bangkok would put the military security command, really the top dogs in security in the Thai scheme of things, in a protective stance. They would be looking into the shooting, but it was probable that little of what was learned would see the light of day even within Thai police or the Justice Department circles that the DSI operated under. Neung would have to go outside of normal channels. Of course, "normal channels" in Thailand is a relative term. Any bureaucrat worth his salt in Thailand worked hard to develop connections with powerful allies, in the police, the military or the political realm just in case the normal channels let him down. During his years of service in the military, prior to his transfer to the DSI, Neung had a tough, rising-star general officer as his mentor—General Savin. Over the years as he worked his way up the ladder in the DSI, Neung and the general had maintained their relationship. Neung provided the general whatever inside political and national security information the general might be interested in. The general was there as a potential force of influence should Neung ever be in need of it. The previous year the general had received a warning from Neung that one of his business relationships outside the military was about to go sour. The information, and work by Matt, helped the general to turn his back on a profitable yakuza connection, which could have hurt him politically if it had become public. The general and his key staff were grateful to both Neung and Matt. Neung would go to his army connections to find out what ISOC was doing.

Neung's plan was to speak with Tommy, he and Matt's buddy from their days of U.S. Army Ranger training at Fort Benning, Georgia. Tommy and Neung had both been nominated to take the course which usually included a small number of officers of U.S. allied forces including Thailand. They had met Matt on the first day and been delighted to find an officer who spoke their language as both Tommy and Neung were struggling with English at that time. Also Matt's experience in the ways of the U.S. military had helped them to understand what the goal was of the differing training activities. The mutual encouragement, the never-give-up attitude they shared with each other, was the most important part. The bond in those hard days still held and Tommy, now an Army colonel holding the position of regimental commander of the Royal Guard, was a safe place within the military establishment to start his inquiries.

Neung had thought to meet Tommy at his office at the regimental headquarters, but when he spoke with Tommy on the phone—updating him on the attack on Matt and the possible tie-in to army security—Tommy cut him off and told him to come to the office in the Prakanong district of Bangkok at seven that evening. Neung wasn't surprised. The office Tommy referred to wasn't an office at all but an apartment Tommy kept for his *mia noi* or minor wife as the Thai called the women the men kept as consorts outside of marriage. Tommy also used the apartment for occasional meetings with Neung, Matt and a few other close friends when sensitive matters had to be discussed. The *mia noi* would not be in attendance during the meeting, but out on a shopping expedition. One of the requirements of the position for a *mia noi* was an understanding nature. She would do her shopping, have dinner with a girlfriend and take her turn in a beauty salon until receiving the message she could return home.

When Tommy admitted Neung to the apartment, Neung was at first surprised to see another man waiting, but then recognized him and understood why Tommy had called him in. The man was Major Chirawat, the aide to General Savin. Major Chirawat was the go-between for those who wanted to get a message to the general or a favor from him. If possible, there would be a willingness on the general's part to assist Neung and Matt in the current matter. There were no secrets in Thai military circles that were kept from the general. It was very probable he would lead the next coup. He would have knowledge of whatever considerations ISOC might have on the matter. At the same time, under no circumstances could the Army be embarrassed.

Tommy's relationship with the major went back to their academy days when Tommy had taken the cadet under his wing and guided him through the demanding first year at the academy. It had become a lifelong relationship and a useful one for both military men.

Tommy welcomed Neung and then, waving to the major who had risen to his feet to greet Neung, said, "I thought it best to bring in Major Chirawat and see what the general might think of what has developed."

Tommy turned back to the officer and addressing him by his nickname, Od, told him to take a seat.

Tommy and Neung also sat down at the table.

"Od, why don't you go through some of the things we discussed prior to Neung's arrival. Bring him up to date."

"Yes, sir. Well, first of all, the recovery of a weapon stolen from the Naratiwat armory in 2004 caught the attention of the senior staff at ISOC as I understand you've discovered."

Neung nodded and indicated to him to keep talking.

"As you might be aware, ISOC is not one entity open within itself to all officers on all issues. It is compartmentalized. I won't go into the details of the organization, but there are several units each with a differing focus. When the information came back on the M-16 and the description of the two shooters as being dark and possibly Southern in appearance, the group working on issues relating to the separatist movement in the South took the lead, but then something happened."

The major shifted in his seat and glanced back and forth between his two senior officers. This was a clear tell that he was embarking on disclosures which could get all of them in trouble if not handled properly. He was nervous about it, but he said nothing directly and continued the briefing.

"Apparently someone at the very top, with knowledge across all operations, decided to take the matter away and assign it to another unit."

Again the major paused, clearly nervous, and then plunged ahead.

"There is a unit in ISOC which has the responsibility of coordinating with the U.S. government in their operations against terrorist groups around the world, specifically Al-Qaeda. This unit is the lead on this case."

Neung interrupted, "Does this mean that the shooters weren't from the separatist groups in the South?"

"No, sir, not necessarily. The complicating factor is that Al-Qaeda representatives have made contact with the Southern separatist groups and our fear is they are both training them and using them for special chores. The attempted hit on Khun Matt may have been one of those special chores."

"I'm sure you understand our government's role in assisting the U.S. anti-terrorism effort has been extensive and includes cooperating with the extra-legal rendition and detention of suspected terrorists. Thailand is just one of many countries providing this sort of assistance and we have made some of our military bases available, specifically the air bases. ISOC would have the responsibility for the coordination and the selection of sites and military airfields which could be used."

The major paused but neither Neung nor Tommy had anything to say. They both had heard though background sources about the detention of Al-Qaeda suspects in Thailand and the use by U.S. government contractors of extreme interrogation methods at those sites. How that passive support by the Thai government tied into this matter was not clear.

The officer watched their reaction closely and knew he had to take them a step further, but now he was on extremely sensitive ground and was hesitant to be too definitive in his statements.

"The Thai government is possibly cooperating, here in Thailand, with a U.S. covert operation against Al-Qaeda." He stopped there. It was clear to Neung and Tommy there was no more to be said as far as he was concerned.

Neung shook his head, this last bit, and its potential implications, was a bombshell. He was appreciative that the young officer was trying to be helpful, but with a look at Tommy trying to gauge his level of support, told the major, "I just don't see where this is going. Are you saying somehow Matt bumped into an operation against Al-Qaeda, based here, and became such a threat to the operation one of the parties involved put out a hit on him?"

The major smiled, and showing instincts that would serve him well in security matters and the intelligence field in the future, said, "No, sir, I am not saying that. You are."

Neung sat back, his first thought was *damn smart-ass kid*, yet he appreciated the smart-ass kid being right. Od had just laid out the trail. It was Neung who had closed the loop. Also, in a moment of clarity, he understood only he himself, due to his recent work with Matt, could say just what it was he had been involved in thereby attracting the attention of either Al-Qaeda or someone involved, Thai or foreign, in a covert operation against them.

Tommy, who had been silent all along, decided to step in and take the major off the hook.

"Od, we appreciate what you have provided. We will handle this information very discreetly. You may go now."

The major nodded, showing his relief and got up and left the apartment. Neung and Tommy were left looking at each.

Neung spoke first. "Tommy, I think you want to stay out of this. The top generals will be very unhappy if an ISOC operation is brought into the open. You and your dad don't need to be in the line of fire."

Tommy had been thinking the same and was relieved by Neung's clear comments. Tommy's dad was a two-star major general, but he was not involved in, and avoided, politics. He was not the type people meant when they referred to the top generals who might be capable of mounting the next coup against the government.

Neung went on. "Let me do some reading through our files. If ISOC has joined with an agency of another country to mount an operation targeting Al-Qaeda, then it has to be with the Americans. It's a normal part of our operations to track what the CIA is doing here, both their activities undertaken with our permission and those without. Now that I know what to look for, the tracks of this operation should be easy to find. I suspect it's being run from the very top on the American side. In any case, I'll definitely need to talk a bit more with Matt as to his contacts."

Their session concluded and Neung went back to his office while Tommy phoned his *mia noi* and told her it was okay to return to her apartment.

Chapter 22

The next morning Neung had found out enough that he was ready to speak with Matt. After some thought, Neung had phoned Matt and arranged to meet him at Noi's apartment at ten AM, well after Noi had gone to work. There couldn't be a more secure place to meet for the moment. It was a completely new location and his men already had it under surveillance for Matt's security.

Back at his office, Neung had worked until after midnight going through old files, focusing on surveillance reports and other memos concerning CIA activities in Thailand and cross-referencing against Middle East contacts. It would have gone faster had he been able to call in some of the agents who reported to him, but he couldn't take the chance. They were loyal to him, but when a subject as politically sensitive as national security and joint operations of Thai intelligence with U.S. government agencies was the focus, the temptation for one of the staff to discuss it with an outside patron might be too great.

As he went through months of reports, Neung began to find hints of what might be going on. Sometimes the clues were found in the documents, but also he began to see a trend in the areas where his field staff couldn't report because they had been called off by "higher authorities" or information was provided on a subject of high interest and then no reports were available at all. He found their absence a curious circumstance. In the end, he had enough information and was able to start connecting the dots.

The problem with extremely sensitive information, once you've uncovered it, is how to handle it. This was now Neung's problem. Matt was his friend and he needed to know just who was trying to kill him and why. At the same time, neither Matt nor Neung could take any action putting at risk a covert operation important to both the U.S. and Thai governments and hope to come out of the ensuing mess intact. For Neung to brief Matt at all would have been a violation of security laws except he had not been "read in" himself so he could claim all he was sharing with Matt, if the issue ever came up, were suppositions. A rather thin defense when it came to national security matters.

Matt had welcomed Neung's phone call and request for a meeting. He had found being taken care of and being in hiding got old quickly. This morning he had pushed Noi out the door to go to work at her regular time. After she was gone, he removed the smaller dressing the hospital had given him the previous day and replaced it with a large Band-Aid. He was ready to get on with things. Until he had a chance to touch base with Neung, he had no idea what he should get on with and how.

Neung arrived, knocked at the door to Noi's apartment and waited for Matt to let him in. As he was waiting, he sensed movement behind him and whirled around dropping into a defensive crouch, one hand going to his back for his handgun. Then he saw the door across the hallway had partially opened and an old lady, wearing a loose colorful muumuu style dress, wire-rim glasses and with her gray hair back in a bun, was eyeing him suspiciously. She said nothing as he faced her, just sniffed in disapproval and closed the door. Matt opened the door to see Neung still in a crouch with his back to the door to Noi's apartment. Matt, knowing the nosy neighbor had made her appearance, laughed and invited him in to sit at the small table in the eating area in Noi's apartment and offered him a cup of tea.

"Now you've met Noi's first line of security. That old lady lives for each knock on Noi's door. I don't know who she reports to, but I'm sure you've made her day."

Neung just shook his head and looked around for a second before sitting down, appreciating the plants and flowers, the traditional Thai artwork, the settings in the apartment had all the feminine touches one would seldom find in a man's apartment. He smiled at Matt indicating the homey decor, "Are you becoming accustomed to your new home?"

Matt smiled but shook his head no. "At another time I might, but I've other things on my mind right now. Have you been able to come up with anything?"

"Yes and no. I think I know what you stumbled into and why one of the parties, if not both, might want your activities to be stopped, but I can't say for certain who ordered the shooters to come after you. You should know that what I have is a few islands of fact surrounded by lots of watery supposition."

"Whatever you have it's more than I have now. Please give it to me."

"Well first what we are discussing concerns a covert operation being conducted jointly by the Thai government and your U.S. CIA."

Matt groaned and said, "Oh no, not the damn agency again."

Neung, not knowing of Matt's previous unhappy experiences with agency operations in Iraq, was surprised. "You have experience with these people?"

"Only bad experience I'm afraid. I'm sure there are some great agents, but I've only run into the bad ones. What is the connection here? Were they somehow connected to Yod's death?"

"It's not clear whether it was people they are targeting or people they are running who were responsible and who went after you. I suspect the latter. You remember Choi mentioned the man putting in the order for boys for sex had a Middle Eastern accent and called him regularly over the past few years for boys. One Middle Eastern name that came up in our reports is a Lebanese merchant who resides in Thailand and has been observed by my agents meeting frequently with CIA staff. His name is Bashir Bechara. He has been doing import-export business in Thailand for over twenty years. He imports from the Middle East and Pakistan and frequently has Arab, Iranian and Pakistani visitors. There were some notes about a drug smuggling watch issued on him several years ago and then suddenly nothing, no more reports. About six months later, he started showing up at clandestine meetings with key CIA staff whom we had under surveillance. We researched him and discovered he frequently orders sex workers for his customers from the Middle East. Apparently the more religious his visitors are at home, the more shy they are about going out to public places here to find women or boys to have sex with when they come to Thailand."

"How does that track with the shooters though? I thought the supposition was these guys were from the separatist group in the South."

"It seems Bashir periodically employs staff from the South. We have observed that with certain visitors, one especially, Bashir has employed what our watchers feel are security teams. These guys work in teams of two and seem to be from the South. Now I have to say here it gets a bit shaky as at one point we asked permission to put a trace on these guys, possibly even have an intentional traffic accident just to make them show some ID to a traffic cop. Somebody very high up in Thai intelligence put the brakes on that. We were told to leave it alone. This leads me to believe whatever Bashir is doing, he is protected. Sometimes the barriers put up and the games are played within intelligence agencies are as strong as the external barriers. It's possible that protection of these guys from the South when they come up here is part of our cooperation with whatever operation the CIA is running."

Matt got up and walked over to the window, looking out and thinking. Neung had gotten his attention, if the shooters hadn't already done so. Going after Yod's killer or killers had seemed a simple proposition when he first started. His initial thoughts had been that it was sex traffickers disciplining an unruly recruit and having it get out of control. Bumping up against people involved in a covert anti-terrorist operation added a level of complexity he wasn't prepared for. It was daunting. At the same time, he kept coming back to the mental picture of Yod, a skinny teenage kid, lying naked in a pool of his blood on the floor of the slaughterhouse. The men responsible had to pay for the crime. No operational imperative justified the brutality and indecency with which Yod had been treated. Those involved must pay.

Neung had just watched, quietly understanding the thought process Matt was going through. Matt turned back to him and sat down.

"So you think it was this Bashir or his security people who were trying to get to me the other day?"

"That would make more sense than thinking the Black Face gang murdered the boy and put the hit on you. Neither action is their style. The hit on Choi while you were away in the jungle could well have been these same guys from the South shutting up a source who might have knowledge of the orders their boss put in for sex workers. Luckily, thanks to your giving him a public beating, we had a chance to speak with Choi before they got to him and get what little he had to contribute. So yes, I think the most likely candidates are Bashir's security guys operating under his orders or the orders of Bashir's handler."

"Okay, but does that mean they were the guys who beat and killed Yod?" Matt refused to use the term the boy; he needed to keep giving Yod his identity just to preserve a small level of his dignity. He wasn't an object, he was a teenage boy, and he was a human being deserving respect.

"Matt, we'll never know. Bashir doesn't order the sex workers for himself; he orders them for his Middle Eastern visitors, probably depending on how important they are. It's possible the man who they ordered the boy for became angry with him for some reason and murdered him and they're covering it up for him. Given the sensitivity of this operation, I doubt we'll ever be able to get closer to the answer."

"So these security guys, the foreign visitor and Bashir and his handler, whoever that is, just walk? They are all too important to be touched?"

Neung sighed; this was a dirty business with neither he nor Matt in a position to touch it. "As things stand right now, they are untouchable. However there are some complications that still need to be made clear."

Matt, eager for any opening asked, "What do you mean by complications?"

"As I mentioned, prior to the break in his record in our reports and his subsequent linkup with the CIA contacts, Bashir was a suspected drug smuggler and we were on the alert to take him down at the right moment. Reading the surveillance reports and then other reports we get from the anti-drug task force, Bashir seems to have been given permission to import, possibly through his Middle Eastern visitors who are all given a green light at customs, large quantities of drugs. We have reports from dealers all around town of a Middle Eastern source who is providing steady quantities of drugs."

Matt snorted, disgusted at the cynicism of it all. "So besides sex trafficking and murder, these guys are allowed to profit on drug sales as part of their operation? What are the drugs they're distributing?"

Neung held back for a second, knowing Matt was going to jump on the next line. "They seem to be getting large quantities of Special K or ketamine from Pakistan as well as Ya E or ecstasy. Both are designer drugs and increasingly in demand here in Bangkok."

"Oh, hell, you mean the same drug found in Yod's system? Neung, I know the agency has been involved in some dirty business, including drugs going back to the war in Laos, but this combination of sex trafficking, murder and drug trafficking is too much to justify any operation as being untouchable. Who the hell is running this for the agency? Do you have any idea?"

"Yes, and that's another complicating factor. When I said this was being run from the top, I wasn't just talking about the Thai side. The guy we most frequently find Bashir meeting with is the CIA station chief here in Bangkok. He is a bit of a character all by himself. You know I once went back to the States for a three-week intelligence methods training course sponsored by your government for friendly intelligence services. A lot of the tradecraft reproduced on films by the CIA went back to the cold war and the tactics they employed against the KGB in Russia and some very tough Eastern European intelligence agencies. I was impressed with the disciplined approach to intelligence operations they were teaching. It has always seemed to me the minute one of these CIA guys gets off the plane in Asia, they decide they can forget all that tradecraft training as they are now in supposedly 'friendly' territory. This idiot station chief is a prime example. His number one mistake is thinking he can get away with acting as a case officer himself. He is much too visible and his attempts at clandestine meetings are laughable, the usual hotel room meeting routines are part of his procedure, but only those upmarket hotels with excellent steakhouses, and a number of the safe houses he uses we were on to a long time ago. This guy has an extensive social life including sessions with one supermodel and one super sexy ladyboy using some of the safe houses as his secret sex pads. Apparently he likes variety. Also we are sure he is taking some of Bashir's drug imports, not reporting them and having them resold here in town for his personal gain. He has made significant cash expenditures to sustain his lifestyle which go way beyond any operational funds we've ever seen."

Matt shrugged his shoulders, "I guess I should be surprised but I'm really not. When these guys go bad, they seem to think they're above the law and convention and they really go bad. Does this guy have a name?"

"Yes. This guy has a long record in the Middle East. We haven't shared our information on him with Washington. I think our top guys like having some dirt available they can use at the right time. His name is Jake Chavez."

Here Neung stopped, as Matt jumped up and hit the table with his fist. "Damn it!"

"What's wrong? Do you know this guy?"

Matt slowly sat back down. "Hell, yes, I know him. He's a real bastard. His nickname is the Snake. I ran into him in Iraq in a death squad operation he was running for the agency. I had no idea he was here. He'll know my name. I gave him a hard time in Iraq and he's not the kind to forget."

"Well he's here and this is his operation. I would say he now knows you are here. If he didn't order the hit, he must at least have been aware of it. I'd say you got a real dangerous enemy and, Matt, there is nobody here who can touch him. You have to be careful. They might think they scared you off by attempting to kill you but they also might just be waiting until your guard is down and plan to come back at you then. Don't forget, very little of what I just gave you is provable in terms of hard evidence. This isn't the U.S. This is Thailand. You can be sure our intel reports will never see the light of day."

Matt was still shaken by the news. He paused for a long moment and then looked at Neung and said, "There's got to be a way. No matter how important the operation, he can't get away with the things he's doing. If there is no one here who can touch him, then we have to look elsewhere. Thanks, Neung. Let me think about this."

"Okay, Matt. Think about it. While you are thinking keep a very low profile. Don't go back to your apartment. Give me a list of things you might need and I'll have one of my guys go over and pick them up. Also, think about finding another safe house, this is a hard place to protect and you don't want Noi caught in crossfire. I can give you some options. I don't think the old lady across the way is security enough."

That got a laugh out of Matt.

"Thanks, Neung. You're right. Let me make a plan. I'll call you later today. With enemies like this, we don't have time to waste. By the way could you have one of your guys bring Blue Magic over, along with my helmet, and park it at Jack's Pool Bar? The keys are in a bowl on the side table just inside the front door of my apartment. If I can borrow a small motorbike to use when I leave here, it would be good."

Neung nodded, "No problem. You're thinking right. You need some options for transportation." Then Neung went out the door.

Blue Magic was Matt's motorcycle, a BMW F800R Roadster, a 798 cc bike. He didn't ride it inside the Bangkok city limits though, the city is flooded with a tide of sub-150 cc Honda Dreams and Yamaha Fino motorbikes, and the odds are heavily weighted against those riding large motorcycles in Bangkok traffic. Between the taxis and the motorbikes, every corner is an accident waiting to happen. He rode Blue Magic when he had time to escape the city and tour the countryside. He called it Blue Magic since it was painted blue but also, as he joked with Noi, when he was riding in the countryside whatever blues he might have disappeared like magic. He thought he might need a little Blue Magic pretty soon.

Chapter 23

It had been a difficult conversation. It was one of those situations in which one person felt they were presenting the power of logic and the other was saying, "Damn the logic, what about what I want?"

While Noi had not used those exact words, it was the essence of her rebuttal.

Matt waited until she came home, confronted her shortly after she put down her purse and keys and came over and gave him a kiss. His opening line was the classic couple's lead-in to confrontation.

"We've got to talk."

She sat down next to him on the sofa and took his hand.

"Of course, babe. What's wrong? Can it wait until after dinner?"

Matt knowing there was no soft way to do what he needed to do, let go of her hand, got up and walked over to the small dining table, pulled out a chair and sat facing her.

"There's no time for dinner. We have to assume these people are going to come after me again. I've put you on the spot by coming home with you. I needed the time you gave me to get my head together. It's together now and you can't be near me until this is finished. It's too dangerous. I'm sorry, babe. I've got to go and the sooner the better. Neung's guys left me a motorbike down in the basement. I'll use it to get to my next stop. I'll call you when I can. I'm sorry. It has to be this way. I learned from Neung that these are people even he may not be able to stop."

"Where are you going to go? What are you going to do? Let me help you."

Noi got up and walked over to Matt, kneeling down and putting her hands on his knees, starting to cry softly. She had been very strong until now but nothing in her life had prepared her to deal with murder and the potential murder of someone she loved. Her emotional answer was to get closer, not to go apart.

Matt was overwhelmed; combat was so much simpler, no one cried when you walked out through the wire to start your patrol. No emotions were involved except the palpable sense of fear that rose in your throat as you left the security of the base and you worked constantly to keep it under control. You never wanted it to show. You never wanted to give in to it.

Matt stood up and pulled Noi up with him hugging her, burying his face in the sweet scent of her hair. He had been ready to pay any price to avenge Yod's death, but he was not ready to have Noi become part of the cost of avenging Yod. He was angry with himself for not anticipating the worst and allowing her to be involved. At the same time it was too late for second thoughts. He had to be disciplined and finish the job if Noi was to be safe.

He pulled back and looked at her, still holding her. "I love you. Please trust me. It has to be this way. I have friends who can help, but you can't be involved. These people are ruthless."

Noi said nothing, just looked at him, tears still running slowly down her face. She nodded, once then again. Matt hugged her again, hard, then released her and went to the door. At the door, he paused and looked at her.

"I'll be back. This will be finished. I promise, babe."

Again Noi nodded and then, showing her strength, lifted her head and said, "You'd better keep your promise, or I'll kill you."

She had forced a laugh out of Matt. "We don't want that do we? Goodbye for now, babe." He turned and went out the door.

Matt used the borrowed Honda motorbike to leave the basement of the apartment and go up to the entrance to the soi. He deliberately didn't wear a helmet and paused at the exit to the soi for thirty seconds to give any observers a good opportunity to see it was him. The danger, of course, was if a competent sniper were positioned within eyesight waiting for a shot at him, he would have been dead. No shot was taken so he rolled out into traffic. He wasn't worried about being followed. He knew plenty of in and out routes to disclose whether he was being tailed and to lose a tail if necessary. In the crazy world of Bangkok traffic, the options included going up a one-way street the wrong way or riding on the side walk brushing pedestrians aside. Neither action would be noted as being unusual.

Matt had spent the day making calls and preparing his next steps. He hadn't yet told Neung his plans. Matt knew he needed help and the help he needed had to be above and beyond the reach of the Snake. The problem was, as Neung had pointed out, much of what Neung had shared with him was supposition based on surveillance by Thai intelligence, not hard evidence he could lay before any higher authority. In Thailand the Snake was working with ISOC, there was no higher command he could go to. The answer in one sense was simple then. He had to go outside of Thailand. However, right now, he needed to stay alive.

He went first to Jack's Pool Bar. Blue Magic was waiting for him there, dropped off by one of Neung's team. He gave the agent waiting there the keys to the Honda and then, taking time to pick up a cheeseburger to go, got on Blue Magic and headed up the road. While he was waiting for the food, Da came out and said hello and asked what was up. She had loved Blue Magic from the first time she saw Matt ride in on it and had gone out and gotten an older model BMW bike herself. She had teased Matt by calling her bike Black Magic, saying it was magic the way pretty girls, seeing the bike, wanted to jump on the back and hold tight to her for the ride. Matt told her he was going to be out of town for a while and asked if she would keep in touch with Noi. Da had smiled, a bit of a crocodile smile, and said she would call right away.

From Jack's place, Matt rode over to what would be his new home while he made his travel arrangements. He was going to a place where he could conceal Blue Magic and few questions would be asked. It was called the Lucky Hotel and was located less than a mile away on Sukhumvit Soi 26 between Sukhumvit and Rama IV roads, two main business avenues. The setting was a typical love hotel: rooms rented out were normally used for the short rental periods it was deemed required for the act of "love," two or three hours at most. The exterior of the hotel turned its back on the world and was all concrete block, two stories high on four sides with just a narrow entrance for a car to drive in. It was designed so that when cars entered from the road they immediately turned left into the courtyard entrance so you couldn't see directly in from the street. The rooms were sited over parking spaces with large drapes at the entrance that could be pulled into place after the car, or in this case, Blue Magic drove in. This effort at security was to protect the identity of whatever prominent politicians or public figures needed a secure and quiet place to bring their current lady of the evening. The Thai sense of a man's right to enjoy life in this regard is so strong that such fortresses of love are scattered all over metropolitan Bangkok and even into the countryside. The love hotel concept fit well into Matt's need for security. Food was available within a short walk to a number of street stalls along the soi and he could pay one of the houseboys or maids to run out and pick it up for him.

The rent for two hours was twelve bucks, but Matt negotiated and paid for two days in advance at a much lower hourly rate. An unusual procedure for the love hotel but one that, for enough money, the manager was happy to accept. Matt was using cash provided by Neung. He wanted to avoid using either his ATM or his charge cards for now.

It was a long and somewhat noisy night. Matt had phoned Noi and let her know he was safe. On the phone she alternated between being angry at him for not staying with her and then warning him to be careful. She didn't push for details of the threat he was under or his location, she accepted his evaluation and didn't question the reality of the threat with the ambush he had survived being proof positive. He didn't give her any details of his plans, just promised to phone the next day. After the phone call Matt was left alone to confront himself. It was clear why he had become a target. He had pushed hard for answers about Yod's death and those threatened by his push for answers had turned out to be very dangerous people. The questions he wrestled with: why did he get involved in the first place and why was he pushing so hard? He hadn't expected these people to be so dangerous to him, Noi or anyone in his vicinity. It made it all the more important for him be clear minded as to what motivated him.

A year earlier he had been drafted into the search for a U.S. research scientist who had gone missing in the jungles of Northern Thailand. He had gone along and investigated the matter initially as a favor to a former Ranger buddy working in intelligence in the U.S. and then tried to back out of the case as he came to believe it was something for the Thai and U.S. governments to handle. The killing of another research scientist Matt had met convinced him to help solve the case. The killers had obviously wanted to learn what Matt was up to and had ambushed the scientist to try and get some answers. Matt felt responsible for leading the killers to an innocent party. It was that direct connection between his contact with the scientist and the man's subsequent murder that spurred him on. He felt responsible.

Now again it was a personal angle driving him. He knew Yod. He had helped train the boy in Muay Thai. Yod was an innocent party, a boy left on his own and taken advantage of by others.

In the end, it came down to Matt's glorified image of the father he never really got a chance to know. Those who grow up living with both parents come to realize that however good their parents appear, they are still human with faults and foibles. It takes the absence of a father, much as Matt had experienced, and the need to fill that absence with a belief the father figure is a hero, to create the inner desire and drive for him to rise to a level he imagined his father would approve. Matt's father's death at the hands of terrorists only heightened the young boy's need to believe in the heroic image and increased the strength of that belief. His desire for an American education, entrance into the military and volunteering for airborne and ranger training all grew out of his desire to measure up to the father he never knew.

He didn't feel he was responsible to right the wrongs of the world, but when those evils came to his doorstep his reaction, which needed little prompting, was to take action to eliminate the evil presence. When it came to crimes against those he knew, it was a black-and-white world for him. His training and experience just meant he had more tools with which to confront the criminals and he felt more responsibility.

By the time morning came, Matt was clear in what he wanted to do. The plan was simple if limited in hope. If no authority in Thailand could rein in the Snake and bring Yod's killers to justice, then Matt must go outside of Thailand, back to the U.S.

There was one contact he wanted to make, one conversation he wanted to have before he left the country. He needed to speak with another ex-soldier who had had dealings with the agency nearby in Vietnam and Laos. The agency, before Delta Force and the Ranger units were organized post-Vietnam, had frequently called on Special Forces units to assist their undercover war operations. Matt needed to have another talk with John Scales, the former Special Forces trooper who had experience in both Vietnam and the dirty CIA war in Laos. John may have some insight into what buttons to push to get the agency's attention. Matt made the call and without disclosing his location, made arrangements for John to be walking down Soi 26 from Sukhumvit road an hour later.

Matt had gone out to the street a few minutes early knowing John would walk through at the very front edge of the agreed time slowly checking things out. The soi was a nice break from the usually bare side streets of Bangkok, most of which would just be termed alleyways in the West. Beside the Lucky Hotel, there were several small upmarket boutique hotels along with some residences and small shophouses. There were actually sidewalks on both sides so pedestrians didn't have to fight the traffic and trees growing on both sides, providing a shady, cool feeling to the soi. John soon appeared, dressed all in black as usual, but wearing a loose shirt over the belt, a sign to Matt that he was carrying his sidearm. John knew of the attempt on Matt's life and understood this was now a situation requiring some measure of security. John was a bit surprised when Matt stepped out of the Lucky Hotel entrance way and waved him into the love hotel but he never missed a beat, asking no questions until they were up in Matt's temporary room.

John looked around the rather spartan room decorated with a mirror on the ceiling over the large bed and couldn't help himself. He turned to Matt with a small smile and said, "This is good, Matt. I guess this is what they call going to the mattresses."

Matt laughed; you could count on old soldiers to take a skewed view of everything especially as things got more dangerous. It was a manner he was used to and comfortable with.

"Not for long though. I just need to keep a low profile until I can get out of country."

"Well, Matt, this should be a good story. I would guess it has to do with your investigation into that young boy's murder, doesn't it?"

Matt nodded and proceeded to bring John up to date including his plan to leave Thailand by land going through a border crossing into Cambodia and then booking his planes from there back to the U.S.

Even an old hand, such as John, was taken aback by Matt's story. He had sat down on a chair at a nearby dressing table while Matt sat on the bed telling his tale. When Matt had finished, John shook his head.

"I'm beginning to learn that what's remarkable about you is your ability to get into very unusual situations. I just hope your ability to get out of those situations is just as remarkable."

"Old soldier, that's what I'm hoping you can help me with. You were exposed to agency operations, especially the mess they created in Laos, their export of opium to Thai generals and then how they turned their back on the Hmong hill tribe people they had recruited to go to war alongside them. Any advice on what it takes to get these guys to go straight? There has to be some way to bring pressure on the Snake to give up Yod's killers."

John got up and walked the room, his laconic, joking manner gone. He turned to face Matt and spoke slowly and intensely.

"Bringing pressure on the agency is a dangerous game, Matt. I do believe you are right to go back to the States as soon as possible. Even there, be very careful who you contact until you get the lay of the land. The new national security laws in the U.S. mean you basically have no rights if the government decides you are part of a terrorist threat to national security and they only need the slightest of pretenses to act. Keep quiet and keep a low profile until you have all your support systems in place."

John continued walking around the room thinking. Matt just let him go, waiting and hoping there was some positive aspect of his trip that would occur to John.

"First I would say don't threaten the agency. Don't ever say you'll go public. That is anathema to them. They'll react like rabid dogs and just come after you as a threat to security. That of course means their job security mostly."

"I've no intention of doing that. It would just muddy the waters and make it harder to get the justice I want for Yod."

"Have you a contact in the agency or in Homeland Security anti-terrorism?"

"Yes, my best friend who I served with in Afghanistan. He lost his leg to an IED blast, left the service and ended up working with an anti-terrorism unit in Homeland Security."

"Okay. That's your starting point, but don't go to him at work or in any official sense. Call him at home and arrange a private meeting. Brief him. You'll still need a contact in the agency though. Those guys still think and act as if the rest of the government can't be trusted. The agency will only listen to someone in the agency. You've got to find that person whoever it is. Give him the story, be sure you are pitching it as your desire not just to have justice done but to protect what you presume is an important operation from mishandling by an agency staffer who has gone off the ranch. The working guys in the agency want to do the right thing.

The problem is the higher they climb the more pressure they get to provide the NSC and the White House the results they want and the reports they want to hear. The nonexistent weapons of mass destruction in Iraq are a good example. The working guys knew they weren't there, but the management said yes, they are there; it's a slam dunk because that's what the White House wanted to hear. Get to the right level of working guys and let them scare the top guys. Be sure they see you as being a patriotic American who is on the agency's side and can be trusted."

Matt waited, but that was what John had to offer.

"Thanks, John. I appreciate your input. My instincts from the military are to approach things head on yet I understand the land of spooks is a different world."

"I wish I could offer you more, Matt. Most of my contacts back there are all retired or dead."

Matt got up and shook John's hand.

"You've helped me a lot. Now I have to get over there and start looking for the way into making contact with someone who will give me a good hearing."

"When are you off?"

"Later tonight. I'm going to go to Cambodia through the border crossing at Poipet first thing in the morning and then on to catch a plane out of Phnom Penh. I think it's best to stay away from the airports here in Bangkok. I have no idea what sort of contacts and pull this agency guy has. Best to assume the worst and play it safe."

"Good luck, man. Watch your back."

With that John left and Matt started packing his bag. He was traveling light and would buy whatever clothes he needed in the States.

Eight hours later, after most of the short-time occupants had departed, Matt left the Lucky Hotel. Riding a motorcycle through the night on Thai roads is a lottery with death. Once out of the city the roads were unlit and truckers would occasionally park their trucks on the side of the narrow roadways with no lights or reflectors to warn oncoming motorists. It was normal for Thai motorcyclists to run on the edge of the shoulder. Periodically the newspapers would report a fatal crash at night when a biker ran full speed into the back of a parked truck.

As Matt rode Blue Magic through the night, he was focusing solely on the two-lane highway. The countryside was dead black, broken only occasionally by the lonely beacon of a dim light burning in a farmer's shack off in a field. The two-lane country roads were lined with trees, and the branches had grown out over the highway. The successive passage of trucks with fourteen-foot high clearances had trimmed the branches hanging down but had left drivers the menacing visual effect of riding down a dark tunnel with just a narrow center strip of night sky and stars visible above. Matt's subconscious mind would have to work on the problems he faced. His conscious mind had to be completely absorbed in the job at hand, surviving the night ride. Matt normally loved riding on Blue Magic, and the cool night air was comfortable, but he was aware there might be an unmarked obstacle around every curve. He had timed the two and a half hour ride to the border crossing so that he would arrive around seven AM. The border crossing would open at eight and he wanted to ensure there was time to properly coordinate his crossing.

By the time Matt arrived at Poipet, he was totally exhausted from the tension of the ride. He had arranged with Neung to meet one of his agents at the border crossing and turn over Blue Magic and the sidearm Neung had loaned Matt to replace his own which was still held by the Lumpini police. Thankfully a two-man team was waiting. Their pickup truck was parked at a roadside food stall a few hundred meters from the bridge crossing the border. Matt had time for a cup of tea. Then they loaded Blue Magic in the pick-up truck and locked the Sig Sauer in the glove compartment. One man stayed behind to watch the truck and the other escorted Matt through immigration. Arrangements had been made on the Thai side, and on the Cambodian side money talked. As he got into the car he would take through the Cambodian countryside to the airport at Phnom Penh, Matt started to relax. He wasn't sure what flights he would take, but there would be flights to

Hong Kong from Phnom Penh and from there a hundred options were available going back to Washington, D.C. The difficult first step was over.

Act II—Washington, D.C.

Appointment in Samarra

A servant to a rich Baghdad merchant goes to the market and encounters Death there, who gestures at him. Convinced that this is a very bad omen indeed, the servant rushes back to his master in a great panic and begs him for a horse so that he can ride to Samarra and escape whatever calamity will befall him should he stay in Baghdad. The kind master gives the servant a horse, and goes out to investigate for himself. When the merchant finds Death and asks him why he frightened the servant so, Death replies: "I wasn't trying to scare him, it is just that I was so very surprised to meet him here, because I have an appointment with him tonight in Samarra!"

—*Adapted From the Babylonian Talmud, 9ᵗʰ Century AD*

Chapter 24

As the United Airlines flight from Tokyo turned into the landing pattern at Dulles International Airport, Matt looked down at the varied colors of autumn leaves in the Virginia countryside with mixed feelings. He was relieved to finally be with friends and to confront the problems he encountered in his search for answers to Yod's death. Through the long hours of the flight, the awareness had slowly grown that the Snake was a well-placed part of a secretive network in the government and could have, through back channel communications, put out an anti-terrorism alert of some kind on Matt. It wouldn't declare Matt to be an outright terrorist but something more in line with describing Matt as a "person of interest." However the effect would be the same as painting him as a terrorist. Matt would be detained and questioned and every aspect of his activities in Thailand and previous military service would be examined and doubted. Unlike the American tradition of being innocent until proven guilty, the statutes passed since 9/11 to implement the war on terrorism had granted the authorities the ability to treat people as "guilty until proven innocent." He could survive being detained and questioned, but those procedures and disclosures would drag his quest to find and punish Yod's murderer into the mud. Furthermore, as John had warned, if the agency management came to think he was a threat to the security of an important operation, his standing as a result of his distinguished military service record would offer little protection. As the saying goes, just because you're paranoid doesn't mean they aren't after you. The Snake was really after Matt and he decided he had to proceed based on the worst assumptions.

As he deplaned and boarded the airport bus, Matt looked around him. Another negative possibility hit him. He was with mostly businessmen returning from sales trips to Asia or making sales trips to the U.S., students, both Asian and Western on school travel and some family groups, possibly immigrants, making their first landing in the U.S. Almost all of them had hand luggage and he was sure they had checked in bags also. He was carrying only the gym bag Neung's guys had taken from his apartment. He fit into no group and it occurred to him that at his age, his tan skin color, his shoddy appearance after thirty hours of travel, and being resident in Thailand, he might well fit into some drug courier watch profile the Drug Enforcement Agency had. His mission might well be over before it started, not due to the Snake, but due to the enforcement issues involved in combating America's voracious drug habit.

As people rushed to get off the airport bus and proceed down the hallway to immigration, Matt, who normally moved through checkpoints at a fast clip, often at the head of the crowd, decided to hold back. He was nervous and he didn't want to be in the front of the crowd or in the back. He wanted the immigration officer who talked to him to be a bit tired from having checked a good number of people through already and to feel the pressure of having to deal with a great number more lining up to come through behind him.

As he waited his turn in the U.S. citizen's line, he looked to the back of the immigration booths trying to see if there were senior officers on the lookout for anything special. He couldn't spot any but there were certainly officers scanning the crowd. Were they looking for him? Had they spotted him? Were they just waiting until he was through immigration to confront him?

This suspense was all new to Matt. As a military officer in uniform, he had breezed through all U.S. entry checkpoints before, usually receiving a "Thank you for your service" greeting. Now, at his turn, Matt walked up to the immigration booth and handed over his passport and entry card. The immigration officer looked him over for a second and then put the passport onto the electric scanner. Then the officer, noting how long he had been overseas in Thailand, asked what he did there. Matt answered that he worked as an environmental consultant to the Thai government which seemed to satisfy him. He stamped the passport and said, "Welcome home."

Okay so far. Matt took the entry card and passport and, skipping the crowded baggage carousels, went to the customs line. He scanned the area behind and around customs looking for agents watching the crowd. Again no sign of watchers, but certainly they were there. Matt handed his card and passport to the customs officer who asked him, "Just the one bag?" Matt replied, "An emergency trip." The customs officer just nodded and waved Matt through.

Getting through immigration and customs did not relieve Matt. He was conscious of being in "the land of spooks" as John said. From now on he would have to conduct himself as if they were watching. If he was a person of interest, he wanted to limit their interest to himself and not have it extend to his friends.

Matt had not made contact with anyone while traveling back from overseas. He wanted to find a place to stay and to let Noi know he was okay. Afterwards he would make contact with the man he was counting on, his Ranger buddy Carl Winters.

For now Matt would not worry about being tailed or watched in any way. Acting too suspicious would just reinforce suspicions. He got in the taxi queue and out of force of habit when they asked him where he was going, he said, "Key Bridge Marriott." That was the address he had written on the customs form. From there he could make calls, plans and get some sleep. It had been over thirty hours since leaving the Lucky Hotel including the thirteen-hour plane ride from Tokyo. He was mentally and physically exhausted. If people wanted to watch him, let them watch him sleep.

Chapter 25

It was a crisp fall day, thankfully no rain and clear blue skies as the sun continued rising. Matt had taken the metro rail, the blue line, to the Arlington Cemetery stop. It was a short ride from the Rosslyn station located near his hotel of choice when visiting Washington, D.C., the Key Bridge Marriott. During his years in the military, he had dreaded visiting the Pentagon and encountering the military bureaucracy—an old warrior, friend and mentor, Dave Hackworth, had once dubbed the generals the "perfumed princes of the Pentagon." He was never comfortable staying in a Chrystal city hotel—a commercial area closer to the Pentagon. He found it to be a jungle of high-rise government office buildings with no personality. The open environment offered by the Key Bridge Marriott set Matt more at ease. He liked the view overlooking the Potomac River, Roosevelt Island and Georgetown University and it provided a choice of excellent running tracks. As tired as he was on his first night, he woke up at four thirty AM due to the jet lag and as the sun was rising he was running across Key Bridge and on to the C&O canal. The six-mile run alleviated much of the anxiety he had felt the previous day.

He arrived at the Cemetery early. He and Carl had agreed to meet at ten at the gravesite, but Matt wanted to wander a bit. Whenever he came to the Cemetery, it was his habit to look at other tombstones and reflect on what Arlington Cemetery meant.

It was an impressive sight, the legion of white tombstones marching in formation across the rigorously trimmed grassy hillside dotted with trees. Down below the hazel-hued Potomac River, having slowed its pace from its upstream rush, plodded by. The two shores, Washington, D.C., and Virginia, are tied together by four bridges: Key Bridge leading to Georgetown, the Theodore Roosevelt Bridge extending Virginia's Route 50 over the Potomac, the Arlington Memorial Bridge immediately below the cemetery and the busy 14th Street Bridge closer to the Pentagon. Here above the Potomac, lay the fallen heroes in their serried ranks. Arlington Cemetery is imposing just in its size and geographical layout. The grounds, previously the estate of Robert E. Lee's wife, Martha Custis, and their home together, were confiscated by the Federal government early in the Civil War and cover a broad swath of a gently rolling hillside that runs nearly down to the Potomac River.

If Matt had time when visiting, he would walk over to the northwest corner to the graves laid down at the beginning of the cemetery during the Civil War with simple tombstones dating back to the 1860s. Today he didn't have the time. He instead kept himself to the section with the most recent graves, those from Iraq and Afghanistan, as well as older veterans of Vietnam and even Korea who had survived to be buried in the new millennium. To Matt the story was simple: they were all brothers. He hadn't told his mother, but it was his intention to be buried here. His ticket allowing him entry to the cemetery when he died were his Silver Star and Purple Heart medals—either one of which met the criteria to allow him to be buried here with his brothers. He always had the thought he should have already been buried here. He felt strongly it was wrong he had survived when so many others he had served with, better men then he, had died. Psychologists and others call it "survivor's guilt." To Matt assigning a name to it meant little. He still felt it was the reality. He should be here. Fate had played a trick on him by allowing him to survive. At the same time, he had survived, so he always came back to the same place. Deal with it. Get over it and get on with life.

"Hey, soldier, wake up!" It was Carl, calling him back to the moment. Matt turned around. Carl was working his way up the slope. His prosthetic leg helped him walk okay on flat ground, but going up even a slight rise could be a struggle.

Matt automatically smiled. He just felt right when he was around Carl. Carl was incurably upbeat and had always been so throughout difficult times and places. No matter how bad things looked, Carl would always say, "We're survivors and survivors will survive. Just hang in there and keep doing what we have been trained to do." Somehow he had always been right. Even after losing one leg and a military career he loved, Carl was still upbeat.

Matt greeted him, went over and put an arm around his shoulder. "Hey, combat. Good to see you."

"I knew you would get out here early and look around. You satisfied for the moment?"

"Yeah, let's go over and say hi to Jack."

A few paces further on, in one of the newer sections of the cemetery, they found the meeting place they had agreed on. The tombstone inscription was simple as they all were. The inscription read Cpt. Jack Fletcher, USA, Iraq, SS, BS, PH, and included his date of birth and the date of his death in 2003 in Iraq. He had served as a company commander in the same Ranger battalion as Matt and Carl. They had been with him in the fight in Samarra when he was killed leading his men in house to house combat.

For those who have served in combat and know fellow warriors buried there, the magnificence of the Arlington National Cemetery setting fades as the memories and stories of those fallen warriors come to mind while they slowly walk the hill side. Both Matt and Carl remained quiet, each consumed with his own thoughts as they walked over to Jack's grave and looked at his tombstone.

Finally Carl spoke, "A good man."

"A damn good man. He led the way."

"And he paid the price. Are you going to join him here?"

Matt was surprised at the question but understood. Carl lived and worked here in Washington, D.C., and would see the cemetery frequently. Thoughts of eventually being buried here would naturally come to mind. The cemetery was filling up and had restrictions on eligibility for burial. Both men were eligible due to their combat awards.

"I don't know. I've thought about it. My dad could have been buried here, but his family wanted him buried up in Boston. I've never seen his grave. In any case, let's not rush the process, okay?"

"Okay. Let's get going. I've got a quiet place we can talk. I need to get clear on your story and I need a cup of coffee."

Carl led the way down to the parking area where he had left his car. Matt noted the disabled license tags and again felt a twinge of guilt. He had both his legs. There was no reason he should come out of Afghanistan in one piece and Carl should lose a leg, but that was the way it was.

Having only one leg didn't bother Carl's driving. He drove back out on the intersecting roads going between the Memorial Bridge from Virginia and over to Washington, D.C., turning back towards Virginia and the Rosslyn office area next to the Potomac. He went into the Rosslyn area and then turned left taking Wilson Boulevard going further into Virginia.

Matt asked, "Where are we going?"

"I'm heading up to Clarendon. It's become a nexus of government offices, some CIA, some Homeland Security and others ever since 9/11. The Bush administration expanded the intelligence and security community so much there was no room to park us all in government buildings and the government had to go to commercial sites for office space. My office is up in that area, but don't worry. I'm not going there. We'll keep this off the books for now. There is a nice old diner a bit of a ways from my office. No one will be there at this time of the morning, or if there is we'll know someone is tailing you."

Matt sat back and relaxed. He might not know how to conduct himself in the land of the spooks, but it seemed Carl, in the past several years of work, had gained some insights.

The Clarendon area was a Washington metro rail success story. In the 70's when the metro rail was built in Northern Virginia, the Clarendon area was a run-down relic of the 20's building boom with many empty and shuttered stores. Slowly things had changed after a metro stop at Clarendon was opened. In the late 1970s and 80's, the Vietnamese boat people arrived exercising the energy of immigrants and opening restaurants and shops along the streets and for a while the tag "Little Saigon" was applied to the area as had happened in many other urban sites in the U.S. The Nam Viet restaurant in particular became a stopping place for many notable veterans of the Vietnam War and its dynamic owner, Toi, befriended all. The area was dominated by highrise apartment and office buildings, most catering or selling to the government. Many of the old restaurants were gone replaced by places such as the Hard Times Café and those pubs or sports bars serving the thirty-something professional crowd who had no memory of the first Iraq war much less the Vietnam War. The Silver Diner, Carl's choice, was one place that had remained through all the changes, still standing as a monument to the 1920's.

Once inside, Matt thought The Silver Diner was a great choice of a place for them to have a quiet talk. As a traveling soldier, he had always looked for simple old style diners in which to eat. Not having a home made a place that felt homey all the more appealing.

Matt and Carl settled into a booth away from the door. The diner was not crowded. There were only two other patrons, both seated at stools at the counter and some distance away from their booth.

While they were waiting to place their order and get their drinks, Matt and Carl had a chance to talk a bit and catch up on personal matters. Carl looked good. He had the muscular upper arms and chest of those who had to assist their walking either with crutches or wheelchairs, but he had also managed to control his weight. He wasn't in the running, fighting trim he had been as a Ranger, but then none of us are, Matt thought. It turned out Carl was in a relationship. This was great news to Matt. Carl had been in a somewhat shaky relationship when he had been wounded and lost his leg. It turned out the difficult times of going through rehabilitation, both mental and physical, at Walter Reed had been more of a burden than the girl was able to carry and they broke up. Initially, Carl had been bitter and Matt had been worried that the experience had soured him for life. But it hadn't. After time, Carl's positive energy returned and he got on with life. Unfortunately, dating for the handicapped isn't an easy process. Even if someone wants to go out with you the thought surfaces, "Why are they doing this?" No one wants pity and it's not an emotion to build a relationship on.

In Carl's case the relationship had grown out of his ability to turn a negative into a positive. As he became capable of using his new hi-tech leg, wending his way through life and driving his handicapped equipped car, he remembered the guys he was in the hospital with while undergoing rehabilitation and started a long process of volunteering, going back and talking with the soldiers and mentoring them through the rehab process. Many people volunteer for a short time. There's only a few who have the stamina to stick with it for the long run, especially when the people you are trying to help are wrestling with PTSD as well as the "why me?" syndrome. This was tough work and Carl became a standout in performing it. He came to know all the medical staff and those involved in rehabilitation, both military and civilian. Often times, they would sit together after sessions with patients and have a cup of coffee. He became friends with many. Eventually, he and one of his female rehab friends, a physical therapist, decided they were so comfortable together they would try dating. The dating evolved into a romance lasting a year now to the point where they were discussing moving in together.

Matt was, as they say in the military, pumped.

"Man, that's great to hear. Life goes on doesn't it?"

"Yeah, Matt, life goes on and it can be good. How about you, have you settled on a girl now or not?"

"I'm good. At least I think I'm good. Her name is Noi. We've been together, more or less as you are, for over a year now and I'm not interested in anyone else. She's great. The problem I've got is this business I'm involved with is pretty nasty and, without thinking, I might have dragged her into it by staying at her place while the bad guys were looking for me."

"Let's talk about that. Give me the story. Why are you on the run?"

So Matt unloaded. Carl got the full story with no omissions. If the story needed editing when relayed further on, to someone in the Agency for instance, Matt would rely on Carl to do it. He felt Carl needed every detail.

Carl's immediate response wasn't encouraging and was couched in his usual military speak.

"Whoooeee, you talk about walking into the proverbial shit storm, this is it, buddy."

"Yeah, I know. That's why I'm here. I see no way out of this in Thailand. I'm hoping you can help me find a way out of this mess through your contacts here in the confusion capital."

"Well, you know my philosophy: Where there is a will, there is a way. We need to do some serious thinking about what that way may be. For the record, I have no detailed knowledge of the operation you say the agency is running in Bangkok. Sources and means are just not disclosed outside the agency. I do get the intelligence product with an identifier that may say it's from a high level, reliable source that has graded well in the past, etcetera. We are all aware that much of the intelligence we get on terrorists is collected outside of the Middle East when these guys travel and of course Bangkok is one of the places they are comfortable traveling to."

Carl paused while the waitress poured him some more coffee. Carl had learned of the Snake previously in Iraq when Matt let him know of the run-in he had with him.

"For what it's worth, I don't think the Snake has sent anything back on you. The last thing he wants to do is to call any attention to his operation. The whole idea in the field is to have Washington thinking things are well oiled and going smoothly. Now what will happen when we ask somebody to lift up a rock in the agency and see what's underneath? That I don't know. You will definitely be a person of interest then. We have to be very careful and find just the right person to sit down with. You know the agency is divided into two sides: the Operations side which does dirty tricks, handles agents overseas and collects intelligence; and the Intelligence side which provides tasking, analyzes the information and prepares the reports for the Washington community including the White House. I know most of the intelligence analysts working on the counterterrorism front, but I don't know any of the operations people and I'm sure a lot of the intelligence people in the agency don't either. The operations staff rigorously protects the identities of those who work in the field."

Matt asked, "Would anyone over at the Defense Department be useful?"

"No, the agency really has no regard for Defense Intelligence. There are sixteen, count them, sixteen intelligence agencies in Washington, D.C. The DIA is pretty much at the bottom of the list. The agency operations side might want to use military units to implement their plans in difficult settings, much as you learned in Iraq, but they will not respond to inquiries from DOD in any serious manner especially when it might touch on sources and means of collection."

"Well, what do we do, Carl? I'm really at a loss as to how to go but somehow we have to let the right people know what this guy is up to. His lack of control is not just hurting innocent people. I know 'collateral damage' is not a big concern for these people, but from what I learned of his tactics and personal conduct, he is putting an important operation at risk. The agency should care about that."

"They will, but the whole danger is possible over-reaction on their part. Let's not get you squashed along with the Snake. Matt you have to understand something. This town is politically toxic. If there is the slightest hint that a secret operation has been disclosed, it will be like blood in the water for the sharks. There will be a feeding frenzy with journalists, politicians and other government agencies going after the administration and the CIA and you will be chum in that bloody water. What we do is this. First, you stay where you are at the hotel, there is no sense running around trying to hide. If the security people want to find you they will and it's best not to act as if you have something to hide. All of this must be done outside the usual channels with no official record. Let me get in touch with a good friend from the intelligence side of the agency who works with the Counterterrorist Center and see if he has some names on the operations side he would consider to be open to approach. As for you, don't be seen talking with anyone else in town, right now you may be a danger to whomever you talk to. If and when they ask you who else here in town you told this story to you must be able to say no one. I'll phone you on your mobile when we have something. Got it?"

Matt smiled at the clear direction from an old Ranger buddy, "Yes, sir."

Carl gave him a grim smile and then said, "Matt, one more thing. They may accept my story, but the security guys may decide they want their hands on you immediately for their own form of 'debriefing.' If, when I phone you, I say something about you buying the coffee, disregard whatever else I say and get out of the hotel as fast as possible, don't even check out. I'll find you or someone will contact you later, five PM each night, at the bar we closed down that time on the hill, the Dubliner. Remember it?"

Matt was a bit dismayed because Carl felt the option to continue on the run might be necessary, but rolled with it, "I remember. I got it."

Carl called for the bill and told Matt how to take the metro rail back to Rosslyn and his hotel. He would drive over to his nearby office and get started on finding the right name to talk to.

Chapter 26

In one sense, standing by and waiting for developments from Carl was a relief to Matt. He knew he wasn't at the top of his game. Jet lag hits everybody and the eight thousand eight hundred miles and twelve-hour time difference between Washington, D.C., and Bangkok meant this was about as bad as it could get. He would need to rest up and ensure he was alert when the time came to deal with whoever Carl was able to contact at the agency. He wanted to do something, anything to move things along, but the no local contact rule made it difficult.

In the end he decided to call Noi even though it was eleven at night in Bangkok. At least he could reassure her that he had arrived safely and things were under control.

It rang several times before Noi answered.

"Hey, babe, it's me. I just wanted to call and let you know I'm in D.C. and everything's okay."

"Thank God you called. I've been going crazy with worry. I couldn't focus all day at the office. People kept asking me what was wrong and I couldn't say anything. This is no way to live."

"I know, babe. I'm sorry. We'll work things out here and I'll be back soon, okay?"

"Okay. I don't mean to whine. This is just more drama then I'm used to."

Matt heard someone talking in the background.

"Who's there with you?"

"Oh, it's Da. She's been really nice. She offered to let me stay with her for a few days and I was worried about people watching my apartment so I accepted. It's smaller then my place and her bed is barely big enough for two. She has been really sweet and has been cooking for me. I hope you don't mind. She said you suggested she look after me while you were gone."

MURDER IN THE SLAUGHTERHOUSE

Matt paused for a second digesting the news. He had asked Da to look after Noi as a bit of a reflex action. He hadn't thought they would end up bunking together. However, this wasn't really unusual for close Thai girl friends. It seemed best for Noi to have someone close. It was his fault he had dragged her into the violence and danger of his quest to find Yod's killer.

"No, that's great, babe. I feel better with you having someone close by and I understand you certainly can't go to your mom's place."

They talked for a few more minutes with Matt reassuring her things would work out and he would be back soon and their life would be back normal.

After he hung up, Matt remained sitting on the bed next to the nightstand the phone was on, thinking about how his desire to give some meaning to a boy's death had spun in so many unexpected directions. Now he was on the run, possibly from his own government and his girl was bunking with an attractive male-role lesbian who was being "really sweet." He shook his head and had to laugh at himself. He had reassured Noi that things would work out. Now he needed someone to reassure him the same.

Carl would be trying to arrange a private meeting with one of his agency contacts that night. Matt would just read and watch TV until he got a phone call. Hopefully Carl could get him some answers and be in touch with him tomorrow or the next day.

Chapter 27

The next morning, Matt went for another early run. This time he decided to go down to Roosevelt Island and use the trails around the perimeter and through the forest crisscrossing the island. At points along the trails, he felt as if he was in an isolated national forest, not in the middle of a major city. The crisp bite of the cool autumn air as he ran and the explosion of fall colors in the trees were a tonic to his spirit. Matt was getting over his jet lag and starting to feel a bit more human and functional. After cleaning up and getting breakfast—one of the things the Marriott did well—he decided to head out and do some shopping. The amount of clothes he had stuffed in his gym bag was limited and he knew just looking like someone who had it together and was reliable would be important when he met whoever it was that had to accept his story. He had to avoid giving doubters any reason to reject him or his version of events in Bangkok.

The weather was unchanged from the previous day. It was clear and crisp, with blue skies and temperatures in the sixties. Matt was greatly enjoying the contrast to the heat of Bangkok. It was about eleven when he was walking from the Rosslyn metro stop towards the Marriott. He had a couple of plastic bags with clothes for a few more days and a carry bag a bit more dignified then his old gym bag. There was a lot of traffic on what was essentially a small roundabout in front of the Marriott parking lot. As he walked towards the Marriott, there was a plaza on his left, an open space above the roads located between the Rosslyn office buildings and the Marriott, as a sitting area for pedestrians. Matt detoured through it and decided to sit for a moment and take in the view. Just then his phone rang. It was the call he was expecting from Carl.

"Hey, Carl, everything okay?"

"Things are fine. I just wanted to get back to you and confirm I'm arranging a meeting. Just stand by at the Marriott and I should be in touch soon."

"Thanks, Carl. I greatly appreciate this."

"No problem. I appreciate your paying for the coffee yesterday."

Matt paused but then caught himself. "No problem, buddy. It's your bill next time. So long for now." Matt hung up.

Well, Matt thought, this shouldn't be a surprise. At least he had some warning from Carl. Whoever Carl had contacted must have thought discretion the best course and protected himself by informing the security people at the agency of the contact. It was probable that security staff met Carl when he arrived at work and told him to help bring in his friend. He had no choice but to appear to do so. As security forces do the world over, they would prefer to go the strong-arm way of course. Detaining and questioning Matt was the priority.

Matt was still sitting gathering his thoughts when he saw the two black Ford Explorers emerge from the GW Parkway, circle the roundabout, swoop into the Marriott parking lot and screech to a stop at the front door. There was no baggage to be unloaded, rather two men dressed in black suits jumped out of each vehicle and raced into the Marriott.

Matt didn't react immediately. There was no reason to. He was just sitting and enjoying the sun as far as any observer was concerned and by turning and running he could bring attention to himself. His first thought was they should really label the Explorers with big signs, U.S. Government Security; it couldn't be any more of a giveaway. His emotional reaction was despair. These had to be government security people and their search had to be for him. This was proof Carl's effort to contact friendly ears must have gone bad. He remained still, just taking a few seconds to turn off his mobile and to take out the battery. He wasn't sure how extensive their efforts to track him would be but best to take no chances. Matt's second emotion was relief. He had the forethought, before going out shopping, to take all his funds, passport and other key documents with him. All he had left in the room was his gym bag, bath items and old clothes. He had used his charge cards that morning so he still had plenty of cash left. Now he even had clean clothes and a new bag to put them in. He could survive in the city, or in another city if he chose, for quite a while, at least until Carl got in touch with him and let him know what was going on.

It was time to move. Luckily the best way to move was close at hand. The metro rail, with the exception of the security cameras installed at various points, told no tales. He pulled out a Washington Nationals baseball cap he had brought for running on sunny days, put it on to give himself a bit of cover and turned and went back down towards the Rosslyn metro stop. He would go into the city. He had promised Carl he wouldn't contact anyone else directly but it seemed that, in the situation he was in now, he would need help in staying underground. There was an old friend who would definitely not be known to anyone who might be looking for him: Ray Parker a friend from his days as a patient at Walter Reed Army Hospital. Ray was uniquely situated to help Matt with a room he could hide in until he had some further contact and guidance from Carl.

An hour later, Matt was sitting in a room at a Florida Avenue rehabilitation and transition center for alcoholics, part of the program of the Coalition for the Homeless. Ray had arranged the room. Ray was actually a friend to all the guys undergoing rehab. He was a disabled Vietnam vet having lost his left arm to shrapnel wounds in the war. He had undergone some bad years afterwards—doing drugs and drinking, living on the street until in the late 80's—he pulled himself together with the help of counselors from the Coalition. He had stayed on ever since as a counselor himself, becoming a senior figure at the Coalition. When the wars in Iraq and Afghanistan erupted, Ray had decided to volunteer at Walter Reed and see if he could provide a positive voice to those who were fighting to overcome their injuries, the emotional ones as well as the physical ones. One trick he became famous for was the steady supply of ice cream he provided on his visits, becoming known as the "ice cream man."

* * *

Ray had responded immediately and without questioning Matt as to the source of his troubles. He told the other staff that Matt was a disabled vet in rehab and authorized him a room for a few nights. Matt, for his part, would help to clean up around the center and serve the meals. It was a low price to pay, though Matt decided he would make a donation of whatever cash he could spare when he left. Now he had to wait to see if Carl contacted him. Of course he would, it was just a question of how and when. The security guys coming up empty-handed at the Marriott would put a watch on his room. When he didn't show up eventually, they would go back to Carl and tell him to make contact and set up a meeting with Matt. The security folks were scared now and wanted their hands on Matt. When he was wandering loose, they didn't know who he would meet with and what he might say. Their number one fear was he would go to the press. That would be a disaster. Their number two fear was he would go to a politician. That would be a disaster of lesser proportions, but still not acceptable from a pure security-is-everything point of view.

Chapter 28

Carl wouldn't be able to comply with the wish of the security people. Matt couldn't be contacted by phone since he kept it turned off. He and Carl had set up the fallback meeting at the Dubliner. He thought it ironic the fallback meeting place Carl had chosen was the Dubliner. One of the best pubs in Bangkok was also named the Dubliner and frequently visited by Matt. Sited across Sukhumvit Road from Matt's office in the Emporium complex, it provided him a handy place to meet visitors. As Carl had pointed out, they shared good memories of the Washington, D.C. Capitol Hill version from their days in the service.

He went up to the Dubliner at five on the first day, had a cup of tea and stayed for twenty minutes. No contact was made. Matt was not surprised since he believed Carl would be under observation himself and it would be hard to organize an alternate on short notice. He decided that starting with the second day after the raid on the Marriott he would go up to the Dubliner at four forty-five and stay until five fifteen. On the second day, he arrived at four fifteen to just look over the neighborhood. Then he went over to a bookstore at nearby Union Station to kill time for a while.

Matt was sitting in a side booth at the Dubliner at five on the third day drinking a cup of tea and reading a guide book to Washington, D.C., when the contact was made. The pub was largely empty but was beginning to see the first waves of an influx of twenty-something Capitol Hill staffers. By and large they were aspiring government policy wonks from colleges all over America, drawn to the flame of power projected by the center of their universe, Washington, D.C. Young and loud and wanting to let all the other junior wonks know what important things they were working on, they paid little attention to others in the pub.

An exception was a very fit looking woman, age thirty-something, wearing running shoes, form-fitting jeans and a black turtle neck sweater sitting at the bar nursing a cup of tea. She had short brown hair and very little make-up. Matt had noticed her when he came in fifteen minutes earlier. She waited until five, walked over and sat down across from him without asking. Matt looked at her, was sure she was from Carl, but decided to let her say whatever it was Carl had told to say to introduce herself.

"Hi, Matt, I hear Rangers lead the way. Is that true?"

Matt smiled, that opening line could only come from Carl.

"Yeah, it's true, even sometimes when it seems to make no sense."

"I'm Deborah, Carl may have told you about me."

"He did. He seems to be very happy to have found you. He said you two are a great couple."

Deborah's eyes shone at that statement.

"We're a good couple. Carl is a very positive guy. I think you know that."

"I know that. He kept me positive through some tough times. I'm sorry if I've brought you and Carl any problems with this visit. I just didn't know where else to turn."

"Don't be sorry. He wouldn't have it any other way and from what I understand you're trying to help clean up a very dirty situation."

"Well I haven't achieved anything so far. Does Carl have any ideas on how we can get past the security guys at the agency and talk to someone with an open mind?"

"Actually, yes. Tomorrow you think you can go for a run on the C&O canal?"

"No problem. It would be good. I need to run out some of these worries."

"Carl wants you to take just your running gear. Have a taxi drop you off at the grounds of the old Glen Echo amusement park off of MacArthur Boulevard at four PM. From there you can run down the road to the C&O canal at Lock 7. Run north along the canal until you come to the Great Falls visitor center parking lot. It's about a seven-mile run, give or take a bit. Carl says you won't have any trouble with that. Run up the exit road going out of the park. Carl will be waiting for you there along the exit road at five."

"Is Carl okay? I didn't get him in trouble, did I?"

"He's fine. Don't worry, Carl's got enough friends in and around Homeland Security that the agency guys can't push him around. In any case, they still want to handle this, whatever it is, discreetly. Here take this."

She handed Matt a new mobile phone.

"Carl thinks he has the security guys at the agency going along with him for now, but these precautions are just in case they don't keep their word. In case things get jammed up, you can call him on this. I should go now. Good luck tomorrow."

"Thanks, Deborah, I look forward to getting together with you and Carl after this is resolved."

"Me, too. Take care."

With that Deborah left. Matt waited a few minutes to let her get clear and then left also. Tomorrow would be a big day.

Chapter 29

Matt had complete faith in Carl yet he understood Carl was dealing with people who made their own rules. At the same time, he needed to get the attention and ear of someone who could make a decision in the agency. This meant taking the leap of faith and exposing himself, putting himself in their hands. Hopefully Carl had been able to prepare the ground so that a hearing, not an interrogation, would be the order of the day.

The Great Falls park area on the C&O canal was a public enough area that he could jog through without looking out of the ordinary. If things seemed too spooky or out of order, he could just keep running and circle back later.

It was another beautiful fall day, clear and cool, and the jogging and biking traffic on the canal path reflected such. It was a long, very gradual ascent from the end of the canal in Georgetown as the trail along the canal followed the course of the Potomac River flowing down from the Harper's Ferry and Antietam area over seventy miles away. There was a bit less traffic at the lock point on the canal where Matt started near Glen Echo. Matt had to periodically pass some joggers and then jump out of the way of bikers overtaking him, but it was still a pleasant run. At one point the path went under what was called the Cabin John Bridge spanning the Potomac and carrying the traffic of the eight-lane beltway going around the capital. The path was bordered by forest covering the ground between the canal and the Potomac on his left side as he ran along. Twice he saw deer taking shelter in the trees. Migratory ducks, mallards, were swimming in the area of the canal past the Cabin John Bridge. Except for the worries he was carrying, it was an idyllic run and Matt felt at peace with his decision to come back to the U.S. and tackle the problems posed by the Snake head on.

Matt ran slower as he approached the locks leading up to the Great Falls center. Here there were quite a few people; many seemed to be tourists and family groups, walking along. The road access and parking area made this a popular hiking and picnic point.

Matt slowed to a walk the last few hundred yards. He was a bit ahead of schedule and the area was somewhat crowded so he decided to look around carefully before moving ahead. He saw the parking lot off the path across a small wooden bridge and crossed over to it. No one standing around or any evidence of surveillance. He just kept going. He saw the exit road and starting running again, up the long hilly way with forest on both sides of the road. This was not the running track and it was difficult going up the hill therefore he had the road to himself. About one hundred and fifty yards up the road, a cabin appeared in a clearing on his left. There was an old cannon parked in front near the road appearing to be of World War I vintage and several cars were parked in an area off to the side of the cabin. As he pulled even with the parking area, he saw a door on one of the cars open and Carl stepped out and waved to him. Matt jogged into the parking area and stopped to catch his breath. Carl was smiling, possibly a bit amused since Matt was breathing hard after the uphill run.

Carl gave him a towel to dry off with. "Hell, Matt, I didn't think a little seven mile run would give you any trouble."

Matt was getting control of his breathing now.

"It didn't. The last little bit on the road up the hill got my attention. We don't have hills in Bangkok. It's a bit like New Orleans I guess, just one flat piece of city on a river delta."

Carl handed him a T-shirt and told him, "Here put this on after you dry off. We can't afford you catching a cold."

Carl turned and started leading the way into the cabin.

"Come on inside. There's someone I want you to meet."

There was a ramp leading up to the entrance door on the side. Just inside the door Carl stopped, picked up a pen and started writing in a journal kept on a stand next to the door.

"Welcome to Cabin John VFW Post 5633. I'm a member here and need to sign you in as a visitor. I've signed in another visitor who is waiting for us in the conference room. Let's go back and say hello."

Carl led the way past a bar that faced the door through which they had entered. There was a woman tending the bar and two older men sitting there and talking. They exchanged hellos with Carl as he walked by. Carl explained, "That's Marty and Mike, both Vietnam vets. There are over a hundred members here, most of them are Vietnam vets but there are guys from Iraq and Afghanistan joining up nowadays."

Carl led the way through a sitting area with a big fireplace and past a small central hall. The walls had newspaper cuttings going back to World War II and the Korean War along with insignias of differing military units, the 1st Cav, the 25th Infantry Division, a Marine Corps decal, a framed Ranger tab and other evidence of the shared heritage of the members.

Carl paused at the door to another room and turned to Matt, "This is the conference room. It's not used much and we'll have it to ourselves to talk with our new friend. I think you'll like him."

Carl opened the door and walked in. A tall wiry brown haired man, possibly a few years older than Matt, stood up from the conference table and some papers he had been going over.

Carl looked back at Matt.

"Matt, I want to introduce you to a man of reason. He is why we've hopefully been able to escape the mindless clutches of the security guys. This is Rick Chance. Rick, this is my Ranger buddy I told you about. This is Matt Chance."

The man smiled and stepped forward holding out his hand. "Actually I've heard a lot about you, Major Chance. I'm sorry it's taken so long to meet you."

Matt was completely taken aback. He had been prepared for many things, but not this.

"Your name is the same as my dad's. Does that mean we're related?"

"I'm Richard Chance, Jr. You and I have the same father. I am your older brother, or half-brother, by two years. I was thirteen when Dad died and I guess you were eleven then. As I say, I'm sorry it took so long to meet you. Grandpa Chris told me he went out to California to meet you when you were in school."

"He did. He was a great guy. We had a good talk and he did a lot to make me feel like I had a family."

"Well, I think you can understand, my mom could never accept you, but Grandpa did. He said you were a lot like Dad and that's good enough for me. In some ways we've taken similar roads following the family path of national service. My career has been in the agency, on the operations side, and I'm aware of your service record. You got a lot to be proud of. Dad would have been proud of you."

Matt was more than overwhelmed. He was incapable of saying anything. He wanted to say something except it was too much of a surprise. He'd known he had an older half-brother but had never felt comfortable to go and look for him. Now his brother had come to him. He just nodded.

Carl motioned them to sit down at the table so Matt went over and took a seat.

Carl decided to explain the basis of the meeting.

"Matt, first let me apologize for making you go through some security steps in coming to this meeting. Even though Rick had negotiated internally that the security guys would stop trying to find and detain you, neither of us was really sure they would keep their word. Rick and I also took some unusual steps coming here and it appears we're clean. Rick will be in charge the rest of the way."

Rick looked down at the papers in his hand and then up to Matt.

"Matt, to cut to the heart of things, the issue is so sensitive it is only myself and the top guy in operations who are aware of it. I approached him after I got the story from Carl. He has given me some special powers. I have authorization to bypass all normal agency channels and enlist help from wherever in the government I think is necessary."

"Thanks, Rick. I appreciate that but, as Carl has told you, right now I'm involved in a bit of a mess an agency guy has helped to create. Do you see any way out of this?"

"There's a way out, Matt, but this is going to be a sensitive operation. The Snake definitely has a record of leaving a lot of collateral damage and questions behind on his assignments. He's had his defenders at the top of the agency, but people have grown increasingly aware that he is a cancerous tumor. We want to remove the tumor, but we have to do so without killing the patient, that is the very important operation he is currently involved in."

"Can't you just call him back into Langley?"

"There's some doubt that he would come back if he smelled anything wrong, if he sensed any doubt or suspicion on the part of management in Langley. He has friends within the agency who might tip him off if they hear his work is being questioned. He has no real assets here in the U.S. His two divorces have pretty much cleaned him out. He has no children or real family ties. His overseas assets are thought to be considerable. He knows this is his last assignment. If he thinks things are going wrong he may just cut and run to a country that won't extradite him. We can't have that."

"Then what do we do?"

"Well, the ugly but inescapable answer is we mount an operation in Thailand to relieve him of his responsibilities in a covert manner. This is where Carl's connections here, your background in the military and your connections in Thailand can be of real help if you are willing. All of this will have to be outside of normal agency channels and by that I mean the covert operations channels. We will essentially be mounting a black operation inside the agency. The Snake is the master of his world in Bangkok. He will sense anything going on in his sphere of influence. The operation must come from outside yet still be coordinated with the Thai military security and intelligence system."

"Who goes where and who does what?"

Rick laughed. "You military background is showing. Okay, those are the key questions and we have a lot of details to work out. The biggest issue is how do we get assets, including you, into Thailand and in place to take the Snake into custody and get him out of Thailand quietly. Your buddy Carl here has come up with an idea which may provide the vehicle for doing so."

Matt looked at Carl, raising his eyebrows, questioning how his friend had the answer for what needed to be a black operation that even the agency staff focused on Thailand wouldn't be aware of.

"What is it you have in mind, Carl?"

Carl smiled, "Not really so difficult when you think of it, but I understand you've been outside the military operations mode for a couple of years now. You know about Cobra Gold don't you?"

"Only because I saw the name in the Thai press last year. How does that fit in?"

"It's the annual Thai-U.S. joint military training exercise which has been held in Thailand every year since 1982. It's been the major vehicle for improving Thai-U.S. cooperation in the military area. It's kicking off in a few weeks. U.S. and Thai military are already deep into meetings planning and coordinating the military exercises that will be part of the training. There will be about nine thousand U.S. personnel involved and units from Japan and Okinawa."

Matt looked at Carl and shrugged as if to say so what?

"The details need to be worked out with some friends in the Pentagon, but let's just say for now it's the vehicle of choice for our operation gaining hidden access to Thailand. The U.S. military have clearance to take people and equipment in and out of Thailand without going through the normal immigration and customs channels. Security concerns within the exercise will be accepted as the reason for overlooking the introduction of some people and activities that normally would come under scrutiny. Our ability to operate covertly will require we have the leadership of the U.S. Defense Department Joint Special Operations Command on board. I believe it can be arranged."

Rick stepped back in. "I think, Matt, that's about all we can cover for today. Carl and I are going to have some meetings at the Pentagon in the next few days with the people involved in planning Cobra Gold and some staff at JSOC, the special ops staff. Forgive us, but you can't be involved right now. You need to continue to keep a low profile for a while. However we definitely are going to need you involved once we get the details worked out with the Pentagon. Now, as much as I would like to stick around and talk a bit, I think we'll have to save that for later."

Rick got up and shook Matt's hand again, then looked over to Carl and said, "I'll call as soon as possible." Turning back to Matt he said, "I know we have a lot to talk about. There'll be time later." Then he left the room.

Carl asked Matt, "Forgive me for springing that on you but it was at Rick's request. He said you were aware of him but not of the work he has been doing."

"It's okay. It's not a complete shock and I'm glad someone who knows of me is in a position to help."

"How would you feel about bunking with me for a few days? I've got an extra bedroom and I've got your clothes and other gear here from the Marriott. We can swing by later and pick up the rest of your gear from wherever you are staying now."

"Sounds like a plan to me. You guys have given me a lot to absorb."

"Take a shower in the bathroom across the hall and change your clothes into whatever I brought along here. Then we'll go out and offer to buy a pizza for the guys at the bar. They're a good crew. You should meet them."

Chapter 30

The next few days were agony for Matt. The one thing he had great trouble doing was doing nothing. He was running every day and Carl had gotten him into a local gym in the Bethesda neighborhood where he lived so he could practice some Muay Thai moves. However, none of the physical effort really calmed his nerves. At least he had an update each night when Carl came home and briefed him on that days efforts and how the top-level support was coming together. The biggest holdup was the operation being kept from the mid-level managers at the agency. This meant the coordination had to be done with only a few of the top people at Homeland Security, the Department of Defense and specifically within the Defense Department, the operators in JSOC. Rick's written commitment from the agency's top operator would carry the day in each place. Getting to the top guys, busting into their crowded schedules took time, especially when you couldn't provide details to the gatekeeper's questions as to why this meeting was necessary.

One thing giving Matt some mental relief was his phone calls home to Noi. He called her the first morning he was at Carl's after he had gone to work. She answered almost immediately.

"Hey, babe, it's me. How are you doing?"

"I'm doing okay but I'm glad you called. I've really been worrying about you."

"No need to worry. There are friends helping out here and I will be back soon. How about you? Are you still staying with Da?"

"No, I've moved back home and am back to my regular schedule at work. Khun Neung called me and told me things were okay now and I could go back to my normal life. Also Da calls almost every day looking in on me. She's really sweet."

"We're going to get back to our normal life, babe. I promise. I'll be back and things will be wrapped up soon, okay? Please be patient a bit longer."

"I will. I'm waiting for you. Come home quick, okay?"

"I'll be home soon, babe. Bye bye."

After hanging up, Matt made a mental note to thank Neung for looking after Noi. That made a big difference. He could work more freely here without having to worry about home. Of course he would still have to find out just what Noi had meant when she said Da was "really sweet." He liked Da but had never seen that side of her. It was possible being a tomboy that she only showed her sweet side to women.

The suspense was lifted on the third day when Carl came back from work with the good news.

"Well, Combat, it looks as if we are getting ready to go operational. You and I are invited to a meeting tomorrow at Andrews Air Force Base. A secure conference room has been reserved and Rick will be chairing a meeting with some JSOC people. The goal is to agree on the team we take into Thailand, the means of transportation and the timing. I would say we are a day, maybe two at the most, from liftoff."

"Man, that's music to my ears. I've been going crazy.

"One thing you want to think about is how we coordinate with the Thai military and with their intelligence once we are on the scene. They will want an explanation at the planning meeting and must be assured we, meaning you, have the contacts outside of normal channels to convince the top Thai generals and intelligence guys to go along with our operation."

"Can I give people a heads-up now?"

"Not on the operation in any sense, but you can tell them you need them to be available to come to a meeting within three hours' drive from Bangkok any time after the next forty-eight hours. That will have to do. We'll contact them once we are on the ground and where that will be still needs to be determined though I expect we'll know after the meeting tomorrow. We're expected out at Andrews at nine AM."

"Okay. Let's sleep on it then."

Chapter 31

Andrews Air Force Base is primarily known to the nation as the President's airport, the home of two VC-25 aircraft—the military version of the 747—otherwise known by the call sign Air Force One, the President's official plane when the President is aboard. To the military though, it has the important role of being the nearest air base to the Pentagon able to handle very large airplanes—cargo or passenger—thus a lot of significant military traffic flows through Andrews. In addition, Andrews is home to a diverse range of support aircraft, medical, cargo tankers and a wing of F-16 fighter aircraft.

Rick and the military coordinator for JSOC had chosen a secure conference room on the base as the place to bring the team together for the initial operations briefing for several reasons. They wanted to stay away from the Pentagon itself and all the questions arising by bringing in non-military people and Delta Force members who would normally be seen down in Fort Bragg, not in the Washington, D.C. area. A second reason was in planning the logistics of their entry into Thailand under the cover of the Cobra Gold exercise it had been obvious that Andrews would be the logical departure point for using military transportation.

Carl drove around the beltway from Bethesda to the exit leading to Andrews. With the busy early morning beltway jam, it took over an hour for the trip. At the gate into Andrews, the Air Force liaison had arranged for both Carl and Matt to be on the clearance list. The Air Force military police sergeant on duty checked them in and gave them badges to wear while on base and a map and directions to the building holding the conference room.

Even though Carl and Matt were twenty minutes early, they saw Rick standing in front of a whiteboard talking with an

Army colonel. Four Army sergeants in combat fatigues were seated at a table on the side of the room.

Carl and Matt nodded to the NCOs and walked over and said hello to Rick who greeted and introduced them to the colonel.

"Carl and Matt, this is Colonel Paul Richardson of the Joint Special Operations Command. He is the point guy for arranging military assistance for this mission and he will be going along all the way. I have provided Colonel Richardson your background."

Turning to Carl he said, "Carl, we need you to brief these men on the position of Homeland Security on what we are undertaking and of course we depend on you to keep your top guy in the loop."

Carl nodded with a bit of a sad grin, this was his life now: deskwork and briefings. His combat days were over. Moments like this with the guys who would be going into battle drove it home. "I understand, Rick."

Rick turned to Colonel Richardson. "Colonel, you know all the parties here. Do you want to make the introductions and give the overview? Then Matt and I can brief on the details of what we expect to find and do at the target site."

The colonel nodded and waved towards the table and said, "Please take a seat."

Turning to include the NCOs in the discussion, "Gentlemen, you all know the routine, everything that is discussed and disclosed in this room after this point is classified 'Top Secret.' This is a national security matter of the highest priority and sensitivity. The normal penalties of military justice will apply in case of a breach of security. Are we all clear?"

Everyone responded with a firm, "Yes, sir."

Pointing to Rick, Carl and Matt, the colonel introduced them and their agencies one by one. When he came to Matt, he described him as Major Chance, a Ranger officer. At that point one of the NCOs leaned across the table and extended his hand to Matt.

"It's good to see you again, Major Chance. I'm glad to know we'll be working with you on this operation."

Matt smiled and shook his hand. He had recognized the sergeant on the way in but had decided to wait until the right moment to say hello. The sergeant had done it for him. The man was Sergeant First Class Jesus Rodriguez. He had been a Squad Leader in Matt's Ranger Company in Iraq. Matt didn't know he had gone to the Delta Force since then but it made sense. The man was a solid performer.

"Good to see you, Sergeant Rodriguez. I feel better knowing you'll be along also."

Matt turned to Colonel Richardson and explained he and Sergeant Rodriguez had served together in Iraq. The colonel looked relieved. This contact directly reinforced Matt's qualifications for him. Previously, he had been going on Rick's recommendation and Matt's service record. Any past service connection between members of the team would also help bind them together. Sergeant Rodriguez would no doubt give the other Delta Force soldiers all the background on Matt.

Responding to Matt, the colonel said, "Major, you have orders reactivating you for this mission. Once the mission is completed we will cut orders returning you to your medical retirement status. I'm sure you understand this was the best way to include you officially in the mission."

Matt was in the military service mental mode now and only said, "Yes, sir."

The colonel turned to complete the introduction of the NCOs.

"You've met Sergeant Rodriguez, the other members of the team are Sergeant Hunt, Sergeant Johnson and Sergeant Kim."

The Delta Force was established in 1977 as part of the Special Forces in response to prisoner and hostage rescue requirements that had faced the military during and after the Vietnam War. The lead officer at the time of formation was Colonel Charlie "Charging Charlie" Beckwith, a legendary Special Forces officer. Delta became part of the Joint Special Operations Command formed in 1980 when the integration of the armed forces quick response capabilities was necessary to avoid catastrophes such as the failed Iran hostage mission— Eagle Claw—which came apart in the desert in Iran in April of 1978. One didn't just raise his hand and volunteer to become a member of one of the three rapid response squadrons comprising Delta Force. To be accepted into Delta, a soldier had to have completed Airborne and Ranger training and assignments and served in Special Forces before being given a chance to try out. A good combat record was helpful yet it was not enough by itself. Besides the three squadrons of Delta soldiers, the other quick response team under JSOC is Navy Seal Team Six, who will forever be known as the slayers of Osama Bin Laden. To say a competitive spirit exists between the two testosterone-fueled units would be a vast understatement. The Delta teams considered themselves the best of the best and had proven their worth many times over. Their inclusion on this mission was tribute to the flexibility possible in Delta mission assignments and the high priority this mission had been given.

Rick had reached out to the Pentagon's JSOC and its Delta Force as he felt he needed to compartmentalize this mission outside the normal agency owned Special Operations Division and its own Special Operations Group (SOG) as much as possible. The agency's SOG included the men pictured wearing long beards, riding horses and calling in B-52 strikes against the Taliban entrenched in the mountains of Northern Afghanistan in October 2001 in the initial phases of the war there. They recruited many of their members from the Special Forces and Delta troopers. That would have normally been the first place Rick would have turned for operators such as this mission required, but he felt there could be no telling where within the agency the Snake had contacts. It was best to be overly cautious.

Colonel Richardson continued the briefing.

"Gentlemen, the logistics of this trip are we'll be going from here at Andrews to Travis Air Force Base in the San Francisco area. From Travis we go over the Pacific to Yokota Air Base near Tokyo and then down to the Thai Air Base at U-Tapao south of Pattaya in Thailand. We'll be going in under the cover of being part of the military support for Cobra Gold, the annual U.S.-Thai joint military exercise. The primary coordination of Cobra Gold is in the hands of the Navy and they are working with the Thai Naval Command at the Sattahip Naval Base nearby the U-Tapao Air Base. We're still looking at what types of aircraft we'll be on, but we have the highest possible priority for this one and I believe we'll be able to hitch a ride on a C-135 cargo plane for the trip to Travis and also for the trip to Yokota. From there I'm afraid we'll be on a C-130H going down to U-Tapao as that's a better fit with the air support normally given to Cobra Gold."

The Delta guys were all smiles at the realization they would be on the C-135 for the longest legs of the trip. It wasn't civilian travel or a charter, but depending on how it was fitted it could be a fast, comfortable flight. They all just shrugged their shoulders at the mention of the C-130H, the rugged four-engine turboprop plane on which they lived much of their lives. Cold and uncomfortable, it would still get them where they had to go.

The colonel turned back to Rick while still addressing the NCOs.

"Once we are on the ground, the operational lead will be with the Agency representative. Rick, do you want to outline how we plan to proceed?"

Rick handled the rest of the briefing, identifying the goal of the mission as the "repatriation" of a U.S. government official who had become a security risk. This caused raised eyebrows amongst the Delta guys, their mode was more to kill terrorists or to rescue people from terrorists rather than to arrest someone, but they would do as they were told. Rick and Carl then reconfirmed to all that the mission was cleared at the highest levels in the agency, Homeland Security and the Pentagon.

Rick turned the meeting over to Matt who told them they would be met on arrival at U-Tapao Air Base by representatives of the Thai Army and Thai intelligence who would help plan the isolation and detention of the subject as well as coordinate the relationship with the military and intelligence side of the Thai government.

When Matt was finished, he turned the meeting back over to Colonel Richardson.

"Okay, soldiers, that's it for now. The mission has effectively started. You're restricted to the base tonight. You may call your families and loved ones and let them know you'll be gone for a week or so on assignment. You know the drill: you can't tell them where you'll be going. If you want to say it's not to a combat zone to put their minds at ease that's acceptable, but nothing more. Of course say nothing to anyone here at Andrews. If an officer pushes you on this, refer him to me. We may have a plane at noon tomorrow but that, as you know, depends. It could be a couple of hours earlier or a couple of hours later. Be here with your travel kit, including civilian clothes as I briefed you before, at eight AM tomorrow. You are only authorized to carry sidearms. If we need more weapons, they'll be available in country."

With that the colonel concluded the meeting.

Before leaving with Carl, Matt went over and talked with Sergeant Rodriguez again and introduced himself personally to each of the Delta soldiers. If they were going on an operation together, the more they knew him and the more comfortable they felt the better. These guys were warriors, they didn't need handholding, but building trust within the team was always important. The fact that he and Sergeant Rodriguez had been in combat together would be a big help. They would all grill the sergeant thoroughly about just how capable Matt was and how he handled being under fire.

Chapter 32

On the ride back home with Carl, Matt asked him what he thought.

Carl took his time answering.

"What I think, Matt, is there is a hell of a lot hanging loose here. Normally before getting on a plane, these Delta guys would know all there is to know about the target, the support they'll receive and the area they are going to go into. This time the team will be dependent on the briefing they receive at whatever air base they go into in Thailand to get the mission details. This is not a military mission. The planning time is very limited. This is more like organizing a posse in one of the old Western movies and heading out into the mountains after the bad guys. It's not a comfortable situation."

"Yeah, I know, yet I think Rick is right. This has to be compartmentalized as much as possible and organized outside of the agency without letting anyone other than the top guy know what's going on. If the Snake finds out what's coming it will make things much harder and he might well get away. That means official channels of communication are out until we have the contacts arranged on the ground in Thailand."

"That puts the burden on you and your Thai contacts big time. Once you're on the ground you'll have to plan quickly and execute faster. No offense, but are you confident both these Thai guys will be able to carry their weight?"

"Tommy and Neung are troopers. I've worked with both of them in the past and they will do their part. What do you think about the Delta guys Colonel Richardson has brought in for this show?"

"I think they're all solid. They're standard issue Delta. They're hardcore; they won't hesitate going into a firefight. I would guess the only question is if they're used to situations where they can shoot first and answer questions later. This job

173

looks to be a bit more delicate. Something like police work. You'll have to keep an eye on that. Also ..."

Carl's answer tailed off a bit and grabbed Matt's attention.

"Also what?"

"You remember Sergeant Maxwell?"

Sergeant Maxwell had been a squad leader in Carl's company in Iraq.

"I remember him. A real hard case. I thought he was one of your best squad leaders. What about him?"

"Oh, he was one of the best. No doubt. There was just one thing though: he was always too ready to kill, if you know what I mean. Remember he always carried that twelve-gauge shotgun? He had a dead look in his eyes that worried me. He was a killer. Whenever we got around civilians I felt I had to warn his platoon leader to watch him closely."

"Yeah, so what?"

"Well, this guy Sergeant Hunt you have on your team, I get the same vibe from him. You look at him and he's got dead eyes. He'll be quick to shoot. You might want to keep an eye on him when the time comes, if there are civilians around."

"I understand. Hopefully there'll be no shooting. If we plan this correctly and surprise the Snake, he should come along peacefully. Then the Delta guys become the escort to take him back to the States and the custody of the Justice Department. At the end it can be just a couple of long plane rides for them. I doubt they'll even get a night out in Bangkok or Pattaya as a reward. Once we have the Snake, the plan will be to get him out of Thailand within a few hours."

"Good. Let's hope it all works that way."

Carl drove in silence for a few minutes and the looked over at Matt and then back to the road again saying nothing.

Matt picked up on the body language and finally spoke, "What?"

Carl shrugged as if reluctant to say more and then said, "It's about you, Matt. You seem to catch more of these things than the average guy. You know that, right?"

"Hey, someone I know asks for help, it seems to me I should give it. Is that so bad?"

"No, Matt, it's not bad. It's just that you've got this responsibility thing, this button people can push and you just go into action. It's wasn't an accident that our Battalion Commander nominated you for the Iraq mission the Snake involved us in, you know? You send out these vibes of being the go to guy and people go to you."

"And?"

"And you keep putting yourself on the line and sooner or later the odds will catch up to you, man. I guess I'm just saying be yourself, but be careful."

Matt digested his input for several minutes and miles.

Finally, he nodded, "Yeah, I've thought that myself. I guess that's what my girl is saying, too. I'll think about it."

In his mind he pictured Yod's body lying on the killing floor in the slaughterhouse and young Ben collapsing and sobbing during their talk at Yod's funeral. Some people, some situations, you just couldn't turn your back on.

"It's just sometimes you run into things you feel you can't walk away from, you know?"

"Not really, but that's why you're Matt and I'm a desk jockey at Homeland Security. Just watch your back, dude."

They rode along in silence and then Carl looked over at Matt and laughed.

"What?"

Carl, laughing more now, "Well, maybe what you need is a new look. You're too damn straight. How about an earring or tattoo? They're all the style now and maybe people will see you a bit differently." Still laughing, "I mean, why not give it a try?"

Matt shook his head and smiled.

"I'll think about it."

While Matt was making his preparations to return to Thailand, the Delta team were packing their gear for the trip and making phone calls to their families on the basis Colonel Richardson had outlined for them.

However Sergeant Hunt had one extra phone call to make. He had reached his twenty years of service in the army. He was eligible for retirement and the possibility of a civilian job and two paychecks a month. It was an attractive proposition. He had already made a contact and was working to keep up that relationship. The contact was another Delta NCO who had retired two years previously and was now with the Agency's Special Operations Group. They had discussed Sergeant Hunt joining SOG when he retired later in the year. It seemed to him this was as secure a contact as there could be. Also it would be good to remind the SOG guy that Sergeant Hunt was the kind of guy selected for special missions. He made the call and had a short conversation, just letting the man know he was in Washington, D.C., and just called to say hello. His contact invited him to join him and some of his SOG friends for a beer that night. Sergeant Hunt had to say no. He explained he was on his way out to Asia the next day for a mission. When pushed on the destination, Sergeant Hunt told him it was Thailand, nothing special, not a combat mission, just going to pick up a U.S. government employee who had gone off the reservation in some way. Probably just some Embassy geek caught diddling kids was the way he put it.

When he hung up the phone, Sergeant Hunt's new friend thought about the conversation for a while. Delta Force guys on an operation in Thailand? That was something his old friend the Snake might want to know about. He would send him an e-mail on his private address in the morning. It's important to keep working your contacts.

Act 3—Thailand

"Vengeance is mine. I will repay."
—Romans 12:19-21

Chapter 33

The meeting place was the coffee house on Soi Arab, the same one they had used previously. The narrow soi was fenced on both sides by four-story buildings, the timeframe for direct exposure to the sun, roughly eleven AM to one PM depending on the season, had passed. Now at two, they sat wreathed in shadow inside the dim lights of the coffee house.

As the Camel sat down, the Camel Driver threw a newspaper on the table and said, "We have a problem. Do you want to tell me about this?"

Hamel looked at the story line that the newspaper was folded to display. The caption was eye-catching, "Slaughterhouse Murder." The story went on to describe the scene at which the body of a teenage slum boy was found, his throat cut. Hamel noted the date of the paper was several weeks old.

"This is indeed sad, my friend, but what is the problem?"

"Come on, Hamel, don't play cute with me. This occurred on your last visit. This is the boy I arranged to have delivered to your special room before you left. You can have your fun with these boys but this is not acceptable. How did he end up like this?"

The waiter approached and the Camel Driver picked up the newspaper and put it into the pouch in which he carried things. Hamel ordered an espresso and both waited until the waiter had delivered his coffee and walked away. Hamel sipped at his espresso and settled back in his chair.

"This is regrettable, but was apparently necessary. The boy became somewhat overwrought after we had finished our session. The drugs apparently had some side effects. This can happen. He had been docile throughout. Suddenly he became very agitated and irrational, as if he was experiencing some nightmare. I had trouble handling him and had to call security

179

to take him out. That was the last I saw of him. I can only suppose he gave them more trouble. They panicked while taking him back to his slum and decided to ensure he wouldn't have anything to say when he got back home. I find it somewhat excessive that they left him in a pigpen. Perhaps he insulted their religion and they felt a need to return the insult. They were both very conservative boys."

The Camel Driver was rigid with suppressed anger, he leaned on his elbows over the table to speak as closely to Hamel's face as possible in order to emphasize his words.

"Why didn't you let me know? Hamel, this could be a serious security issue. This puts us both in danger."

Hamel leaned back to give himself some space.

"Please control yourself. The answer is I didn't know. These men were sent up here to act as security for me by my friends in the South. They are part of our network of contacts down there. They must have panicked and turned off their phones. I couldn't contact them when I called to get a report. No one can connect this to me and I am not responsible."

The rage the Camel Driver felt started to edge into his voice a bit.

"You're not responsible? Surely you're the one who gave him your drugs and sodomized him. There are many professional sex workers available here. Your insistence on using young boys such as this puts our entire operation at risk."

Hamel's demeanor didn't change. He prided himself on his control. A relationship including sex with a young boy who he mentored was acceptable, traditional and enjoyable. Indeed, if his need for security didn't make it impossible, he would keep a favorite boy here for his visits to Bangkok, just as he had a young boy he kept with him and cared for during his work in the field in Pakistan. Many men of status, married or not, did the same. To think he would defile himself with a sex worker was abhorrent.

"Again, I say, please calm yourself. This won't happen again and no one needs to know. I'm sure no one near the house saw or heard anything. We can just drop it. I am sure you can find many suitable locations in this large city. Now, let's get on with our work."

The Camel Driver paused and thought for a second. Hamel was wrong. It wasn't so simple. At the same time, the Camel Driver needed to reassure Hamel the contact here was safe. He was too valuable as a source to lose for any reason.

Chapter 34

The flights back to Thailand were, if anything, even more exhausting for Matt than the trip to the U.S. The C-135 flights across the U.S. to Travis Air Force Base in California and then from Travis over the Pacific to Yokota Air Base in Japan had gone smoothly. He had been very impressed with the ability of the Delta troopers to sleep whenever they were given a chance. The C-130 flight down from Yokota was a rougher trip. The plane had been loaded with some cargo: pallets of military supplies for the Cobra Gold exercise had been strapped down along the center of the cavernous hold of the plane and the members of the team were seated in canvas seats hung from the side hull of the airplane. The interior of the plane was cold and drafty and the engine noise loud. The flight had departed at two AM Tokyo time and the expectation was that they would be landing about eight AM Thailand time.

It had been a long boring trip but productive in some ways for Matt. It had given him a chance for private conversations with all the team members. Also it had reminded him of what it was like to live with the men in uniform who had to do whatever dirty jobs society needed to have done. Whether they were military, policemen or firemen, the macho jokes and shorthand language used to occupy idle moments waiting for action would always emerge.

As the sun rose over the Pacific when they were a few hours from landing, Sergeant Johnson began working away on a time chart involving several lines of measurement converging at times, drifting apart at others.

Finally he looked it over carefully, dropped it in his lap and said, "Oh no, this isn't good."

A bit alarmed Matt looked over and asked him, "What is it, Sergeant Johnson? Is something wrong?"

"Sir, the lines are just not converging in a good way. I'm going into a triple down cycle at the worst time."

"What?"

Then Sergeant Rodriguez interrupted, laughing.

"Major, it's just that time of the month. Our man is going to have his period just when we need him the most. He does this every mission. I haven't seen him get this right yet."

Matt just shook his head, looking at the guys for an explanation.

Sergeant Johnson looked up mournfully. "I'm sorry, sir. It's my biorhythms. I should have checked them before I volunteered for this assignment."

Again Matt just gave him a blank look and the other NCOs laughed.

Sergeant Kim, laughing, hardly able to speak, said, "It'll be okay, sir. Just have someone run out and pick up some Kotex when we get to the air base. He'll be fine."

Sergeant Johnson had heard enough. He gave a scornful look to his colleagues and said, "You are a bunch of unscientific fools. The science of biorhythms is proven."

Then, looking to Matt, he gave his explanation.

"Sir, each person's biorhythms start at their time of birth and can be charted according to physical, emotional and intellectual cycles reaching highs and lows over a range of days. The physical cycle is twenty-three days, the emotional cycle is twenty-eight days and the intellectual cycle is thirty-three days. These measure variations in your ability in these differing areas."

He held up his chart for Matt to see the wavy, different colored, lines. "As you can see, sir, they operate independently, but at times they coincide at a peak or at a low. The best time to attempt any challenge, such as an exam, is when you have a triple high. The worst time to undertake something challenging is when you have a triple low. The way this looks I'll be just coming out of a physical low starting the gradual ascent towards a new high when we arrive, yet I'll be going into an emotional low followed in a few days by an intellectual low. This isn't good, sir. I'll be there for you. It just doesn't seem as if I'll have my best stuff."

Matt was just dumbfounded. It took all he could do to keep his mouth from dropping open. The other Delta NCOs saved him by jumping in, laughing out of control, heaping derision on Sergeant Johnson's ideas and offering cynical advice.

"We definitely can't put you on point, Johnny. That's an emotional burden we won't ask you to bear, man."

"Maybe I can carry your extra ammunition, Johnny. That will help you with your physical limits."

Sergeant Kim volunteered, "I'll try to dumb down the hand signals, Johnny. Make them a bit easier for you to understand. We'll get you through this, man."

They all collapsed laughing. Sergeant Johnson had evidently gone through this before. He just sniffed and looked away. Then talking to Matt said, "They refuse to learn. Don't worry, Major. I'll be there for you."

All Matt could say was, "Okay, Sergeant Johnson. I know you will."

As they quieted down Matt sat back and thought, remembering the many times before he had similar exchanges with soldiers going into battle. "This is great. This is what I miss about the troops. No matter what danger they're going into these guys will always find a way to joke and stay loose."

Matt had also been able to have a long quiet conversation with his newly-found brother, Rick.

It turned out they were both baseball fans and both had walked on to their college baseball teams with limited success. Unfortunately, Rick, growing up in Boston, was a die-hard Red Sox fan. When he discovered Matt, following Johnny Damon's career, had become a Yankees fan, he was speechless with dismay.

"Anybody but the Yankees, Matt. I mean they don't have a soul!"

Matt laughed, he had heard this before, "It's all about the quality of play, Rick. These guys play the game the way it should be played and...Derek Jeter!?"

For Matt that statement normally ended all such conversations. He couldn't see anybody questioning the excellence of The Captain's career.

It turned out Rick had two kids: a twelve-year-old boy and a ten-year-old girl. He helped coach his son's baseball team and his daughter's soccer team. Matt was moved. It seemed his older brother was a solid guy all the way around. It left him pondering what his years in military service and his decision to live a single life had cost him.

They hadn't discussed what they would do after arrival in any depth because much would depend on the situation report given by Tommy and Neung who were to meet the plane. Rick had told Matt he would play off of whatever action plan they came up with in the planning meeting. Rick's primary role would be to get in touch with a contact at the Bangkok station who he was sure he could rely on to take over the Snake's position as Station Chief once the Snake was in custody. Then he had to make an introduction to the new Station Chief of an agent he had ordered up from the station in Kuala Lumpur who would be the new case officer for the Camel. Matt didn't need to know the details of any of that and he didn't get any. The American Ambassador would be informed after they had completed the job. She was considered a somewhat lightweight functionary primarily interested in public relations and new dresses in any case. Not a player as they say.

An American military officer who would be their liaison with the Cobra Gold leadership would meet Colonel Richardson who was handling the military side of things. He would find rooms on the base for the team to rest, plan and prepare for the mission as well as assure any back-up equipment, transportation or communication needs were met.

Chapter 35

After landing, the C-130 taxied over to the military side of the air base. The 2011 floods in Thailand had closed the old Don Muang Airport in Bangkok for several months and threatened to close the primary airport Suvarnabhumi. Since then, U-Tapao Air Base had become dual-use allowing civilian traffic, primarily charter flights, as well as military traffic, though both types were limited. At the side of the field used by the Thai military, there was a parking stand outside a hangar for the C-130. Several American military were standing at the entrance to the hangar along with some Thai military and civilians.

As the tail ramp of the C-130 lowered, a wave of the hot, moist air of Thailand rushed in and Rick grunted. "I didn't know it was going to be this hot."

Matt smiled at him, "Actually this is the end of the cool rainy season. You'll get used to it."

Matt walked down the rear ramp of the C-130 and saw Tommy and Neung standing on the side of the group by the hangar and waved to them. Colonel Richardson told him to go meet them and he would go ahead and see to the quarters and lunch arrangements for the team, while Matt and Rick met with Tommy and Neung. The whole team would be briefed after lunch once it was clear just what the situation on the ground was.

Matt and Rick then walked over to meet Tommy and Neung. Rick had been prepared for the introductions and knew just where Tommy and Neung fit in. The surprise was on Tommy and Neung when Matt mentioned Rick was not only the CIA representative on the team who would handle any contact required with the station and Thai intelligence authorities, but was his older brother as well. It was a good surprise because it validated Rick immediately with the two

Thai men. They understood family. Matt was family to them and if Rick was his brother then Rick was family and could be trusted.

Tommy had arranged a conference room inside the military office area of the air base where they could talk in private.

Both Matt and Rick had the same question for Neung to kick off the meeting.

"Do we know what the status is with the Snake?"

"Yes. We have had him under observation twenty-four seven since your call two days ago. It's not difficult to track him. He gave up any semblance of operational security way back when he arrived here. Right now he's at the embassy, which is his normal mode in the mornings. He usually goes out later in the afternoon depending on where his meetings are. Tonight one of his operational staff has booked a room at the Marriott and he has a reservation at the steak restaurant. We're pretty sure he will be meeting with the Lebanese merchant. We've been watching him also and he has a visitor from the Middle East traveling on a Jordanian passport though we think he is most probably Saudi by birth."

Rick looked at Matt, "This isn't good timing. That visitor is most probably the guy we are concerned with. We can't do anything to scare him off."

Matt looked to Neung but spoke to Rick, "This is your call but the sooner we move on the Snake the better. Is it possible to go after him tonight? I mean after he has his meeting at the Marriott with the agent he's running."

Neung spoke up, "My guys are ready to move at any time once we are clear on just what we want to do. I do agree with Matt. Your man may have forgotten his operational security, but you give him too much time and he will smell something's wrong. One thing we have noted, after his nighttime hotel meetings, he dismisses his security and goes on by himself. Sometimes he just goes back to his apartment. Sometimes he meets one of his girlfriends or a katoey for a sex session."

Rick hesitated and then decided. Neung was right. Speed was important; if they delayed, it might give the Snake the time he needed to evade them.

"Okay, when we are finished here I'll need a ride and an escort up to Bangkok. I'll contact the two guys who are going to be taking over the operation and brief them this afternoon and then give you the go ahead."

Matt looked back to Neung and Tommy. This was the critical juncture in several ways. The normal Thai way of approaching a mission as sensitive as this, with such a high possibility of failure or embarrassment, would be to be refuse to accept responsibility, "*mai yom rat pit chop*," as the Thai say, "I cannot accept responsibility." He was asking a lot for them to commit themselves to the solution of what was essentially a foreign problem. They had nothing to do with creating the problem and would get little benefit or recognition even if it was successfully addressed. There was no upside, except that of helping a friend in need, but plenty of potential downside if things went wrong.

Tommy and Neung were looking back at Matt and both understood the thought process he was going through. For both of them though, Matt was family. They were prepared to go the extra mile. As usual, it was Tommy who spoke first.

"Matt, I've cleared this with our Internal Security Operations Command. The ISOC people responsible for contact with the Snake and coordinating support for the operation against Al-Qaeda see this as a problem the U.S. CIA needs to address. The sooner the better. They have only two concerns: nothing hits the public light of day and the operation running the contact with the Al-Qaeda courier continues. Also no Thai military will be involved in taking this guy down. You will have to do that on your own, though we can provide logistic support and run interference with the local cops if necessary."

Then Neung chimed in, "That is the same message I have from my top guys. Our agents will lead you to the targets, but once on the scene it's your guys who will have to handle the action if a problem arises. We don't see the Lebanese merchant as a problem. He will cooperate once he understands there is a new boss he must deal with. He is completely invested in Thailand. He can't really cut and run. Your station chief is an unknown factor to us. You know best what he is capable of and how he should be approached."

Rick had been observing all this. His bureaucratic instincts, honed by years of fighting the internal fights at the agency, were "go slow, go slow, go slow." That was the mantra to avoid blame. "Let's study this a while longer." How many agency meetings over the years had ended with that proclamation made from whoever was on high at the moment? At the same time, he realized what Neung had said about moving quickly was operationally correct. They were here to take the Snake into custody and get him back to the U.S. where he could be addressed under the new anti-terrorism laws. Essentially it was the illegal rendition of a U.S. citizen, but nobody would know about it. As the agency evaluated the situation at the moment, the needs of homeland security required it.

"Okay. Let's go for it tonight."

The plan evolved. It was decided to wait before moving on the Snake until after the early evening meeting in the hotel room. Rick and the case officer brought up from Kuala Lumpur would be waiting with two of Neung's agents in a closed van in the parking building of the Marriott. When Bashir came back to the parking garage to get into his car to leave the hotel, they would pull up, assist him into the van and drive off to a nearby safe house to brief him on his new reality.

Meanwhile the Snake would be kept under observation. He normally dismissed his security guards after the meetings and proceeded on his own, driving his own vehicle rather than an embassy car. If he went back to his apartment, they would intercept him there using uniformed Thai police, supervised by Neung's agents, with the Delta troops and Matt in the background stepping in to make the grab. If he went out on the town, they would follow and wait until he had finished his partying and was alone.

Once they had him in custody, they would go straight to U-Tapao Air Base and back to the U.S. on military flights.

Chapter 36

The Snake was uneasy. He was used to being in total control of his world. He was the spider in the middle of the web. If there were faint vibrations, he would feel them and know how to respond. If anything was going on, he would always know. Yet now he felt twinges of uncertainty. The message from the CIA's special operations guy was both too little and too much. It was too little information on which to make a decision and too much for him to ignore. He was aware of the Cobra Gold exercise and not really concerned with it; it was a military matter. It was just a standard training exercise. Having Delta Force guys come out to participate was unusual however. They could be here to train Thai troops though it would be more normal for regular Special Forces troops to do that. The Delta guys were normally involved in anti-terrorism activities and his office should have been informed if that was the case in Thailand. He had gotten the military attaché to check on it and at first the guy said he knew nothing. Then several hours later, he called back to say apparently there were some "special" troops coming in but he had no assignment for them and it had come as a surprise to the officer acting as liaison for Cobra Gold also.

The Snake sensed danger and he wasn't going to wait to see exactly what form the danger would take. He was pretty well set for life. He had reveled in this last assignment as the soft post he deserved after all his years of doing the dirty jobs in ugly places. He'd made substantial sums of money here, primarily from the drug trade, not the tens of millions he had been able to hide away during the years in Iraq yet a good addition to his retirement nest.

He made a couple of calls back to key friends at Langley. These were people who could get answers and would let him know what was going on so he could best protect himself.

Meanwhile he decided to go off the charts for a while. As Station Chief he couldn't just disappear, unless he meant to keep on going. He could let his number two man know he would be out of office for a day or two and was not to be contacted unless it was an emergency. Then he would go underground and wait to see what happened.

First he had to keep the meeting with the Camel Driver. As Station Chief it was extremely irregular for him to be running an agent in this manner. That choice opportunity had fallen into his lap shortly after his arrival when the Thai intelligence people approached him and suggested not punishing Bashir for his drug smuggling, instead turning him against the jihadi groups to which he was providing service. The Snake had jumped in and claimed the operation as his before anyone could say otherwise. It kept him in the limelight back in Langley and provided other benefits the agency didn't need to know about. He wanted to keep this operation on track in the hope he would be able to continue to reap more profit as it developed. He was sure the importance of the operation in tracking Al-Qaeda leadership would also provide him bargaining chips down the road if he needed them.

After the meeting with Bashir he would go underground and relax and let things play out. When he was sure he was secure, he could emerge. If not, he had options and resources.

Chapter 37

There are within the boundaries of any major city sections of wasteland. They could be the sites of long-dead factory projects left to go to ruin, possibly an area used as a river flood plain or a truck or rail cargo terminus bypassed by newer development. In all cases these are areas to be avoided, definitely at night but also during the day in many cases. It's expected the mean creatures of the street find corners of the wasteland to call their home and don't welcome visitors from the upper world.

Bangkok is perhaps unique in having such a wasteland sited virtually in the center of the city, surrounded by dense urban apartment dwellings and older hotels. The area is called Makkasan. Roughly a mile long, over a quarter of a mile wide and bordered by an overhead expressway on one side, it is a large sprawl of mostly unused rail tracks, derelict carriages left to rust, empty storage facilities and broken warehouses, all the property of Thailand's most moribund state enterprise, the State Railway of Thailand. One edge of the grounds holds the main depot and offices of the State Railway and a railway museum. Some of the grounds are covered with trees in overgrown grassy areas. One area is essentially just a section of swampland. Ironically, one of the desirable and notable features of the area is derived from the absolute neglect it has received. The rainy season in Thailand runs from June through October. In September through November when the standing water in the swamp area is at its deepest and widest, migratory birds from China—herons—find their way to rest and march through these quiet mid-city waters on their annual trek south.

It is not only people of the street who crave hidden corners to hide, the Snake also found the empty, desolate venue of Makkasan attractive. While he didn't dream of moving into an abandoned warehouse, he did find a housing unit, separate from other apartments bordering the wasteland, and had arranged through a go-between to have it purchased and fixed up as his own safe house. It had fences and alarms to protect it from criminal intrusion and was isolated to protect it from the curious. Inside he had put together his own pleasure dome. No one from the station had ever visited or seen the inside of this special hideaway. When the Snake came here, it was without official security. He also was careful to practice his tradecraft in this most important of areas. He made sure no surveillance teams would ever track him here. He was only accompanied by whatever women he was enjoying at the moment and free to ply them with drugs and do with them as he pleased.

For the watchers from Thai intelligence, the hotel meeting was normal. The Snake and the man they knew as the Lebanese merchant arrived separately. The Snake came an hour in advance of his contact. The meeting lasted no more than thirty minutes, after which the Lebanese merchant departed for the parking lot and was met by the team in the van without incident. He would be busy for the next two hours meeting his new controller and being interrogated as to just what he had been up to and just what differences existed between the Snake's reports—especially in the area of payments received in cash and drugs—and the reality according to his agent. Rick had promised Matt he would get the real story on how Yod came to be murdered.

Matt and the Delta team were waiting in a separate van. Their job was to back up the Thai police who would stop the Snake's car when the time came and then step in and take him into custody. The team members were all dressed in civilian clothes consisting of khaki cargo pants and black shirts worn loose to cover the sidearms they carried.

The Snake had gone to eat his steak and wine dinner, enjoying the best of both, alone.

After dinner the Snake drove over to a private hostess club on Sukhumvit Soi 24. This was one of his regular haunts and the watchers had not been surprised by this stop. He had a relationship with two of the hostesses, one a beautiful young woman and the other a beautiful young katoey who stood near to six feet tall, often taking both of them back with him for the night.

After an hour, the Snake came out with just one hostess, the beautiful young katoey. All was pretty much running according to normal, but this was when the watchers were to be surprised. The Snake headed in a new direction. He drove to the parking garage at the Landmark Hotel on Sukhumvit next to Soi 6. The watchers saw him drive into the parking area. Two stayed and watched the exit of the garage and two went into the hotel, checking to see if the Snake had booked a room or was going to one of the night spots. After an hour they had nothing. They called to the watchers outside who reported the Snake's car hadn't come out. Only two cars had exited, both driven by Thai men who were alone. They went into the garage and checked to find the Snake's car parked there and it hit them: Somehow the Snake had given them the slip.

Matt and Neung were still in a van with the Delta team waiting for directions on where to intercept the Snake when the word came. The Snake was gone.

They didn't know it, but the Snake had gone to his Makkasan den. He would wait and watch and, if necessary, as soon as possible, make his next move out of country.

Chapter 38

The next morning they met in a safe house—a private residence—the new Chief of Station, previously Jake's number two man, had provided for their use as an operations center. The official story being given out at the embassy was the Snake had suffered a mild stroke and was in private medical care and seclusion for security reasons.

The depression amongst the team was so heavy it seemed to clog the air in the room as they sat and reviewed what might have gone wrong. Rick was there along with Matt, Neung and the Delta team members doing a post-mortem. The Delta guys were sitting back. Their body language clearly saying they were here for the action, not the think tank process of deciding what the next step should be.

Half of the operation had gone well. The Camel Driver had accepted his new case officer without qualm or protest. Actually he was relieved, Jake had scared him. The new case officer was more normal, more bureaucratic. He might press as hard as Jake had for intelligence results but he wouldn't have the near crazy intensity Jake had shown him only too often.

Now the problem for Rick's team was finding Jake. The new Station Chief was talking with the security men and others who had worked closely with Jake trying to find leads. So far he had come up empty except for one lead. One of the security guys admitted Jake had ordered him to leave a car at the parking garage earlier in the day. No explanation had been given but that was par for the course, Jake didn't give explanations. Also a woman's dress and shoes had been found in a public bathroom at the hotel. The katoey had arrived as Jake's female companion and after washing her face, changing clothes and tying up her hair had left as the male driver of one of the cars the watchers had seen departing with Jake hidden from sight, probably on the back seat floor.

Jake's phone was off. There was no way to track him and putting on a police search was out of the question. It would only ensure the hunt became public which couldn't be allowed.

It seemed there was nothing to do except wait for leads to emerge from the discussions being held with the agency staff at the embassy.

Matt was sick. He thought they had made the best plan possible and moved as quickly as possible yet Jake had evaded them. Somehow he had been tipped off. He raised this with Rick.

"Rick, this isn't an accident. Somehow he got word we were coming after him. How could that have happened?"

Rick shook his head. "Matt, you'll learn there are no secrets, but you're right. I thought we had this pretty closely held. No one at the embassy knew, so no one there could have told him. In any case we can do a witch-hunt later. What we need to do now is focus on his contacts here to see if anyone might have an idea of where he's gone to ground. The new Chief of Station will let us know what he gets from the staff. We need to look in other directions."

"What other directions are there?"

Rick thought for a while and then said, "Actually there is one person who had a lot of face time with the Snake the station chief can't question."

"Who's that?"

"The agent he was running. I spoke with him yesterday. My concern was primarily to put him at ease and lock him into his relationship with his new case officer. Except for some general background on what Jake was up to, we didn't discuss the Snake in depth. It's not the best thing to push him too hard right away. Now, we have no choice. I'll have his case officer set up another meeting today and I'll grill him on possible places where Jake can be hiding."

It was agony for Matt and the rest of the team. All they could do was wait. Setting up a meeting with an undercover agent isn't a matter of a simple phone call, even in the modern age of instant messaging. The possibility existed that he was directly involved in activity with the Al-Qaeda courier he was handling. Some protocols had to be followed involving what seemed to be normal customer inquiries at his outlet and allowing time for Bashir to respond.

Matt had not yet phoned Noi to let her know he was home and safe for now. Simply because it would be a lie. He was home but couldn't really be sure how safe anything was. This process of bringing in the Snake could get messy and he didn't want to mislead her. It was best to just focus on the job at hand. Personal needs could wait.

It took until mid-afternoon for Bashir to come to the agreed meeting place. It took another hour of careful grilling by Rick and the new case officer before they came up with a possible lead. Rick called Matt and asked him to get the team ready and request Neung to attend the meeting.

Rick had still not returned when Neung came over. He waved Matt into a back room indicating he wanted to talk privately.

"Matt, we've been so busy trying to catch this guy we haven't had a chance to catch up on some things that happened while you were gone."

"What is it?"

"Well, I think you want to talk with this man we're chasing to be sure, but two bodies turned up in Chonburi last week. An anonymous caller tipped off the police at the port the bodies were the two men who killed the boy at the slaughterhouse. No other information was given. Also one of the men had wounds on his leg which indicated he may have been the guy you shot during the ambush attempt."

"That doesn't make any sense. Why should someone kill them and tag them as the killers?"

"It may make sense in one way. If these guys were working with what was supposed to be a secret operation and did something this stupid, maybe the leaders of the operation wanted to make an example of them. Since control has changed, maybe your brother can get the whole story out of the agent they're running."

Neung stopped and grinned at Matt, "You could say that as far as the Thai police are concerned it's now a dead issue."

Matt couldn't help but smile and shook his head, "I think you've had one too many English language lessons."

Then Matt went silent for a minute.

Neung was right; the whole focus had become the hunt for the guy in charge, the Snake. The original cause, Yod's murder, was being forgotten. He didn't want that. He would speak with Rick. He needed to be sure the two guys who had been killed were really Yod's murderers.

"Thanks, Neung. I'll speak with Rick after we catch the Snake."

When Rick returned, he explained to the team and Neung what they had come up with.

"While it may not be the answer, there is one possibility. We checked the list of safe house locations that the Chief of Station gave us. Then we asked the Snake's agent to go through all the safe house locations in which he had met with the Snake. He came up with one place which isn't on the station's list. That's where we'll start tonight."

He looked over to Neung.

"We'll need help. It would be good to have the place checked from the street in advance. Also any advice you have on how to take control of the neighborhood when we go to make entry later on would be appreciated."

Neung was careful in responding. Depending on the location, an armed raid on a private house could be a bombshell.

"What address did he give?"

"He said the Snake had a secret house in an area called Makkasan. He had it fixed up as his pleasure palace complete with a hot tub, bar and facilities for entertaining his women. That's why it isn't on any official lists. Our man only went there one time. It was at night and the Snake was alone for the meeting. He had the impression there were some women in the back room while they were talking and the Snake finished the meeting and pushed him out quickly."

"Makkasan is a big area. Did he give you anything to narrow it down a bit?"

"Yeah, he gave the name of a second-class hotel a block closer to the central city from the house. He said the Snake's place was directly across from the rail yard in a pretty abandoned area."

"That's enough. We'll find it. I'll have my guys take a look. It's best if we go in after dark. That area should be deserted."

Rick then asked Neung and Matt to meet him for a private conversation in a separate room at the house. Neung gave Matt a look that said, "What's going on?" and followed along.

"There is a development you should be aware of. I made some calls back to Langley and got some disturbing news."

Rick paused, knowing he was giving out information that would cause concern, especially for Neung.

"It's not completely confirmed, but it seems we may not be the only team looking for the Snake."

"What do you mean?"

"What I mean is the rumor at Langley is the agency's Special Operations Group sent some guys out here on their own to pick up the Snake. He has operated close to that group over the years and they may want to protect him and get him special handling back in the U.S. or..."

"Or what?"

"Or they may be out here to close his mouth. The Snake knows where all the bodies are buried. He has the goods on highly placed people not only in Langley, but also throughout the government apparatus in Washington, D.C. A lot of important people would be very happy if he just disappeared."

Neung gave Matt a very cynical smile and addressed both Rick and Matt.

"My goodness. You guys make Thai politics look like a walk in the park. We would never dream of killing off the opposition. It's much easier just to buy off the system."

Rick nodded sadly, "We'll have to tell the team at some point, but for now let's just execute the raid on the Snake's hideout tonight and get him safely tucked away. It seems we're in a race and I want to win it."

Chapter 39

Rick, Matt and the Delta team soldiers were waiting in a van as they had the previous night. This time they were in the Makkasan district, a few blocks away from the target house. Neung's agents had scouted the house during the day. There was no sign of activity and no car in sight. They waited until it was dark at eight. Neung had gotten local police to block the ends of the road leading to the house but the area was so isolated there was no traffic.

When the team approached the gate, they were ready to blow it if necessary to gain entry. It wasn't necessary. The gate pushed open at a touch. Matt had planned on leading the way in, but the Delta team, now equipped with M4 assault rifles, pushed him to the back. "This is our job, Major."

The front doors, two beautiful and expensive pieces of rosewood, were locked and they kicked them in. Matt had to admire the precision with which the team went about their jobs. They covered each other and went room by room, each calling "Clear!" as soon as they were sure. The house seemed to be empty. Finally a call came from the back, from a bedroom. "Back here!"

Matt went on back and looked in. There was a king-size bed in the middle of the room, the headboard against one wall. There was a door leading to a large bathroom on one side of the bed and the other side of the room had two glass doors leading to a large wooden hot tub built into a wooden deck. The room wasn't empty. Sprawled in the middle of the silk sheets on the bed was the katoey escort who had gone with the Snake the previous night. In perhaps an unconscious attempt to give her some dignity, Matt found himself thinking of her as a woman. She was nude. Her tall, model-slim body was lying back with her long, curly, dyed brown hair spread over a pillow. One hand was thrown above her head in a posed look, the other hand was thrown out to the side. The fingernails were long and carefully decorated. Her legs were spread open and you could see she hadn't taken the final step to womanhood of having her penis removed as it hung flaccid between her legs. Her silicone breasts, at least the right one, pointed upward even in death; the left breast had imploded when the bullet that killed her passed through on its way to her heart. That breast had become a pitiful wrinkled pile of flesh with a nipple as the silicone had run out. She would have been devastated; her strongest wish would have been to die with the appearance of a beautiful woman.

Matt walked closer and looked at her face. It was heavily made up. Her eye shadow had run a bit from both eyes. Was she crying at the end? Had she been begging her lover not to kill her? It hit him then that she was very young, maybe only five or six years older than Ben, the boy at Metta whose wish was to blossom into a woman such as this.

Jake was gone.

"Jesus," Said Sergeant Rodriguez. "This is a first of a kind event for me. I've never seen a guy like this."

Sergeant Kim said, "I guess the pretty boy outlived his usefulness. This Snake is one tough bastard, isn't he?"

Matt finally found some words. This was not what he anticipated, but he was learning it was what you should expect from the Snake. He moved quickly and he moved hard. He had done to the katoey what he had tried to do with Matt. If someone becomes an obstacle, eliminate him or her.

"The lesson is the guy is ready to shoot and kill. Keep it in mind when we get close. We want him alive but let's not take chances."

The Delta team guys didn't need the reminder but they all nodded their heads.

Neung walked through the door and his reaction was the pragmatic one Matt had learned to expect from him.

"We've got a mess to clean up, haven't we?"

Neung walked around the room quickly and then took over. He turned around and addressed Rick.

"The assault team should get back in the van. Nobody has seen them yet and it's best to keep it that way. You and Matt have twenty minutes to go through things to see if you can find leads to where this guy ran to hide. I'll have a team come in and clean up and they will give a report on what they find. We'll move the body to a love hotel, there is one just a block away. We can create a cover story for the discovery of the katoey's body and his death there. Good enough?"

Rick and Matt both nodded. It was a relief to have Neung take charge of the scene. This couldn't be allowed to go public. "Good enough."

Chapter 40

The team meeting at the safe house early the following morning was again a scene of depression. The mentality of the Delta team was of soldiers used to hitting fixed targets and getting the job done. They weren't police used to adapting to the evasive tactics of criminals they were chasing. Matt thought he had to give them a pep talk and keep them focused on the job, catching and bringing in the Snake.

They had gone over some maps found at the Snake's hideaway. The maps covered all of Thailand and some of Cambodia and didn't really give them a focus on the next place to look. It was time to brief the team on what the direction and process would be and they didn't have much to give. Rick had one idea he had gotten from a late night talk with the Station Chief. He just needed to run it by Neung to see if it made sense.

Before the meeting, Rick and Matt, whose newly discovered relationship had gone well until now, had their first major disagreement and argument.

The disagreement grew out of their differing professional backgrounds. Rick, as a career officer in the CIA, wanted to hold back information from the team. That was the normal mode of operation in the agency, to compartmentalize information. Matt, with primarily a military service background as an infantry officer serving with Ranger units, felt the men deserved all the information they had.

Rick told Matt he was not going to bring up the intelligence he had received: there was probably another team from the agency looking for the Snake and was most likely here to kill him.

Matt's response was immediate.

"That's bullshit!"

Rick was surprised. He felt this was his operation, his area of expertise and he had not expected any pushback from Matt.

"Matt, that's just good operational sense. We need these guys to stay focused. Why cloud the issue by raising the possibility of a division within the agency on how to handle the Snake?"

"Because this isn't about the agency, Rick, or Washington, D.C., politics. It's about sending men into danger's way and not giving them full information. It may be the way the agency does things. It's not the way the military or I do things. These men are soldiers on a mission. If our latest information is there are some complicating factors posing a danger to them, they have a right to know."

Rick thought it over. It was still his operation. He could overrule Matt or he could trust Matt's judgment. He decided to go along with Matt. It was important to keep the Delta team soldiers committed to the mission.

"Okay. They'll get the full story. Let's go talk with them. We need to make a plan and get a move on."

While they were talking, Neung had arrived to give them an update on what had been found in the Snake's hideaway. Tommy escorted him as Matt had called him and asked him to sit in, anticipating they would need his help. Rick had asked them to attend the team meeting so they could review all the material and come to a decision together.

The discussion between Rick and Matt had essentially finished by the time Neung and Tommy walked in, but there was still a residue of tension in the air. Neung was the first to speak.

"Is everything all right?"

Matt smiled at him, "Everything is fine. Rick and I are just getting to know each other better. Let's go and sit down with the team and make some decisions on what direction we go in."

Neung led off by giving a summary of what had been found by his agents when they cleaned up the house.

"We came up with several unregistered weapons: sidearms and an M4 assault rifle. As we go after him we must presume he is well armed. There was a large supply of drugs, mostly ecstasy and Ketamine. We also found some maps and background material of Cambodia and the Thai border areas with Cambodia and Laos. I think it's safe to say he plans to go across the border probably into Cambodia by land. There, with sufficient cash, he can buy anything he wants and make his escape to anywhere in the world."

Matt asked him. "That is a tremendously long border area. Is there any indication of specifically where he might want to cross?"

"No, there were no specifics in what we found in the house."

Here Rick spoke up, "The Station Chief mentioned to me the Snake's most recent trip outside of Bangkok was a long weekend visit down to Chantaburi over a month or so ago. Does that make any sense in terms of where he might run?"

Neung nodded, "It might. Chantaburi is also the Thai province bordering Battambang so that makes sense. I don't think he will try to go across one of the established border crossings to Cambodia near Trat that have immigration checkpoints. There is a national park, Khao Khitchakut, north of Chantaburi from which he can reach the border using back roads. It's a mountainous region and there are several back roads where you can cross the border illegally, but it's not easy especially if it's raining and it rains a lot down there."

Matt chimed in, "I know the park. I've done work down there. I know the people. It can be tough going on the roads outside the park especially when you get close to the border. Not many foreigners go down there. If he is going that way, we should be able to track him."

But leaving Bangkok would raise new issues for Neung and Matt thought he should get that on the table.

"Will you be able to help us if we take the hunt down there?"

Neung gave him a rueful smile. Matt knew what the limits of Thai bureaucracy were and he had hit on the main point. Neung wouldn't be allowed to operate with the same impunity outside of Bangkok as he had to date inside the town.

"The answer is yes to a limited extent. I can go along and have some agents on the ground to assist you. Let's just say we won't have quite the same clean-up capability we do here in Bangkok. If things go wrong, such as the mess we cleaned up last night, we'll have to brief local officials. It's best if things are finished cleanly. Another lead we have is the car being used has

Bangkok license plates. That will help us to track him if he is down there. Chantaburi is a small city. We should be able to find sign of him if he has been there. Should he go into the jungle, it's up to your team to track him and get him. My agents aren't trained for that sort of work."

Neung paused for a second and then added, "Also you must understand, under no circumstances can my men or I go into Cambodia. I strongly recommend that you don't try. You must remember Khmer Rouge are still running the country, though they now use differing political labels. The political leadership have their roots in the killing fields. Your team may well disappear quickly if the wrong people on that side get a hold of you. Stop at the border."

With that they turned to planning the logistics. Using the guise of operating as part of the Cobra Gold exercise, they would call on Colonel Richardson to stage a helicopter lift for the team and Neung, together with his agents from the Air Force side of Don Muang Air Base to Chantaburi. Tommy would arrange the Thai military clearances. It was a four-hour drive to Chantaburi. They had to assume the Snake was already there. They worked out the rest of the logistical details including having the team change back into combat fatigues and gear. The Cobra Gold cover was now the operational mode. With that they were told to be ready to go in twenty minutes.

Rick had one more announcement to make. He told the team about the probability of someone in the Agency having dispatched a team from the Special Operations Group to get the Snake.

Neung just looked at Matt and shook his head. He had always thought the American operators were organized. He found this internal conflict quite amazing. Matt returned a look of agreement.

Rick's statement brought a strong and quick reaction.

"Sir, if there is another team after this guy, what are the rules of engagement? How do we handle a meeting with the other team?"

"We don't engage them and they won't engage us. We just have to get to the Snake first and then they'll have to back off."

"What if they get to the Snake first?"

"Then I'll have to talk with them if at all possible. It'll be on me. Under no circumstances do we get into a shootout with our own guys."

This produced some muttering from the team and certainly there would be some discussion in private later about the assholes in the agency, but no more questions. Sergeant Hunt was left wondering if this development was going to hurt his chances of getting into the Special Operations Group after his retirement from Delta.

Chapter 41

The move to Chantaburi was quick and efficient. Colonel Richardson, with Tommy's help on the Thai military side, had acted quickly to move away obstacles. The vehicle was a CH-47, the U.S. military's heavy lift chopper. Even though there was no airport or military air base in Chantaburi as it was a small city, there were several Thai army bases in the area with helicopter pads. When Tommy arranged a request from the Thai Army's ISOC, permission to land and discharge "special" passengers at a base just outside of town was quickly given. They arrived before noon.

Two four-wheel drive SUVs were waiting for them. The question was where to go? While Tommy met with the colonel commanding the base, Neung was on the phone arranging to set up an operations base in a house on the outskirts of the city.

Neung had called the police asking them to have a list of foreigners registered at local hotels for him to go over. He sent one of his agents immediately yielding no results. The Snake had been on the run for over thirty hours now. He had to get some rest and it was possible he had found a small backpacker's hostel or even a private home. They asked the local police to check any possible places including making inquires about cars with Bangkok plates. The limited number of foreign tourists interested in coming to the area had to make the search a little more feasible.

Finally, a couple of hours later, they had a few hits from Neung's agents. One of the tourist guide places had talked with a foreigner late the previous day who wanted to hire a guide for a few days. The man fit the Snake's description and when shown a picture of the Snake, the lady in charge said it was him. The only problem was he wanted a male guide and she didn't have one available for him to hire. The agents then talked with other tour offices yet no one remembered talking with such a man.

Neung, Tommy, Matt and Rick met to talk it over. It was getting late in the afternoon. Since Neung's agents were providing all the information based on their pounding the pavement and literally going from door to door in the town, he spoke first, addressing Rick.

"Your man is up to something. If he was just running for the border, he could be long gone by now. This business of hiring a guide doesn't make sense for someone who is on the run. Do you have any idea what he is up to?"

Rick thought for a second, "No, except he might be trying to make contact with someone to get him across the border on some back road."

Matt spoke up, "There are a limited number of roads through the park and a limited number of back roads without immigration controls going into Battambang province. He doesn't really have a lot to choose from. We should be able to cover them."

He looked to Tommy, "I can coordinate with the park authorities. Could you arrange to put a couple of troopers on each of the roads coming out of the park going towards Cambodia? Not to stop traffic, just to observe. They could call you and let you know of any foreigners coming through. Then we could move from here by chopper to the border."

Tommy smiled at Matt. Possibly the only person outside of his chain of command from whom he would take this sort of direction on how to use his troops was Matt. The relationship they had forged in the Ranger course years before was incredibly solid.

"Yes, we can do that. I have a platoon from my regiment en route here now for support. They should be here early tonight and I can have them move into position on the roads going from the park into Battambang first thing in the morning. We'll also have a Huey support chopper down from Bangkok in the morning."

Neung waited to see if there were other ideas. No one added anything.

"Okay. I'll have my agents continue to work places where

this guy might put up for the night or go for food or drink. He has got to have some place to rest if he's waiting on something."

Left to himself for a while, Matt decided now was the time to call Noi and let her know he was back. If he had called previously when he was in Bangkok, she would have wanted to see him and been unhappy when he had to say no. Now, calling from Chantaburi saying he was on an operation with Neung and Tommy, she would accept that he couldn't drop what he was doing and come right over.

Noi picked up immediately. He could tell right away she was in the office by the background noise.

"Hey, babe, it's me. I just wanted to call and let you know I'm back home."

"At last. How are you? Where are you?"

Matt laughing, "I'm fine. Everything's okay. I'm in Chantaburi with Tommy and Neung, just helping them finish this job. It's going to be over soon and then I'll be back in Bangkok. How about you? Is life back to normal?"

"It'll be back to normal when you're really home. Da has been a great friend, but she's not you."

"Ahh, I'm glad to hear that. Just a day or two more and this will be wrapped up, babe. I'm not alone, okay? Other people are handling things and I'm just assisting."

"Okay, just finish up and come home. I'll be waiting."

It had been a good call. Now Matt could focus on finishing the job.

Chapter 42

The Snake was very clear in his mind about what he was doing. His basic plan was to get into Cambodia on one of several back roads he had previously scouted. Once there, his money could buy him whatever sort of support he needed. However when he had called his key friends in the agency to find out just what was going on, they had come back with what they termed a better option. They would send a team to exfiltrate him and get him back to the States free of the constraints being found by Rick's team would impose. Once he was on the ground in the U.S. and free to act on his own there were many contacts, some in Congress, he could call on to protect him from a witch-hunt by others in the government. If possible, Jake preferred that option. At the same time, a man of his experience in the dark passages of human behavior knew better than to take an offer of help at face value. It was his habit, learned from monitoring his own conduct, to always look for the dark side of any behavior that seemed good on its face. In other words "trust no one." He would protect himself with the Cambodia option but it seemed reasonable to invest a day or so, no more, in the agency option.

He had arranged a safe house in the area on a previous trip months earlier. Now he coiled up in his den and waited. Tomorrow's activities would provide the answer as to which option was best. He would wait for his friends in the agency to show their colors.

Chapter 43

The two-man rescue team Jake had been promised by his friends was en route. There are a lot of thirty or forty-something single guys from all over the world coming to Thailand. Many are on a fitness kick, muscle-building or come to learn Muay Thai or just want easy access to the steroids readily available in the market place. The two men fit the picture. They were both extremely fit, one about five ten, the other about six two. Hard bodies topped by hard eyes. They had flown into Bangkok on a commercial flight, rented a car and were driving down to Chantaburi. They had a stop to make along the way. They were going to delay for an hour or so in Pattaya. It was not to experience the delights of sun, sand or sex, though all existed in plentiful supply in the fishing village on steroids, but rather to meet with a supplier.

Thailand is unique in the world as a haven for virtually every mafia organization identified by Interpol. From the Japanese yakuza, the biggest and longest established mafia in country, dating back to the 1950s, to the Russians, the meanest, killing their own kind and other gang members regularly on the beaches of Pattaya, to the Dutch, who killed one of their own by tying a bomb to his body and exploding it—the Thai police decided it was a suicide—and even the Vietnamese. The mafia groups use Thailand as a refuge when things get hot back home and as a source for drugs, passports and other identification documents and guns. They were all available in Thailand and Pattaya—the R&R center for the world's criminals—was a convenient supply point.

What the Special Operations Group guys were after today were guns. They couldn't take a chance on bringing any in but they couldn't undertake their mission without being properly armed. Normally the station could provide their support, but not on this mission. Everything had to be handled through the black market. They had a phone number and had called ahead using a mobile phone newly acquired at the airport in Bangkok. The meeting place was a Thai restaurant at a certain kilometer marker on the main Pattaya highway, actually still Sukhumvit Road, the road in Bangkok which extends down through Pattaya. They used the name they were given, were escorted to a back room, used some of their cash supply and twenty minutes later were leaving with two 9 mm Glocks and two M-16 assault rifles, one with a scope, and sufficient ammunition.

They continued the drive down to Chantaburi. They had the name of a small hotel in which to stay the night. Tomorrow they would follow the directions they had been given to make contact, rendezvous with the Snake and complete their mission.

Chapter 44

Early the next morning Neung phoned Matt and requested a meeting at the team's house. He said his guys might have come up with something. It was raining outside though it was forecast to let up later that morning.

The rain would have cast a bit of gloom over the day even if the team wasn't meeting for the third morning in a row to plan yet another effort to catch the Snake. The meeting room Neung and Tommy walked into was very quiet. Repeated failure has a debilitating effect and the team was in a mood, yet again, to match the weather. They were looking for good news and a positive plan of action to match. Neung gave them something to work with.

"We've got something good to go on. In talking around town, one of my agents got word of a foreigner who had rented a house outside of town in a secluded forest area between the town and the national park. It was rented a couple of months ago and the man paid six months' rent in advance. That sort of payment is a bit unusual around here. This is probably our man."

Neung looked over to Matt and Rick, "How do you want to go after this."

Rick looked at Matt and smiled, "You're the boots on the ground guy. Any suggestions?"

"Yeah. I think we have to split up. We should have one team hit the house and be prepared for the possibility he'll run before we can get to him. I think we should put another team ahead of him on the back roads leading to Battambang to cut him off when he runs in that direction. I know those roads. I'll take Sergeant Rodriguez and Sergeant Jackson with me. We'll link up by radio with Tommy's guys watching the park roads and they can alert us if they spot him. You, Sergeant Hunt and

Sergeant Kim can hit the house. Neung's guys can lead you to the house and back you up, if that's okay with Neung."

Neung nodded, "We can do that."

Matt looked to Tommy, "The rain is letting up. Could we use the chopper to lift us onto the road coming out of the back side of the park closest to access to the roads to Battambang?"

"No problem. My guys are on the road now. Let's give them another thirty minutes to be in position and then you can lift off and join them."

Neung and Rick agreed that they and the other Delta team members would leave immediately to get into position by the house they were targeting and would radio when they were in place. The rain was letting up but the dirt roads would be muddy and slow going. Tommy would stay at the house being used as the operations base and coordinate communications and support by the troops he had ordered down from Bangkok.

Chapter 45

The two special operations guys from the agency were very careful in every step they took. They had survived until now by letting the other guys make the mistakes. They wouldn't start making mistakes now. Their understanding was the Snake was in hiding and viewed their arrival as a rescue mission. They expected him to welcome them and be fully cooperative with their plans to get him out of Thailand and safely back home.

The Snake for his part was relieved they had arrived. When you are on the run, waiting for any reason is the hardest thing to do. When they contacted him by phone the night before to let him know they were on the scene, he felt he was a step closer to getting out of Thailand and back to a place where he could protect himself and negotiate better. He had the goods on a lot of important people. When he started pulling strings, things would happen. He just had to get out of his current situation. He had arranged for the two men to come to his safe house at ten AM. Since they were professionals, he knew they would arrive early to case the scene. He had made sure they would see what they expected. His plan for the three of them to leave Thailand and cross over into Cambodia by back roads had been accepted. Support was to be waiting across the border. Now it was just a question of linking up and getting over the border. He would remain security conscious and take nothing for granted.

The two men did arrive early. The Snake had said ten but they planned to arrive about an hour earlier to look things over. The rain and muddy roads had slowed them down and they were a few minutes later than they planned. They drove past the turnoff to the safe house checking things out and then turned back and parked off the road. They took their weapons out of the trunk of the car and walked through the woods surrounding the safe house to a spot on the edge of the clearing where they could see the house clearly. They were careful to stay back in the foliage so they couldn't be seen. Their main concern was that Jake had been caught or was under surveillance already. They didn't want to walk into a trap.

They were about a hundred yards from the house. The shorter man with the scoped M-16 used it to look over the house and the surrounding woods. The taller man used a pair of spotting binoculars with a broader view that also gave the distance to the target. There was a car parked in a driveway next to the house, otherwise there was no movement.

They crouched down in the woods and waited. Every few minutes one or the other would stand up and scan the house and around the woods. There was no activity.

At ten, they were both standing and watching when the agreed signal was given. The Snake walked out of the house to a covered porch in the front. He was wearing a white Panama hat, sunglasses, a loose dark shirt and khaki trousers. He looked around. The white hat was the all-clear signal. If he had been captured or was being coerced in any way he wouldn't be wearing any hat.

The tall man said, "It's him. One hundred and ten yards. No wind."

The shorter man asked, "You're sure?"

"Yes, damn it. Take him."

The shot hit the Snake in the chest. He had been standing in front of a chair. He flew back and settled into the chair slumped over, bleeding from the chest wound. He was dead.

The tall man turned to the other. "Go get the car and meet me in front of the house."

He would walk across the field. They needed to take a picture identifying the Snake before they left.

They both reached the front of the house at the same time. It was the short man, the shooter, who had been ready to deliver the second shot of a double tap if necessary who first noticed.

"Awww shit. It's not him. We've been set up. That bastard. Let's get out of here."

The man slumped in the chair was the Thai "guide" the Snake had been looking to hire. He had found a man of the right height and weight who had agreed, for a good sum of

217

money, to help watch his house and to greet some visitors expected that morning. He had been told the white Panama hat and the sunglasses were very important and of course they were. The Snake was balding and the hat, besides shading the man's face, covered the Thai guide's full head of hair. He had earned his money.

The Snake had been watching from the woods behind the house, another fifty yards further on. He said nothing when they shot his guide. He just shook his head. Did they really think it would be that easy to take him out of the game?

If this was the way the game was to be played, he would play it this way. If the two men had come out in the open to greet him at the safe house, he would have joined them and they could have made their escape together. Now it was every man for himself and the Snake was ready to run. He had not waited to see what they would do. He had run back to the car he had parked near an access road on the back side of the woods and by the time the two men learned they had shot the wrong man, he was well on his way driving towards the national park and then, through it, to the roads leading to Battambang. He had his own escape plan in place and people in Langley and Washington, D.C., would pay for thinking they could eliminate him so easily.

Chapter 46

The rain had also slowed down Rick and the assault team going after the safe house. Neung's agents had to go over the directions and be sure they were taking the correct road out of Chantaburi. It was after nine thirty when they finally got on the way in two four-wheel drive vehicles, Neung leading the way with three of his agents in the first vehicle and Rick and two of the Delta team being driven by another agent in the second.

It was about ten thirty when they got to the entrance road to the safe house. They duplicated the tactics of the two men who had come previously. They drove past the entry and then doubled back and parked off the side of the road. It was one of Neung's agents who noticed the tire tracks in the mud going off the road nearby and called them to his attention. Neung called over to Rick and the Delta team soldiers.

"Someone has been here before. These tracks were probably made earlier this morning otherwise the rain overnight would have washed them away."

Rick shrugged his shoulders.

"Nothing to do but go see what we have. Let's walk through the woods and take a look."

The Delta team guys took point and led off moving cautiously. Rick and Neung and one of Neung's agents followed along. The rest stayed with the vehicles and waited for Neung to give them the word.

At the edge of the woods fronting the house, Rick and the Delta team guys, Sergeant Hunt and Sergeant Kim repeated the actions of the previous two visitors who had been in this place only minutes before. They didn't have a scoped rifle, but Sergeant Hunt was carrying binoculars. They could all see the white hat and somebody slumped in a chair at the front of the house. Only Sergeant Hunt, using the binoculars, could see the blood.

He turned to the others, "We're too late. This guy has been shot."

Rick and the Delta guys headed straight across the field towards the house while Neung called to the team in reserve to drive in.

At the house, the Delta team guys went inside to clear the house while Rick looked over the body slumped in front. The killers had put the Panama hat back on after lifting it off to discover they had killed the wrong man. Matt had the same reaction as the killers when he lifted the hat.

"The bastard."

Rick did the same as the killers and put the hat back on the dead man's head. Seconds later Neung and the back-up team drove up and the Delta team guys came out of the house reporting it all clear. They all stood in a circle looking at the body.

Neung walked up to Rick asking, "What's the situation? I take it this is not your man?"

"No, the tricky bastard fooled the guys who were sent out to meet him. He must have been in hiding somewhere nearby when they shot this guy thinking it was the Snake. He must be on the run to the border now. He can't have gone too far. We have to go after him."

"Okay, I'll leave a couple of my guys here to talk with the local police and clean this up. The cover story is that we were looking for international drug traffickers and came across this scene. First let me call Tommy and Matt so they can coordinate the effort to block the roads."

Sergeant Hunt was the one to ask Rick about who the killers were.

"Sir, are the guys who did the shooting the other team you were talking about?"

"That would be my best bet, Sergeant."

"Do you think they're still after him?"

"I doubt it, Sergeant. After a fuck-up like this they will probably be heading out of country as fast as they can to make sure they don't get caught up in any investigation. I imagine these guys will find themselves out of work when they get back to the States. However, let's keep our eyes open for whoever may be out there. The Snake seems to have a lot of people who want him dead. Our job is to bring him back alive if at all possible."

Matt and the other Delta team members were in position on the main road between the park and the access roads to Battambang. The chopper had dropped them off at the site where the platoon leader of the Thai soldiers had set up his command post. The rest of the platoon had been broken up into eight fire teams of five each and positioned as watch teams on all the access roads. Their orders were just to observe not to stop. Any foreigner coming through should be reported to Matt and the platoon leader; they would handle intercepting the car and questioning the occupants.

The rain that had been falling earlier had hindered their operation, making it slow and difficult to get in position. Now the rain, falling only lightly, was a friend. It would slow the Snake in making his escape and it meant there were no tourists on the roads. The Snake would be the lone foreigner driving through their area and there had been no traffic on the road at all.

The road itself was a brown dirt slash through the dark green of the forest on both sides. Though the sky was still gray, cloudy and overcast, visibility had improved throughout the morning and was between two hundred and three hundred yards. The road, as were many country and forest roads, was not flat but rolled with the natural topography of the land. Matt had asked the platoon leader to park the four-wheel drive vehicle on the side of the road, just short of the crest of one rise in the road on which he could see several hundred yards both ways. They waited for word.

At first Matt was worried they had made the wrong move. When Tommy called and reported what Rick and Neung had found at the safe house, it only partially relieved his worries. Sergeants Rodriguez and Johnson were relaxed but both visibly, at least to Matt's experienced eye, now in the hunt mode. There was little joking and a lot more attention paid to everything surrounding them. Matt didn't want to sit in the SUV they were using and got out and stood on the side of the road. The sergeants joined him. Their life in the field was often spent in the rain and mud. It didn't bother them. They were more comfortable with their feet on the ground. The Delta guys and Matt were all wearing combat fatigues and the light rain dripped off their circular cloth bush hats. The M4s were slung over their shoulders, muzzles down.

While they were waiting, looking at the roads leading to their site, Matt had an idea he quickly discussed with the Thai platoon leader. He and the two Delta NCOs would be dropped at the crest in the road about one hundred yards away from their current position, closer to the direction they expected the Snake to come from. They would stay out of sight in the foliage alongside the road. The platoon leader and his men would park the SUV so it clearly blocked the road at their present position.

The plan was the Snake, as he drove towards them, would stop as he got to the crest of the hill and saw the military SUV ahead on the next rise in the road. Then Matt and the Delta team would show themselves alongside his car and force him to surrender. If the Snake kept going, the platoon leader and his men would take him prisoner at their point on the road. After they moved into the new position amongst the trees, Matt and the Delta soldiers waited. Though the rain had dissipated, large water drops continued to fall on them steadily from the overhead foliage marking out a sense-dulling jungle metronome. Time slowed to a crawl as it does in all ambush settings. The team members were all professional. There was no talking, no excess movement.

Finally, about an hour later, the platoon leader got a call on the radio from one of his units. A foreigner had driven out of the park and gone by their post without slowing. The car had turned on the road going in their direction. He called Matt. The Snake was coming.

Matt got out a pair of binoculars and watched in the direction they had been told to expect the Snake to come from. A few minutes later he saw a car coming towards their position rise over the crest of a hill one hundred and fifty yards away and go down into the dip in the road. They waited.

The plan worked as Matt had hoped. As he reached the crest where they were in position, the Snake saw the SUV blocking the road ahead and the soldiers standing around it atop the next hill. He braked to a stop. When he did, Matt walked out of the brush alongside the road, five yards away, leveling his M4 at the Snake. The two Delta team members automatically flanked him, standing back several yards to keep a clear field of fire in case the Snake wanted to shoot it out. He didn't.

Matt stopped and told the Snake to get out of the car and keep his hands in sight. For a few seconds time stood still. The Snake wasn't used to losing. Matt could almost hear him calculating all the possibilities in his mind. Matt yelled again for him to get out of the car. The Snake shrugged his shoulders. He would give up.

The car door opened and the Snake slowly stepped out and faced Matt. He held his hands up, looking at the Delta soldiers and then back to Matt.

The Snake was composed, even scornful of all that confronted him.

"Well, Major, I thought you had retired. What brings you out to the woods?"

"I was offered a chance to end your career. I couldn't say no."

"Ah, Major, you are so out of your depth as usual. You are mistaken. I have done nothing but promote the interests of the U.S. government in the war on terror. However let's go through with your charade. I have many friends in Washington who know my contributions and value. They will reward me for my service no matter how mistaken you and a few low-level bureaucrats are."

Matt had kept his distance, now he took a step closer and motioning with his M4, told the Snake, "Turn around and put your hands behind your back. Before you talk with your friends, you'll be spending a lot of time talking with the Justice Department."

As the Snake started to turn, out of the corner of his eye, Matt saw movement further back down the road in the direction the Snake had come from. An SUV was parked on the crest of the hill one hundred and fifty yards away. Two men dressed in black were standing alongside the vehicle watching them. There was a glint of light.

Just as Matt yelled at the Snake to get down the Snake's body jerked backward and Matt heard the shot. As Matt bent down to aid the Snake, a second shot was fired and Matt heard it buzz over his head. Matt sprawled on the ground and brought his M4 around to bear on the shooters but even as he did so, he saw they were back in their SUV and rolling backwards down the hill, using the crest of the hill to mask their vehicle so no shot was possible. Next to him Sergeant Rodriguez was firing short bursts of automatic fire. Sergeant Johnson was behind them and blocked from firing.

Matt pulled himself up and kneeled over the Snake's body. Nothing could be done. The Snake had taken a shot through the center of his chest as he had turned to put his hands behind his back. He was covered with blood. Even as Matt watched, his heart stopped pumping. He was lying in the mud. His head was tilted to one side and his eyes were sightless. The sniper had done a good job. Matt was stunned.

Sergeant Rodriguez came over and said, "Major, I think I put a couple of rounds in the SUV but I don't know if I hit one of the shooters or not."

"Thanks, Sergeant. That's the best we could have done."

At first Matt didn't know what to do. It was an incredible letdown. For the past few weeks his whole being had been focused on catching the Snake, now it was over. They had caught him. The job was done. The man was dead.

However the shooters were still out there. He had to let the rest of the team know.

Matt radioed to Tommy and Neung. The two men in black were heading back towards the soldiers who had been watching the access roads. They should be alerted to stop them. Possibly Neung and Rick and the rest of the team coming after the Snake would meet them on the road also.

With that done, Matt went and leaned against the side of the Snake's car. He felt empty. He had done his best but it seemed it had come to nothing. He had wanted the Snake taken alive. Then an investigation could find out all the background and the circumstances surrounding Yod's death. With the Snake dead much of the impetus for an investigation would be gone.

Chapter 47

U-Tapao air base was only an hour's drive from Chantaburi and was busy with military traffic when the team reassembled there that afternoon. The rain had stopped and a strong sun had created a virtual sauna as the team unloaded the vehicles. They assembled in the same meeting room they had used on arrival three days earlier. It had been an intense period of time. The mood was mixed. The Delta team guys felt they had come and done their job. The Snake's death felt like justice to them. Mission accomplished. Besides they would be glad to get out of the heat and rain they had found in Thailand

Neung and Tommy were relieved the mission was over without anything going public. They had managed to cover up the Snake's killing of the katoey in Bangkok and the shooting of the Thai tour guide in Chantaburi as being drug-related. The police had made sure drugs were found at the scenes of both shootings. There were so many drug-related killings in Thailand no one would notice or question another two. They had carried the Snake's body back with them and it was being prepared for immediate air transport on military flights back to the U.S. An announcement would be made at the embassy that he had died from the stroke he suffered.

The Delta team guys had joked the cause should be listed as heart attack. "He died of a heart attack, an attack on the heart get it?" They all laughed. As long as their team was okay and the mission over, they weren't going to mourn a scumbag being shot. The Delta team, Rick and Colonel Richardson would all fly back on the same flights with the body.

Rick had mixed feelings. This was in many ways better. Having the Snake held and interrogated would have been politically explosive. This was cleaner. Yet, the extent of his many private activities were still unknown and many of his collaborators were walking around in Langley and in

Washington, D.C. There would be an investigation into who had come out from the Special Operations Group at Langley to meet the Snake and who had ordered them out, but there was no chance the agency was going to wash its dirty linen in public. The tension level at the agency in the coming months was going to be very high.

For Rick the most important thing was the agent the Snake had been running, the Camel Driver, was still in place and operation Desert Breeze continued functioning. The operation was too important to be hindered in any way. The Snake was right: the operation was too important to have problems. The issue in the end for the Snake was that he had come to be identified as the problem. Rick had met separately with the new station chief who he had asked to come down and meet him in another part of the air base. They had agreed, now that the Snake was dead, the important thing was for the station chief to let his Thai counterpart know the U.S. government felt all problems were solved and the operation could go on as before, and Matt should no longer be a "person of interest" to either party. Rick and the station chief felt that should be enough to protect Matt.

It was still unresolved as to who the men in black were who had taken out the Snake. Rick was certain it wasn't the Special Operations guys from Langley. As he had told the Delta team, their standard SOG procedure, once things got messed up as badly as they had with the shooting of the Thai guy at the Snake's safe house, would be to dump their weapons in the nearest river and run for the border. He was sure that was what they had done after any chance of a clean, quiet kill was gone. In those situations you just cut your losses and go.

After Matt's call and report of the Snake being shot and killed by a sniper, Rick had listened to Neung talking on the phone. The conversation was all in Thai so he couldn't understand. Somehow he got the feeling from the lack of urgency in their voices that Neung and Tommy were telling their guys to stand down, not to press to catch the men in black. However he didn't raise the issue with them but right before leaving, he did mention it when Matt asked to speak to him on the side.

"Matt, I had the feeling out in the woods that Neung was telling his guys to stand down, not to go after the shooters. Why would that be?"

"I don't know except it's very possible there are people here in Thailand who didn't want the Snake talking about the operation here. He probably wasn't the only one with dirty hands. If that's the case, those shooters were working for a very highly placed person and interfering with them would be a fool's game for Tommy or Neung. It's just that simple."

Rick nodded seeming to accept what Matt was saying. Matt went on.

"Now I've got a question for you. I'll accept what you and Neung say that the two guys from the South were shot and their bodies left in Chonburi were Yod's killers. Maybe they were the same guys who went after me. They got what they deserved. The Snake is dead. What I want to know is what happens to the other guys in that operation?"

"What do you mean?"

"Listen, Rick, I accept you guys are running an important operation here and it has to be protected. At the same time, someone involved was procuring young boys for sex and providing drugs for that purpose. It wasn't the Snake. He might approve it but he wouldn't perform the dirty chores. You have new people on the scene. Is it going to be business as usual? Are these guys going to be allowed to continue to drug and rape and kill children?"

Rick paused for a long time, looking at Matt and gauging his answer. He would have told most people it was none of their business, that gathering intelligence was often a dirty game, but he couldn't dismiss Matt.

"Matt, this is a situation where some of the people we are targeting choose to have sex with boys. It's their cultural background. We can't change that. We can influence what they do and we can refuse to be part of certain activities. It was anything goes with the Snake and that's unacceptable. However, our national security interests demand we get the best intelligence we can and we will always be dealing with ugly people. I can tell you the guys handling the operation now are solid guys. I know them both. I helped to pick them. That's the best I can do for you, okay?"

Matt waited an equally long time to respond to Rick but finally he nodded. At some point you have to accept reality and just hope decent people are in charge.

"Okay, but you keep tabs on them, right?"

Rick smiled, "I will, Matt. I understand where you're coming from."

They both reaffirmed they would stay in touch, with Rick inviting Matt to come to Boston and see a Red Sox game with him and his kids.

"I may take you up on that but if they're playing the Yankees, I'll be pulling for the Yankees."

Then, Matt, Tommy and Neung said goodbye to Rick, Colonel Richardson and the Delta team as they left to board the C-130 which would be taking them on the first leg of the journey home. Matt invited them to come back and visit on their own time saying he would be happy to show them around. The Delta NCOs had said they would like to come and learn more about the "wildlife" existing in the cities, not the forest.

Then they returned to the briefing room. Matt had a few questions he wanted answered. He knew there were some things his friends wouldn't say in front of Rick and the other team members. It was time for the truth. Basically he repeated Rick's question.

"Do either of you know who the men in black were and how they got away without anyone seeing them?"

Tommy answered, "Matt, you know we have a history of 'men in black' in Thailand. We're never going to know for sure who they were, but let's put it this way, there are probably some highly placed people here in Thailand who didn't want the Snake talking to investigators in the U.S. In a sense the Snake killed himself. He had called on our own special operations people to assign a sniper to take you out before you escaped to the States. It's probable that somebody high up decided, since the team was active and you were no longer the problem, the Snake was. The team's orders were changed to take him out instead."

Then Neung added, "As for their getting away clean, the orders we gave our guys were to be on the lookout for foreign drivers not Thai drivers. I think you can understand we weren't about to stop Thai drivers with all the issues that might raise."

He paused, looked at Tommy and added, "Matt, someone high up decided you weren't worth killing. That doesn't mean you're in favor. Leave things as they are."

Matt just shook his head. It wasn't the clean ending he was looking for but it was an ending. The Snake was dead and according to Rick's questioning of his agent, the guys who had killed Yod were dead. This would have to be enough.

"Okay, guys. Let's go home."

They rode back to Bangkok together. Each of the friends absorbed with their own thoughts.

At one point Neung asked Matt, "Can you give me a call and a chance to talk things over before you volunteer for another helping someone out mission?"

Tommy laughed and Matt held up his hands in surrender. "That's it, guys. I promise. No more volunteering."

For the remainder of the ride, Matt just thought about Noi and hoped the journey to the darker side of life he had unintentionally taken her on could be put aside without damage to their relationship.

Chapter 48

Matt had phoned Noi to let her know he was on his way back. She told him she was taking off of work and would be waiting for him at "home," her apartment. Somehow Matt's knock on the door escaped the attention of the old lady across the hallway. The door opened instantly. Noi had been waiting. Not only had she been waiting but she had dressed for the occasion or rather undressed and dressed for the occasion. It wasn't the usual conservative office attire this time. Her greeting was made in a low-cut, black negligee with matching black silk panties underneath. There was no talk, she threw her arms around his head and brought him close for a long passionate kiss. When they paused, her only words were, "I love you. Don't leave me again." Then she kissed him again, and again, now pulling at his clothes. Matt tried to say something and she just put a finger on his lips, shaking her head no and tearing more quickly at his shirt and then his belt as she continued to kiss him, making it clear the talking could wait. Matt managed to help her, stumbling along leaving a trail of his clothes on the floor leading to the bedroom where he finally got to help her out of her welcome home silk. He held her, kissed her, slowly explored her as she guided him and then joined with her, putting all that had gone before out of his mind and submerging himself repeatedly in the scent and feel and taste of her.

Much later as the frantic clinging and physical bonding had ebbed to quieter expressions of love, there had been some discussion. Matt had tried to say he was sorry for what he had put her through but Noi wouldn't accept it.

"You don't need to apologize. I know you were just trying to do the right thing. I'm sorry I haven't been stronger. It's just that I'm not used to people trying to kill the man I love."

"I'm sorry, babe, I'm not ..."

Noi cut him off.

"Don't say that. I know what you mean and that's enough, you can't promise that people won't ask you for help. It seems to be who you are. Just make sure you have others involved helping you from the beginning if it happens again. Okay?"

They lay still for a while and then Noi sat up, her sinuous body half wreathed in the late afternoon shadows of the bedroom. She had pulled the drapes partially closed and had placed lit candles on the dresser near her bed. Their flickering light was reflected in her eyes. Her breasts touched his chest as she leaned close to look into his eyes.

"There is something I have to tell you. Please don't be angry."

"I could never be angry at you, babe."

"No, maybe you can be and certainly you can be jealous but I have to tell you. I don't want secrets between us."

That got Matt's attention. He sat up also as Noi leaned into him, staying close to say what she wanted to say.

"When you called from the States, I told you I was staying with Da and she was being really good to me."

Matt just nodded, now worried about what might be coming next.

Noi stopped looking him in the eyes and just looked down at his chest running her fingers slowly across his pectoral muscles, massaging them.

"Well, I was scared and lonely and needed someone to hug and talk to, and Da and I were sleeping together when I was staying with her. I didn't plan on anything happening, and I don't think Da did either, but when we were lying in bed waiting to go to sleep and we hugged and talked. She gave me a sweet Thai kiss, you know, she just sniffed my cheek softly. Then we kissed on the mouth and she used her tongue and then things just happened. I never made love with a girl before but she's not like a girl, she's like a man. I didn't do anything but I didn't need to, she knows how to do everything. I stayed with her one more night after that. Then I thought I had better come back to my apartment before she got the wrong idea. I'm sorry, babe. It just happened. I don't love her. I like her a lot and she really took good care of me. It was just the moment. Please don't be angry or jealous. It won't happen again."

Matt leaned back and looked at the beautiful, confident woman he had come to love and he had left alone and frightened when he fled Thailand.

"I'm not angry, babe. Yeah, I can't help but be jealous. It's my fault. I got you into a difficult situation and then I left you alone."

"Honey, you have what I need. I'll never be confused about that. Da is a friend, a special friend, if that's still okay with you, but you're my man."

"Give me some time to get used to this, babe, but as long as home is with me I guess that's the important thing, and you know what else?"

"What?"

"Well, I hesitate to say."

"That's okay. We have to be straight with each other. I'll understand."

Matt tilted his head to the side and gave her a slow grin. "Well, being jealous makes me very horny. Could you show me exactly what it was that Da was doing?"

Noi said, "You!" hitting him on the chest. Then she stopped and slowly smiled. "It was something like this," and proceeded to demonstrate.

Chapter 49

It was normal during the school break period at the Metta Home to have special activities for the kids. Many of the kids went out of their slum home on sponsored trips to the ocean or camping at a nearby national forest. For the kids who had been taking music or dance lessons, it was the opportunity for a little extra work and rehearsal and then the time to put on a show. Those invited to the show would be whatever relatives a child might have in the slum community or sponsors, foreign or Thai, who donated to Metta as support for the child and visited and worked to develop a parental support relationship.

Matt was keeping his promise to Ben, the teen boy who felt he was born to be a woman. Ben was part of the dance troupe performing Thai traditional dances and they were putting on a Saturday morning performance. Noi had come along, apprehensive about entering the slum area but also interested to see something of the world Matt had become involved in. They were firmly back together again and the trying experience had brought them even closer.

As they crossed the railway tracks and entered the crowded scene that was Jet Sip Rai, Noi had visibly sunk back in her seat. The littered grounds were an ant colony of poverty with people of all ages walking, running, biking and jostling along a street flanked by a never-ending series of food stalls. Normally it was a monochrome picture, however now that school was out, children with their rainbow display of multicolored T-shirts and short pants added some color relief. Motorbikes, many driven by adolescent daredevils, flitted around Matt's car doing wheelies down the street as he carefully picked his way along. This morning affirmation of life was the slum at its most vibrant, discordant essence.

As Matt and Noi entered the activities room at Metta, it was crowded with kids preparing to perform and a mix of adults, some relatives from the slums, some staff members and some from the community at large. The kids were chattering, nervous and excited at the chance to perform.

Krue Tarn saw Matt enter and came over to say hello. Matt introduced Noi and the two women gave each other gracious *wais* and then did the twenty second foot to head eye scan all Thai women engage in. How are you dressed, what is your jewelry, what makeup do you have on and, implicitly, what is your social status? Judgments were instantly made and wouldn't be revealed until much later. Now all was pleasantness.

Krue Tarn spoke to Matt, "Thank you for coming. It will mean a lot to Ben and thank you for all you have done for us."

Matt had briefed her with a limited version of events, only letting her know the police now understood Yod had not been involved with drugs, his killers had been punished and the games shop, still supposedly off limits to the kids, would not be a center of recruitment for criminal activity. That had been enough for Krue Tarn.

Several rows of folding chairs had been put in place for the guests. Matt and Noi were shown to the front row. As the music started, six teen and preteen girls all in traditional dress came out to the middle of the floor and started dancing using the slow, rhythmic steps and arm and hand movements of traditional Thai dance. The fingers on their hands curved back in the position that Thai mothers tried to achieve, spending endless hours working with their young daughters bending the fingers back. Each girl was elaborately made up and all had performance smiles fixed on their faces.

Krue Tarn was sitting next to Matt. She motioned to one of the dancers, "He's quite beautiful, isn't he?"

Matt was puzzled. He still didn't get it. "Who?"

She laughed at him, "Ben, he's the girl on the end."

Matt looked over, sure enough, through the make-up he could now discern it was Ben, the boy who had broken down crying at Yod's funeral. Ben saw him looking and increased the wattage of his smile and turned slightly, dancing just for Matt. Matt smiled back and nodded. Then he turned to Noi and let her in on the secret. Her eyes widened. She was aware of katoeys in Thailand, and had worked with some, but this teen version, this blossoming butterfly, was new to her also.

After the performance, Matt took Noi to introduce her to Ben. The girls in the dance group were all excited, adrenalin flowing after the performance. When Matt came to say hello, Ben just threw himself in Matt's arms, taking Matt back a bit, but Matt returned the embrace.

"Uncle Matt, thank you so much for coming. Did I do, okay?"

"You did great, Ben, and you look beautiful."

Ben just glowed with the praise. Then Matt introduced Noi as his girlfriend. Ben cooled down instantly giving Noi an appraising, somewhat jealous look, but with a polite *wai*. Then Ben surprised Matt by asking Noi what work she did.

Noi answered, "I have my own computer software company. What do you want to do when you finish school?"

"I want to be an airline hostess. The Thai airlines are hiring us now." The "us" in Ben's comment being the recently publicly-stated acceptance by Thai Airlines of hiring transsexuals for hostess positions.

Matt thought that would be a good place for him to step in, "That would be great, Ben. That means you have to stay at home and go to school, okay?"

"Don't worry, Uncle Matt. I listened to you. I'll finish school."

Then Krue Tarn appeared having heard the last comment, "Finishing school means going to school every day, Ben, doesn't it?"

"Yes, Krue Tarn."

After directing Ben to offer Matt and Noi some of the cakes and tea the home had set up on the side for visitors, Krue Tarn chatted with them a while and then walked them to the door.

"Please come back and visit. Weekends are best as the kids are busy with school and homework during the week. It would mean a lot that someone cares enough to visit."

"I'll be back, Krue Tarn."

This last statement earned Matt a sideways look from Noi. It surprised her a bit. Just what level of commitment was Matt making?

Krue Tarn smiled. "Thanks, Khun Matt. You're a good man. The kids need to see good men."

Then still talking to Matt but looking at Noi, she added, "And you would make a great dad."

"Oh?"

AUTHOR'S NOTE

I have been asked by friends who reviewed the draft of this book about the fate of the children whose plight I described in the Prelude.

The examples used were based very much on the children I came to know while working as a volunteer with the Human Development Foundation, or the Mercy Centre as it is more commonly known, in Bangkok. The two girls, Aom and Nang, were based on two hilltribe girls who were trafficked by their family and sold into the sex trade in Bangkok in 2005. In that case the older girl, fifteen at the time, managed to get to a public phone and call for help to an emergency hotline that was being serviced by counselors from the Mercy Centre. The counselor told her to stay where she was and a staff member managed to bring her and her thirteen year-old sister into the safety of the shelter. They both stayed at the home and completed school. The older girl went to work at a factory outside of Bangkok. The younger girl went on to get a degree from an arts college. She still helps out at the Mercy Centre.

Pan in the Prelude and Ben in the story were both based on a boy who was found in the red light district of Pat Pong in Bangkok in 2007 much as Yod's background was described in the book. That boy was twelve years old, had stunningly attractive eyes and facial features and wore makeup. He let everyone know when he was brought in that he was a girl and he wasn't interested in playing football. Because he wasn't of Thai background and had no identity papers the Centre had to turn him over to the care of a boy's home that the Thai government maintains especially for stateless children. I followed up on him a year later and was told that he was doing well at the government home and going to school. I don't know where he is now, at the age of nineteen, but I am sure he has become a beautiful katoey. I wish the best for him. Thailand is certainly the most understanding country in the world for a transsexual to grow to adulthood.

Joe was not based on a boy who was saved but instead on my knowledge of the many boys and girls who are trafficked into virtual slave labor in the shrimp factories and fishing industry in the Indochina countries.

The reality of social work, even for a volunteer such as I was, is that you have to celebrate the few victories you have while carrying with you the terribly sad knowledge that many, many more children are not saved.

—*Tom Crowley, June 28, 2014*

ACKNOWLEDGEMENTS

There are a number of people who helped to expand my limited knowledge of the world around us and who deserve my public thanks. First I want to thank the staff of the Mercy Centre in Bangkok. These are the men and women, mostly women for some reason, who on a daily basis work to protect and educate the poorest of children. Mercy is truly home to heroes. I also want to thank my friend, "Snowy" or Snow White Orawin Smelser who relocated from Texas to work in Thailand helping first the Thai police and now the UN in working on issues of human trafficking and child sex crimes. Snowy provided good advice and background on those issues. My friend, retired Ambassador and former Secret Service Agent Matt Daley, who has been a lifelong competitive shooter, provided advice on firearms and their use. I thank Lt. General Michael "Mick" Bednarek, Ranger extraordinaire, for his input on Ranger activities in Iraq. "Max" Maxwell, an Englishman much more literate than I, provided excellent advice on editing the very rough draft I gave him to look over. They all advised in good faith, any mistakes are those of the author not theirs.

Finally I want to thank my wife May for being ever so patient with my advanced life crisis and growing mania to learn to write.

This is a work of fiction; all names, locations and events are the invention of the author who is solely responsible for the work.

ABOUT THE AUTHOR

Tom Crowley's origins are in the Midwest American town of Milwaukee, though virtually his entire adult life has been spent living in Asia in positions in the military, diplomatic corps and the private sector until the Asian finance crash in 1997. Living in Thailand at the time, he decided to explore a different path in life and volunteered at the Mercy Centre in Bangkok, an NGO working to shelter and educate street children. Tom has continued with the foundation to this time.

His writing reflects his varied experiences working and living in Asia. He divides his time between homes in Kensington, Maryland and in Bangkok. His recreation is competing in pool tournaments. His two adult children and his wife reside in the U.S.

To find out more about his background and other works visit his website at www.tomcrowleybooks.com

OTHER TITLES FROM DOWN AND OUT BOOKS

See www.DownAndOutBooks.com for complete list

By J.L. Abramo
Catching Water in a Net
Clutching at Straws
Counting to Infinity
Gravesend
Chasing Charlie Chan
Circling the Runway (*)

By Trey R. Barker
2,000 Miles to Open Road
Road Gig: A Novella
Exit Blood

By Richard Barre
The Innocents
Bearing Secrets
Christmas Stories
The Ghosts of Morning
Blackheart Highway
Burning Moon
Echo Bay
Lost (*)

By Rob Brunet
Stinking Rich

By Milton T. Burton
Texas Noir

By Reed Farrel Coleman
The Brooklyn Rules

By Tom Crowley
Vipers Tail
Murder in the Slaughterhouse

By Frank De Blase
Pine Box for a Pin-Up
Busted Valentines and Other Dark Delights
The Cougar's Kiss (*)

By Les Edgerton
The Genuine, Imitation, Plastic Kidnapping

By A.C. Frieden
Tranquility Denied
The Serpent's Game

By Jack Getze
Big Numbers
Big Money
Big Mojo (*)

By Keith Gilman
Bad Habits

(*)—Coming Soon

OTHER TITLES FROM DOWN AND OUT BOOKS

See www.DownAndOutBooks.com for complete list

By Terry Holland
An Ice Cold Paradise
Chicago Shiver

By Darrel James, Linda O. Johnston
& Tammy Kaehler (editors)
Last Exit to Murder

By David Housewright
& Renée Valois
The Devil and the Diva

By David Housewright
Finders Keepers
Full House

By Jon Jordan
Interrogations

By Jon & Ruth Jordan (editors)
Murder and Mayhem in Muskego

By Bill Moody
Czechmate
The Man in Red Square
Solo Hand
The Death of a Tenor Man
The Sound of the Trumpet
Bird Lives!

By Gary Phillips
The Perpetrators
Scoundrels (Editor)
Treacherous (*)

By Gary Phillips, Tony Chavira
& Manoel Maglhaes
Beat L.A. (Graphic Novel)

By Robert J. Randisi
Upon My Soul
Souls of the Dead (*)
Envy the Dead (*)

By Lono Waiwaiole
Wiley's Lament
Wiley's Shuffle
Wiley's Refrain
Dark Paradise

By Vincent Zandri
Moonlight Weeps

(*)—Coming Soon

Made in the USA
San Bernardino, CA
13 August 2014